PRAISE FOR CHRISTINA SHEA AND MOIRA'S CROSSING

"A simple, bittersweet novel about three sisters. The dynamics between them and the other characters of this engrossing book are wonderfully, if painfully, realized."

—*Boston Sunday Globe*

"A fluid, meditative family sage."

—*Publishers Weekly*

"Ms. Shea's style combines a briskly practical surface with a lyrical undertone. It holds the reader's interest."

—*Atlantic Monthly*

"MOIRA'S CROSSING describes the unassailable connection that exists between sisters. In this impressive debut novel, Christina Shea details a passionate story that evokes the varied milieu of the Irish-American experience."

—*Barnes & Noble Discover Bulletin*

"The tale moves quickly and satisfyingly. Far less dark than Helen Dunmore's *Talking to the Dead*."

—*Booklist*

"MOIRA'S CROSSING explores the relationship between two Irish sisters who immigrate to America in the late 1920s and never completely loosen their ties to each other, their past, and a long-ago death that haunts them still. Life on an Irish farm, in a wealthy Boston household, and in a Maine fishing village are all vividly evoked as Shea presents the tale of Moira O'Leary and her younger sister Julia."

—*Kirkus Reviews*

MOIRA'S CROSSING

A novel

CHRISTINA SHEA

POCKET BOOKS
New York   London   Toronto   Sydney   Singapore

Acknowledgments

Hasia Diner's *Erin's Daughters in America* and Carl Frederick Wittke's *The Irish in America* were most useful for background, as was David M. Katzman's *Seven Days a Week* and Lawrence McCaffrey's *Textures of Irish America*. The testimonials in Dorothy and Thomas Hoobler's *The Irish American Family Album*, the exellent *Sheepherders* by M. Mathers, and *On Lupus: The Body Against Itself* by Sheldon Blau all helped to inform the narrative.

I am forever grateful for the exceptional insight and commentary of my two longtime readers, Anna Headly and Jessica Ward Lynch. I also credit my many writing teachers—Rosalie Benny, Daniel Marcus, T. R. Hummer, and James Alan McPherson. I wish to thank my agent, Jennifer Lyons, as well as my editor Diane Higgins. I am delighted to have had the support of my sister fellows at the Bunting Institute (especially R. Manley), in 1998–99. Thanks are also due my sister Sheas (plus Michael), as well as old friends—Liz, Andy, Zsazsa—for never doubting. For his constancy, love, and long hours of single parenting, I thank my husband, Joseph S. Lieber.

 POCKET BOOKS, a division of Simon & Schuster, Inc.
1230 Avenue of the Americas, New York, NY 10020

ISBN: 0-7434-1057-2

First Pocket Books trade paperback printing February 2001

10 9 8 7 6 5 4 3 2 1

Cover design by Brigid Pearson, front cover photo by Christina Angarola/The Image Bank

Printed in the U.S.A.

Everything I write is for my father, David Shea, whose love of poetry was my first inspiration. Moira's Crossing is dedicated to him and to my mother, Rosemary Shea.

MOIRA'S CROSSING

I

In the Fold

(1921–1928)

THEIR MOTHER, Heleen O'Leary, had believed in reason, in spite of her faith. Reason told her that the fire inflaming her joints after her daughter Moira's birth was a warning. Her second delivery a year and a half later and the premature birth of yet another girl, achieved with forceps that left the child's skull permanently misshapen, reminded her that faith was more useful than reason, particularly when she had no choice in the matter.

"A boy?" her husband wanted to know.

"The rooster will do as he fancies," she replied, not unkindly. Although she had never taken to the rural farm life of the Beare Peninsula, Heleen O'Leary was fond of explaining herself in terms of animals. A city girl from Cork, she had grown up poor in the long wake of the potato famine. If there was one thing

Heleen O'Leary didn't hate about the farm, it was that there was food. She was unsympathetic when the children complained between meals, and told them that the hunger in their bellies was the work of wolves. Heleen O'Leary's reticent nature left much of what she said distinctly open to interpretation. Moira and Julia grew up having remarkably little in common, save for a highly animated view of the world, sharpened over time by the memory of their mother gripping the bedposts feverishly one night, a rag clenched between her teeth, and the singularly distressing howl she let out as the midwife reached a hand up into her, feeling for life. Heleen O'Leary died of complications one week after the birth of her third daughter, Ann, who, rejecting the efforts of a wet nurse, nearly starved herself to death. She was brought about on sheep's milk eventually, bottle-fed like a runty lamb.

To Moira and Julia, aged twelve and ten in 1921, the act of mothering made particular sense indeed; they would rear their sister not at all in the way that Heleen O'Leary had raised them, but rather as they wished she had. A curly-haired, lavender-eyed baby with a hot temper, Ann O'Leary was pampered and coddled from the start. It was no surprise, then, once the school year resumed and the job of keeping house full time fell to Moira— as Julia was seen to be the one with scholarly promise—that Ann should make her sister's life miserable. Perhaps they had been too quick to pick up their baby sister when she cried. Ann hollered now whenever she desired attention. Moira was helpless against her. She lifted Ann from the cradle and paced mulishly about the room, on the verge of tears herself. She climbed with the baby into her mother's wardrobe and pulled the door closed. In the muffled darkness, Ann's cries died and she took the bottle. Moira rocked back and forth on her haunches, the cotton skirts against her cheeks, a painfully familiar smell—mother herself. Gone five months now. Gone to God in heaven, she ought keep in mind. Her empyreal soul perhaps looking down right now— and yet it made no difference to the gaping hole Moira felt. Forsaken, alone. She could cry her eyes out for the unfairness of it all. But for the life of the babe in Moira's arms, Heleen O'Leary would still be living! She gazed down at Ann, contented now, lips fixed on the nipple. It disgusted her, a creature so needy. Nonetheless she held Ann close, burped her when the time came.

Kicking free the wardrobe door, Moira stepped into the light of the room and stood at the open window gazing out longingly. She could not see him, nor a trace of his herd, but her father was out there somewhere. She inhaled deeply the moist air, fragrant with apples. Some answer to be found in nature, wasn't there? Where survival was everything and one did what one had to? Yes, certainly. Even if it meant you were heartless sometimes, unkind. She took comfort in the green landscape.

Matty O'Leary came unhinged when his wife was laid in the ground. Nothing too disturbing to begin with; he was forlorn, after all, and the white fleece was a refuge. A good shepherd did not disrespect his animals. Up at four to move the band as usual, but no longer home like clockwork, washing up at the well come dusk, Matty O'Leary stayed out nights with a bottle on the hillside, counting his pearls. The tiny ones, the new lambs, were depending on him. He should wait for the quarter moon to castrate or else they'd bleed to death. He should watch the edge of the wood for predators because the ewes would not protect their young from danger.

Heleen had been a mystery to him. Her silence, her taste for books, her preference for coffee over tea. Looking into her eyes never put him at ease. She would have been a schoolteacher if she hadn't married. But it was Heleen who'd said, time and time again (as if she herself needed convincing), that it was their differences that made them loving. She had had a knack for assuaging Matty's worry. At lambing time he'd be a knot of nerves, too anxious to sleep, pacing the house at night. She'd wander out in her nightgown, a candle in hand, her face aglow. "A little something for luck, then, Matty," flashing her eyes. Right there on the hearth they'd lie. He lost sight of his flock in her skin, soft as a baby's. Her hair shining in the firelight. Holding her with an urgency that was unsettling. "Please, Heleen." A son, he was always thinking.

Matty'd saved his childhood hurley stick for a boy. He'd kept up the farm and the flock with a son in mind. Lord knew, it wasn't that he didn't love his daughters. But he'd grown up the fourth of five boys—each and every precious one was dressed in skirts until the age of three to protect against the fairies. It was boys Matty was accustomed to. A boy he had hoped would carry on his name. A boy he could leave the farm to. To be sure, his daughter Moira was apt with a hurley stick. And quick as a whip. More energy in that child than all the fresh air in the world would satisfy. Your spitting image, people told him, although he never did see it. She had her mother's grace. She was a girl, after all. They were girls all three. What did he know of it, for pity's sake? Just sitting at supper with them, just being in the house alone without Heleen, he found disquieting.

The morning Heleen gave birth to Ann she told Matty she didn't have the strength for her faith. It was a Sunday. The kettle

sat on the peat like a hen on her perch. Overnight Heleen's legs
and ankles had swelled so that it was an effort just to move about.
She was pouring the tea when she felt the child inside and lost
her hold on the kettle, smashing the cups and burning herself.
She was angry then. Pain led her to anger rapidly. She cursed.
"It's Sunday," he reminded. She was on her knees picking up the
broken pottery. "What kind of God is it who asks this much of
me?" Matty did not respond. Again, the baby took her by surprise
and she clutched the table legs and shook her head fiercely, "I
will not pray today." By which he understood her to mean Mass
could wait, he should make haste and fetch the midwife. Five
days later, as Heleen lay dying, Matty tried to strike a bargain
with the Lord. But as he begged for mercy in exchange for his
own eternal devotion, it became clear to him that he would lose,
in the way that one admits the worst about oneself.

A shiver raced up Matty's spine. He threw the empty bottle into
the sky, stumbled down the hillside and into the cluster of sheep,
which parted round him, flowing by on either side. The sheep
began to circle, keeping him at the center, quite unwittingly, it
seemed. Yet they would not allow him to burrow obscurely into
the fold as he wanted to, as he had witnessed each one of his
sheep do, from time to time, spooked.

Matty O'Leary had often said one had to be crazy to tend
sheep. This was a boast in happier times. Crazy, full of fury. The
silence on the mountainside was that big, that complete; a calmer
man could not endure it. Francis O'Leary, for instance, who by
right was next in line (Joseph and James both having perished in
the war), had married up, and wanted no part of the farm. He

and his bride had plans to emigrate. "It's yours, Matty," he'd said. That was five years ago. And now, the silence had become unbearable.

Clouds clung warmly to the mountaintop. Flies buzzed about the flock grazing the red clover. Matty was, at long last, dozing off the drink, curled on the ground beside a rock. Heleen was just a girl, wasn't she? With thick, straw-colored hair that fell to her waist. Pointing a finger at him, or was she beckoning? He couldn't be sure. She disappeared too quickly. Odd how her death had even compromised his dreams. To Father Riley, the parish priest, Matty had many times divulged his longing for a son—as if it were everything. But after seven miscarriages in as many years, Heleen had been too weak to bear a child. Father had warned Matty not to let desire get the better of him. Though wasn't that precisely what one's desires were designed to do? It was his own fault, his own doing: the child, then the blood that never ceased flowing. Matty shuddered in his sleep, wrapping his arms around himself. The day Heleen died there had been sunshine, giant sheeplike clouds dispersing, and she had begged Matty carry her outside so that she could feel the warmth on her face. She was startling to hold, made of rags. He did remember this: Blood was life. Standing at the edge of the meadow with Heleen in his arms, terrified. "Sunshine shouldn't be this precious," was what she'd said, although it took him a moment to make out her words. Even her voice was weak in the breeze.

Matty awoke to the sound of bells. The collies were barking. His heart pounding. A ewe bleated, brushing past him. He reached out and caught her by the haunches. He pressed his body up against her furiously, filthily. Seconds later, the rain began to fall. He felt the wet drops on his face. He saw what he was doing.

He let go the sheep and she scrambled away, shaking her head. He had tied that bell around her neck to predict bad weather.

Something was amiss. Moira noticed immediately. "Trouble with the flock, Da?" she asked, and saw how his eyes dodged hers. He walked over to the basin. "Water's cold as ice," she warned, and would have offered to set the kettle but he'd already plunged in up to his elbows. He bid her cut a wedge of soap for him and began to scrub like mad. Moira looked on uneasily, until it dawned on her to bring a towel. "Before you drown yourself," she said, urging it on him.

She would have assumed he was home only to replenish— feed the dogs, fill his belly, change his socks. Then Ann began to cry and Matty reached into the cradle. Moira stood and stared.

"Supper's coming, is it?" Matty asked.

Moira shook herself, hastened to fill a bowl of stew for him. She moved the lantern to the table and set down his stew. She took the baby, who just then spat up. Moira wiped Ann clean, remarking, "I'm afraid I haven't the knack for mothering." Matty looked at her, his eyes glistening. Her heart skipped a beat. Biting her lip, she met his gaze. "Perhaps I ought come herd with you instead, Da? Couldn't you use the company?"

He scratched his whiskers. "Bottle's no help," he admitted.

"No," she said, "I wouldn't think so."

"Long day's work running sheep," said Matty.

Not near as long as a day spent housekeeping, she was thinking, but she said only, "Yes. I won't complain."

Moira wandered down the road to meet Julia coming home from school. "There's been a change in plan," she told her. "You're too smart for school. You're a fox in a chicken coop." Julia allowed herself to be convinced. The school yard had become unbearable without Moira there to protect her. Julia's oddly shaped head and shy demeanor made her an object of ridicule, and her effortless good grades never came as much relief. A house to hide in, a fire to stoke, and the chance to read her mother's old books while Moira worked in the fields with her father and Ann was napping: Julia could fathom it.

As for the demanding task of child rearing, Julia shared none of Moira's anxiety. She simply knew that she was doing Ann an enormous favor. The fact that Ann took the favor completely for granted didn't matter, since Julia reveled in her martyrdom. She'd cut Ann's fried bread into perfect squares, spreading the jam smooth and clear to the corners, and serve it on a tin plate that invariably would be sent sailing across the room. Julia'd listen for the clang of the plate against the hearthstone, indicating that Ann had had her fill. She'd leave whatever it was she was doing to wipe up the jam stains—on her hands and knees in the grit, tiny pebbles embedding themselves.

If she wasn't a martyr (at times, it did get tiresome), she was her mother. Heleen O'Leary pushing the rickety pram through the mud. Julia tried to picture how it must have been: Moira toddling alongside, shoelaces untied, and she, herself the baby, struggling to hold a bottle of sugar water steady. Impenetrable gray sky, a sudden glimpse of her mother's placid face (purple scarf blowing), and the sound of her own, infant voice protesting the wet, the mist in her eyes.

To O'Rourke's for meal and sugar, then on to the butcher's for a bit of flitch. Julia fit the groceries in around Ann's sleeping body and wheeled home again singing "Dance to Your Daddy," "Shelly

Kee Bookey," and "Three Gray Geese," nothing so dreary as her mother used to sing. She learned to collect the morning eggs like Heleen O'Leary—at daybreak, in her stocking feet, so as not to disturb the princesses. She slipped her hand beneath the feathers, holding her breath, always amazed at how the hens just slept. Back outside in the growing light, she counted brown and white, and felt glad when brown won out, since brown eggs came of a peaceful hen, her mother'd said. Julia also shed the skin from the turnips in one fancy spiral, though it would take some time before she could do so blind, the way her mother used to, gazing out the window, barely aware of herself.

Julia was a better cook than her mother had been. Matty said so. He was home for supper every noon now. Moira and he traipsing dirt into the house. Julia grew to hate this hour—the sound of their spoons in their bowls, their bottomless cups of tea, smell of the fields in their clothes. To say nothing of how they talked while they chewed. Or her constant fear that their conversation would wake the baby. It was shearing time; they'd clipped half the flock that morning, which meant Julia would spend the coming days carding and tolling the wool. A job she near enough hated for the odor of it, as well as for her memory of the way the work used to make her mother's fingers swell. Her mother had spun wool, too. She steeped it in turnip juice to color it if she had plans to weave it. Julia sighed. It was never-ending toil, the life of Heleen O'Leary.

Julia was in the bog digging turf one morning when she heard a bicycle bell and tires rubbing to a halt on the road. She turned to see Agnes Scully stopped on her bicycle. "The child's too young to be up on her feet," Mrs. Scully called out. She frowned at

Ann, who was toddling along the embankment collecting stones. "It's foolishness to let her walk before she's a year. Her legs will be bowed."

"But I didn't encourage her," said Julia, resting on her spade. "She learned quite on her own."

Agnes Scully clucked her tongue disparagingly and pedaled off. She lived in the next house down from O'Learys'. But Heleen and she had never been very neighborly. Widow Scully wore her grief on her sleeve, Heleen had criticized. The following day, Julia caught sight of Agnes Scully walking up the pathway. She was dragging along what appeared to be a crude wooden cage. Commonly known as a playpen, Agnes Scully explained. She had purchased it secondhand at a church bazaar years ago. "Stowed it away along with thoughts of children when Donald died." she sniffled shortly. Julia peered at the playpen curiously. Mrs. Scully pushed it into the house through the open doorway. She smoothed her skirts and gazed thoughtfully about the house. It was perfectly tidy, which she found surprising. She eyed Julia guardedly. She did not take after her mother, apparently. Agnes Scully knew firsthand how Heleen O'Leary had kept house, as she and Mary Kelly had been the ones to tidy up the O'Leary house before the wake. They'd scrubbed until the calluses came out on their hands. The dirt had been so dreadful, Agnes Scully grimaced just recalling. If she had not been acting as a servant of the church, she could not have endured.

"Now put the child in the pen and go about your business," Agnes Scully said. "It won't do to have her running about on her own." Julia did as she was told. Ann stared out through the bars. Agnes Scully scooped up a toy and held it out to Ann. Ann batted the toy away. "Suit yourself," said Mrs. Scully, and then to Julia,

"She'll come 'round to it eventually." Julia smiled uncertainly, staring at the floor. She assumed widow Scully would take her leave now. The kettle began to boil, and Julia rushed off to it. Agnes Scully said she wouldn't mind a spot of tea. Julia brought out the tea tin (giving it a hopeful shake) and one of two china cups, turning her back to rub off the dust. Agnes Scully sat at the table, looking on. She remarked that by all appearances Julia was managing the house quite capably. The compliment pleased Julia. For an extra touch, she decided to spread a square of linen over the table before setting out the cups.

"Your mother, as you may well know, had her head in the clouds," said Agnes Scully, picking up her teacup. She went on to relate how she had once come to call upon Heleen O'Leary and found her sitting on the step reading a book, a basket of wet laundry sitting there beside her and the baby, Moira it must have been, crawling in the dirt and chicken feed at her feet.

Julia could feel the anger spilling into her cheeks. She set the teapot down roughly on the table and a good bit surged up out of the spout and onto the linen cloth she had spread out.

"You'll scrub until you're blue," remarked Agnes Scully. "I myself would never serve tea over linen, not even to the Pope."

"Soak the spot in vinegar first, before the wash," Julia said quickly.

"Vinegar?" said Agnes Scully, skeptical.

"Works for diapers, as well." Julia went on. "It's what my mother used to do."

"Is that so?"

Julia nodded, although that wasn't the truth. She'd gleaned the tip from a housewife's column on a square of newsprint in the outhouse.

"Well I always felt Heleen was clever, even if she was peculiar," Agnes Scully said, and cleared her throat.

Fishing net, suggested Agnes Scully when she heard that Ann was climbing out, fishing net tied tight across the playpen top. It might have worked, except that in her frustration Ann would rock the playpen back and forth so violently that it toppled over, collapsing in on her. Julia felt it was too dangerous. She returned the playpen and threw away the fishing net, which was frayed from Ann's chewing. As Julia saw it, the problem with Ann walking was not that it would bow her legs (an old wives' tale, no doubt), but that she could hurt herself in a fall. Ann was an emphatic, willful child who resisted having her hand held. There wasn't a cautious bone in her body. She would reach for something and her legs would wobble. Falling on her bottom was startling, but it didn't hurt. Falling down facefirst was something else. Ann's skull smacked the edge of the table and Julia thought of apples. How an apple dropped from a tree bruised instantly. How the worm squirmed its way to that soft, sweet part. Julia picked Ann up to comfort her, saw inside her halting mouth—the tiny teeth she was cutting, a tongue quivering—and braced herself for the scream. Too close to say; Julia's heart ached.

Perhaps Ann could do with a harness," suggested Matty.
"A harness?" said Julia.
"Like your mother used with you."
"I don't remember a harness."
Moira piped up, "Oh I do."

Heleen O'Leary had fashioned hers out of rags, but Matty suggested scraps of leather, so as to make it more durable. He brought the scraps in from the barn and lay them out across the table. Julia looked on as Matty measured around Ann's middle. Ann was smiling obligingly, tickled. A lump rose in Julia's throat. "She isn't a dog, you know."

Matty paused. "You said you were at wit's end, didn't you?"

Julia sighed. "It seems strange is all." She watched her father knot the leather together. "I don't ever remember a harness."

"Well then," said Matty, "what you don't remember won't hurt you."

"You didn't like it much," Moira recalled.

Julia scowled. "I'm not a fool."

Ann wasn't either. When Matty went to fit the harness on her, she put up a terrible struggle, kicking and biting with her new teeth. They tried to bribe her into wearing it. Piggyback rides? Stories? Fruit roll? Ann stubbornly shook her pigtails, until, without thinking, Matty suggested, "An ice cream?" Ann, who knew of ice cream from overhearing her sisters' longings in front of the sweet cart on market day, was suddenly eager to wear the harness. She toddled to the end of the line, then back to the table where, she gathered, she would soon see her treat.

"Da, whatever possessed you?" Julia hissed at him.

Moira admonished, "You can't just make her an empty promise."

Matty rubbed his whiskers, looking troubled. There was an ice house in Glengarriff, there even used to be one in Ardgroom, Fisher's Ice it'd been called (until the chimney, struck by lightning, caved in on the adjacent house). As far as Matty knew, the ice manufactured locally serviced the butchers and grocers; there wasn't a confectioner's around for miles. Once a month on market day, an ice man came with a sweet cart from Bantry, selling bricks of ice cream wrapped in newspaper.

Matty began to pace. Ann scampered along after him chanting, Ice, ice, *ice!* Moira looked at Julia, who shook her head in disgust. Matty wheeled around suddenly. "I'll go to Bantry!"

"Beg your pardon, Da?" Moira couldn't believe her ears.

"That's twenty miles going, another twenty returning," Julia said doubtfully.

"If Macaffrey loans me his horse I'll be home soon enough," Matty replied.

They watched him from the window, walking down the road. Ann, confused, had begun to cry. "Hush now. It's for you he's going," Moira told her.

"Fetching your ice cream," Julia added. "Imagine that. All the way to Bantry for Annie!"

The forms were somewhat spoiled by melting, but it was only Matty who seemed to mind. He had selected each one carefully, amazed by the assortment of molds displayed on the confectioner's wall. Several minutes' earnest deliberation (and the clerk prodding him all the while that the shop was set to close) led him to point to the hare, the curlicue snail, and the butterfly— for Moira, Julia, and Ann respectively, spending more money than he'd intended (as well, to have the ice forms parceled in crystals and straw), but surely one daughter wasn't more entitled.

It was their silence that told him they were pleased. Moira and Julia hovered over their bowls with big eyes, delighting in each bite. Ann behaved less reverently. Refusing a spoon, she shoveled the ice cream greedily into her mouth, then burst into tears because her hands were cold. Once she'd licked clean her own bowl, she began grabbing for her sisters' bowls. Matty couldn't help laughing. He gazed with satisfaction out the window, remembering there was the mare still to see to—a rubdown, to warm up those bones. The horse was fairly exhausted by now. Macaffrey's piebald mare had never so much as had to trot with the milk cart. She wasn't accustomed to a rider and Matty hadn't sat in a saddle in several years himself, but they'd gotten on just fine, spent the better part of a day on the road. He'd dug his heels in—Giddyap, old girl—and felt nostalgic for the pair he used to own, a sturdy broad-backed bay he'd called Bobbie and her foal, Two Socks, with splashes of white on her forelegs. The spring before Heleen passed away proved to be a desperate lambing season and, to make ends meet, Matty'd sold the one horse and then the other, splitting up the pair even though he knew it was bad luck to do so.

Julia was a convert. If she needed to hang out the wash, all she had to do was tie Ann's harness line to the post. If she wanted Ann close, she simply reeled her in and looped the excess line around her own waist. She fixed the supper with Ann in the harness. She gardened and swept the house. She also found that by tightening the line at the right moment, she could offset a fall. Pretty soon she didn't know how she'd done without the harness. So, too, any resentment she felt toward her mother for using a harness vanished. Heleen O'Leary had been smart, after all, resourceful.

Not all farmers' wives of her generation knew how to read and write, but Heleen O'Leary hardly had been typical. Matty used to say that Heleen would rather read than eat. And it was true:

she thinned the broth to save pennies for the purchase of books on the rare trip to Bantry or Cork. The books she safeguarded in an old hope chest, which had sat undisturbed at the foot of the bed since her death. Heleen had been vigilant, possessive, letting the lid fall shut on busy little hands. So it was not without trepidation that Julia first muscled up the hope-chest lid. The air was so stale inside the chest she choked on her breath. But surely her mother's books needed dusting! Julia gently lifted out a book, wiping the cover with her sleeve. It was an encyclopedia of knots. She leafed through it shyly, pausing over the pages of illustrations demonstrating various configurations of practical rope tying. She dug out a second book, an illustrated compendium of wildflowers. Then a third, the subject of which was herbal remedies. Feeling more and more certain of herself with each new title, Julia had had no idea that such useful books existed. Lying across her parents' bed, browsing a stargazing guide for the amateur astronomer, she was filled with the power of her finding, a godsend to be sure.

From her mother's books Julia learned extraordinary things: to sew clothes, make and use a slingshot, cure chicken foot rot, cane chairs, and perform simple surgery. Her favorite books tended to be those concerning either medicine or religion, subjects she deemed most valuable to everyday life. She saw no conflict in their distinctly divergent doctrines; the study of medicine elicited in her a taste not for truth but for mystery, whereas the greatest mystery, the mystery of God, assured her of an essential truth.

Julia left one of her mother's books within her little sister's reach one day and Ann tore out the pages. It was Julia's own fault. Her shame wore the face of her mother, the same way it did when she hesitated at the butcher's block. (She would compensate by bringing down the hatchet more forcefully than was necessary—and the cats went dashing after the flying fish head.) Julia smacked Ann soundly, and one more time to show she meant it. But it only made her feel worse. She gathered up the damaged book, pressing it impulsively to her breast. Ann was bawling. Julia gazed at her thoughtfully. A freckle-faced orphan with pumpkin-colored braids. Ann was going on three years now, and she was clever, everyone agreed. Julia would make it up to Ann. She would teach her to read.

In no time at all, Ann's hostility for books and how they diverted her sister's attention vanished. She became so fond of books and reading that she wanted to do little else. As long as Julia was devoted in her teaching—for Ann could detect insincerity—the reading lesson went smoothly. At the end of a long afternoon of puzzling out letters and studying corresponding pictures, Ann began to yawn and gaze distractedly about the room. Julia encouraged, "Tired little lioness," and Ann's eyelids fluttered. She went off to her nap without a struggle.

The reading fever was spreading. Evenings after his tea Matty came, timidly at first, later more resolute, and stood blocking the lantern light with the Bible in his arms so that she really had no choice but to notice him. He aimed to read the word of the Lord, he said. An ambitious goal, certainly, since he was ignorant even of his ABCs. And he was hardly the quick study that Ann was, his mind set deep in its ways. But what he lacked in aptitude he made up for in sheer will. He clenched his fists, pursed his lips, as if it were quite painful. At long last, sounding a word out. Julia sighed with relief and Matty glanced purposefully at the Bible, a beacon for him (he'd stood it on end in the center of the table). Then crossed himself—as if his hardscrabble progress were an act of God. Which was as good an answer for it as any, Julia felt, and she couldn't help thinking of Job. She had never seen such determination before, such tireless struggle. He told her over and over how grateful he was and what a fine teacher she'd make if she was ever inclined that way. She had all the patience her mother before her had lacked, said Matty. Julia shook her head. "Oh no, Da, it isn't the case," because it wasn't patience; it was pity. Heleen O'Leary simply never felt sorry for anybody.

Thank goodness for sheep, was all Julia could think when Matty, eyelids drooping, called it quits for the evening. At long last, Julia was freed. She read by lantern light deep into the night. Sometimes she read aloud to Moira, curled beside her and Ann in the bed, unraveling her braid, but Moira was hardly the impressionable reaper of knowledge that Julia was. "Dreadful boring," she'd declare, rolling over, restlessly drawing the quilt up. She was no less judgmental of books that interested her—mainly wildlife treasuries and a volume of world geography. She listened impatiently, shaking her head at things that did not sound right, disagreeing readily—as if denying the authority of a book was the reader's real purpose, Julia thought scornfully. She watched her sister drift off in the low light, blond hair fanned out behind her on the pillow, legs and arms parted like a runner's.

The mountains of the Beare Peninsula were steep and rugged, making for muscular sheep. Sheep that ran faster, farther, and, in the hands of a good shepherd, herded themselves. Sheep were thoughtless animals, though extremely alert and driven by greed; they could run for miles after a rainstorm, sensing something lush. Only if they were strewn like a spoonful of barley across a kitchen floor should Moira send the dogs out. He was teaching her to be patient, mainly. Everything else she could learn by instinct. And by his example. Matty marched along, coaxing, gathering strays. The soles of his shoes were worn through to the feet. The wind tousled his hair and whipped his cheeks. He whistled and the dogs crisscrossed back and forth, slowing the herd. Slapped his cane against a rock and the dogs ran circles around the band, tightening the mass. It was the dogs that would keep her company over the course of the day, Matty claimed, excusing himself partly. And she gathered from the easy affection he showed them and the gentle way he spoke to the dogs that he found them trustworthy, which was surprising since her mother had often complained that Matty even scrutinized the wishbone before taking hold, that Matty trusted nothing, nobody.

Up and down the peninsula, coursing races in the foothills was the sport of Saturdays. Spectators placed bets on which dog would catch the hare and swallowed profits in the pub that same afternoon. The owner of the winning dog earned a tidy sum. It was only the dog breeders who saw a steady income; they weren't exactly rich men, but their dogs were well fed. Theirs were the only purebreds in the area, so it came as a surprise to everyone when one of Matty O'Leary's dogs brought the hare home stunned but alive one Saturday. A curly coat and the soft bite of a setter—people said the dog ran on a wish, wishes and desire, was no other way those little legs carried her. She returned victorious week after week.

Perhaps Matty pushed his luck. He frequented the pub, he was privy to the gossip. And people were talking: "You never know, Matty. There's some out there who depend on their winnings. Ought to keep that dog of yours out in the fields with the sheep where she belongs." He didn't heed the warnings. And so one morning he found the dog poisoned. She was curled in a corner of the barn, eyes rolled back in her head, muzzle coated in foam. There was a pool of vomit on the floor and the untidy remains of a beef bone.

The culprit was never found out, although Matty suspected everybody. O'Rourke, the grocer, whose English setter became the local favorite once Matty's dog was gone, seemed a likely candidate, but they had no choice but to continue purchasing flour and sugar from him. Matty accused Michael Flynn of the deed one night at the pub, but Flynn denied it outright, resenting the allegation. They might have come to blows over it except that they were both too drunk to manage.

Matty was at the pub every night now. Sometimes Julia waited up for him, presenting herself seated at the kitchen table reading the Bible when he staggered in. In a grave voice, she uttered aloud certain hard-hearted passages from Job. He retreated to the bedroom. She listened keenly for his snoring, then went and hunted down his strewn trousers and rifled through the pockets for whatever coins he'd left unspent.

Father Riley, the parish priest, was sweeping the church walkway, his bald head shining in the afternoon light. His spaniel bounded up barking as Julia, with Ann holding her hand, approached the gate. She'd come, she said, to speak with him about her father. "I'm at wit's end, Father."

"How so, child?"

She hung her head. "You see, he lost his champion courser. I know it's gambling, Father. But he loved the dog. Now he's turned to the drink. He's drinking away every penny. The same as when Mother passed away."

"I see," said Father Riley.

Matty O'Leary was not a devoted parishioner. He attended Mass sporadically, and Father couldn't recall the last time he'd heard Matty's confession; certainly not since his wife passed away. But Father felt tenderly toward the daughters, Moira and Julia, who, having learned from their mother pride and disdain for charity, dressed their little sister in ill-fitting clothing and left the roads to harden her feet. The girls came to church every Sunday, scraps of ribbon in their hair to set the day apart from other days. Father Riley promised he'd speak to Matty. He wandered into the pub just before closing. It was not unusual for the priest to share in a pint, although he rarely stood at the bar. Perhaps this was why Matty noticed him. Their elbows were all but touching.

"Evening, Father."

Father nodded. "How are your girls, Matty?"

"Oh you know how it goes, Father. They're grown so quickly."

Father Riley was the only person in the village who wore eyeglasses. It was always a bit disconcerting to fall under his gaze. "You're doing them a disservice, returning to the drink," Father Riley said. "Take your troubles up with the Lord, Matty."

Matty noticed the grin on Tommy Healy's face behind the bar. Tommy cleared Matty's empty glass away. The color spilled into Matty's cheeks. He'd come to the pub for a bit of peace. "The Lord is no better than the tax gatherer to me," Matty grumbled bitterly. "He's done nothing but take."

Father Riley sipped his pint. "Perhaps it's the only way He knows to get your attention, Matty."

. . .

In the spring of 1926, Matty O'Leary's herd was one hundred head deep, thanks to a successful spring lambing that had produced a record number of twins. Matty saw his luck returning. Every year, he flushed his flocks in the green foothills to fatten them for breeding. What with the size of the flock this year, he decided they should split the band to move it. It was particularly difficult work maneuvering the herd down the mountain. Since Matty was no longer able to traverse such steep terrain effortlessly, he reserved the two seasoned dogs for himself. That left the dog he'd acquired to replace the Border collie that was lost to coursing. An edgy one-year-old mongrel who minded when it suited him, Moira said. So Matty enlisted Julia and Ann to assist Moira. Now Moira was even more disgruntled. "They'll only get in my way, Da," she moaned. Matty was done listening. "You ought to be happy for the help. What with the weather showing no mercy, it'll be rough going."

But Julia lacked endurance, and Ann, five years old by this time, considered this project an imposition on her and tagged along at a snail's pace. What was more, Ann had crackers in her hand so the dog kept straying off to her. Moira's cajoling only made matters worse, of course. It was hopeless. The sun already high in the sky. Unseasonable warmth. Sheep feeling the heat, lumbering along in slow motion.

"Oh, why don't you take her home, Julia," Moira complained. "I'd be down the mountain by now if it weren't for the two of you."

Julia hustled to catch up. It was true, she was hardly a natural. She didn't like having to run so much. And she found the animals

intimidating, unpredictable—despite what Moira said about fear
being their only conscious sense. If she tried to drive the sheep
in one direction, they were more than likely to scramble off in
the other. Sweat rolled down Julia's back. She gazed dryly at
patches of hawkweed and daisies, the lavender shadows cast by
protruding rocks. A bleak, relentless mountaintop. She felt tired
and bored, and if it weren't for her father's orders, she would
have quit.

The herd had narrowed out through the grassy pass, and the bulk
of it was just coming down off the ridge, when Moira noticed the
swelling. The sheep were resisting taking the corner. She pointed
out the trouble to Julia. "They'll bottleneck," she said. "They'll be
all over the mountain." Julia looked on uncertainly as Moira raced
back and forth, pressing the herd. She whistled to no avail for
the dog. Tried to charge the mass herself. But the herd wasn't
budging, grown tense and quiet suddenly. Moira cursed; she'd be
fine if she had a good dog alongside. She shouted to Julia to run
back up the ridge to get a look ahead at what was worrying the
sheep, but changed her mind watching Julia grope her way.
"Never mind, never mind. I'll go," handing off her stick as she
dashed up the incline.

From the top of the ridge, Moira saw how an older ewe had been
singled out, how efficiently the two wolves took her down, nipping at her heels before tearing her throat. And at that moment
she heard her sister scream. She turned to see the herd erupting,
animals scuttling backwards in panic. Some packed so tight in
line that they lost their footing and were sucked under. Sheep
spilled out in all directions. Some scrambled toward the em-

bankment, a few bolted into the forest, but the largest number turned around and charged back the way they'd come.

Ann was picking flowers in the field when the ground began to rumble. They shouted at her to run, but she didn't. She must have frozen in fear, but, from a distance, she simply appeared stubborn, standing her ground as the spooked herd stampeded toward her. When the herd was within twenty feet of her, fear finally touched her and she made a vain attempt to flee. The white fleece surged over her.

Julia reached Ann first. She was frantically blowing air into her. Moira came up behind her. She looked anxiously at the hundreds of hoof marks, the daisies Ann had picked scattered about, and said, "It was wolves," by which she meant something more.

Julia was counting the seconds. She eyed Moira.

"Wolves," Moira repeated, her heart in her mouth.

Moira carried Ann down off the mountaintop while Julia went in search of Matty. By the time Moira reached the house, her legs were trembling uncontrollably. She lay Ann down on the grass and went to the well, stood there a moment looking down in. Her head was spinning. She lowered the bucket, drew it up full, slow, nearly letting go, and drank in swift, anxious swallows. Breathing hard, her belly aching, she glanced over at Ann and tossed a stone to shoo the chickens.

In the meantime, Julia had found her father on the southside of the mountain, moving his sheep through the foothills. She had called out to him.

"What is it?" Matty demanded, his heart seizing up at the sight of her. Even at a distance, he could see the horror on her face.

"It's Ann," she panted, and she told him what had happened.

He listened, dumbstruck. Wolves? It made no sense to him. Not by day certainly, not with the land cleared for grazing. He'd witnessed a clap of thunder turn a flock on its heel like that. Turn and stampede for all they were worth right over the side of a cliff. He had seen sheep unnerved by rays of sunlight piercing the clouds. If a man felt the weather in his bones, a sheep felt it in its heart. He peered up at the sky, but it was perfectly still. He said to Julia, "I'll go for Father Riley. You follow your sister down."

Father Riley was the first to say there were no more wolves in Ireland. No dragons, no snakes, no wolves, no longer. He walked in circles, swinging a censer. Clouds of smoke hovered over Ann, breathing but unconscious on the bed. Julia and Moira knelt at her side, Father Riley leading them in prayer. Matty, having excused himself ("I'm too wrought up for it, Father"), paced back and forth biting his fingernails, glancing now and then at the bed. They had changed Ann's clothes and washed off the mud. She wore her nightgown, her curls combed down around her shoulders.

Moira felt sure of what she'd seen from the top of that ridge. Certainly it was unusual, but impossible? Why, that was like denying the existence of the Devil, or God even. Father Riley made the sign of the cross, over and over, stirring the smoke. "Are you quite sure you're telling the truth, child?" he'd asked her. The village had grown in recent years, the potato was back, apples lasted through the winter; everywhere evidence that nature was tamer. In the old days, the nearest church had been fifteen miles. "I watched with my own eyes, Father," she'd replied. Her mind went rushing back over the events on the mountain—to the wolves and sheep, a sacrifice, she now realized, since people doubted what she saw.

The scent of incense lingered. Father Riley gone home—only a stone's throw, they shouldn't hesitate should the situation change during the night. He promised to send for a doctor. He also would have the spare bed from the rectory brought up to the house. They sat hunched over their soup bowls. The kittens came out to play in the quiet, scampering about the room. Matty said nothing about putting them out. After a moment, Julia noticed that she was the only one drinking her soup. She looked from her father's face to her sister's, thinking to herself how they were so alike, both intent on feeling responsible, and she said "It's not your fault" in an exasperated tone, getting up to clear the bowls.

Matty rubbed his hands over his tired face. "If anyone's to blame, it's me."

Julia snapped. "No, Da!" Slapping the washrag down. He was thick as molasses. She steadied her voice. "It was an accident."

"It *was not* an accident," Moira asserted. She'd told them both already what it was. She wasn't changing her story.

"But how could it have been wolves?" asked Matty.

"Count head for yourself, Da. You'll find one is missing."

He didn't know her for a liar. "Incredible," he said, shaking his head.

"Does it so much matter?" Julia asked. "You heard Father Riley. Don't ask why of God's will."

"It wasn't God's will!" shouted Moira, sick of it, angry now. "It wasn't God at all, but something else."

Julia was losing patience. "There isn't anything else."

Matty got up suddenly, taking his coat from the hook. They knew where he was headed, but he said so anyway, "Going for a pint—come fetch if there's change."

Moments after he left, Ann gave a great sigh. Moira and Julia rushed to the bed and stood there, expectantly watching Ann's sleeping face. After a while, when there were no other unusual exhalations, Moira said, "Perhaps she's pretending."

Julia turned away, going for the Bible. She sat in the rocker, flipping pages idly. Out of the corner of her eye she watched as Moira reached out and plucked a strand of Ann's red hair. "Doubting Thomas," Julia hissed. Her heart thumped self-righteously. She turned to the thirty-seventh psalm, and read out loud for her sister's benefit. " 'He is their strength in the time of trouble. And the Lord shall help them, and deliver them: He shall deliver them from the wicked, and save them, because they trust in him.' " She looked at Moira, who gazed serenely away.

Moira was no longer a child reciting the Lord's Prayer at her mother's bedside over and over; her words could have turned cream into butter. She'd felt betrayed when her mother died. God was decidedly *un*trustworthy, Moira had realized. Though she'd suspected as much, quite honestly, noting the attention He paid such things as the weather, the number of lambs each spring, her mother's health, and other uncertainties.

"What if I don't trust God?" Moira asked suddenly.

Julia shook her head. "But you do. You have to!"

She did not understand Moira; she felt this acutely. After all, the stampede might just as well have been her *own* fault. Julia didn't know the first thing about sheep. What with chaos breaking loose and Moira abandoning her to dash up the ridge, she had had no idea what to do. As for wolves, she herself hadn't seen any, and further had no opinion as to their likelihood. But the ownership of blame seemed incidental. Julia viewed life as a test. Not quite in the vein of Job (her ambitions being more modest), rather, like Heleen O'Leary, for whom a howling stomach had been a wolf. Hardships, such as hunger, were clues to God—His intention—and, subsequently, Julia's own purpose, which, given the burdens of her life thus far, seemed very important indeed. This wasn't to say that unexplained tragedy wasn't confusing— she glanced over at Ann—but God was known for His inscruta- bility.

The doctor came by carriage from Bantry. He pulled up a chair at Ann's bedside and listened to her steadily thumping heart.

"She's in a deep sleep," Julia offered.

"Ought to starve to death if she doesn't wake up soon," he said, scratching his head. He left with the last two bottles of Matty O'Leary's Christmas whiskey.

"No cause for worry," Julia said, watching from the window as the doctor's hired horses carted him away. "I'll see to her myself." She searched determinedly through her mother's books of veter- inary medicine and herbal remedies, rising from her chair occa- sionally to study the patient, note changes: the movement of the eyeballs under the lids, the apparent luminosity of her skin. When Matty and Moira came in from the fields, expectant, hope- ful, knowing the doctor had been there, Julia scolded, "What did you think he would do? Wake her?" Ann was too strong-willed for that.

A stomach catheter was procured from the barn and disin- fected. Matty pried open Ann's mouth and Julia inserted the feeding tube, inching it down her throat.

"There are two passages," Moira reminded her.

Julia nodded.

Ann's coughing and sputtering subsided once the tube was in place. Matty steadied her head on the pillow. The pump was started. After a moment, Ann's lips closed softly around the tube and appeared to suckle.

"What is it she's feeding on?" Moira wanted to know.

"An elixir," Julia told her, mysteriously. Milk and molasses, boneset and dandelion ground to a pulp; she could only pray that it would have a nourishing effect.

"She's wetting the bed," remarked Moira.

"So she is," said Julia excitedly.

Julia changed the sheets. She changed Ann's clothes. She bathed her and rubbed her body with bee balm. Ann appeared so content, so unblemished, that it was quite easy to imagine her waking at any moment, as if from a nap—stretching out her chubby arms and legs. And once awake demanding a slice of bread with jam, her dolly, a story, every bit of Julia's energy. Indeed, it was extraordinary—this silence, this utter peace and quiet. Julia spoke to Ann in a whisper. "You take your time, Annie."

Agnes Scully brought a loaf of soda bread. She had learned of Ann's misfortune from Father Riley, and had come as soon as she'd gotten the loaves baked. Julia asked should she set the kettle. "Don't trouble yourself," replied Mrs. Scully. Julia showed her to the bedside. Agnes Scully crossed herself, "She's like an angel," which was the same thing people had said of Heleen O'Leary laid out dead.

Julia reckoned that if widow Scully knew what had happened to Ann, the whole village must know by now. Sure enough, the

Eagens and the Harnetts came knocking that same afternoon; O'Rourkes, Flynns, and McDermotts next day. They claimed they came to offer prayers, but you'd never have known it by the gallons of tea she was pouring or the regular racket they were making. "This is not a wake!" Julia said sternly after Michael Flynn asked if there wasn't a drop of spirits about the house to warm his tea. She held the door open while everyone shuffled out, and stood watch until they'd walked clear past the cabbage and potato bins. "Just like her mother," she heard one of them say, by which was meant she was standoffish, arrogant, though Julia didn't mind a bit—Heleen O'Leary, smarter, better than any of them.

Mostly, Matty missed Ann: her love of attention and affection (the gleeful way she would race toward him, arms outstretched), the demands she made on his time evenings after his tea. A hundred and one more urgent things, but he lumbered about the room on his hands and knees with Ann sitting up top, shouting giddyap pony. He hardly knew what to do with himself now. Besides drink, and pace back and forth across the floor until he grew dizzy. He was moved to take the Bible down from the mantel. He hadn't had a reading lesson in months and was rusty. He had never developed the skill of reading to himself, so it made sense after a while to move his chair closer to Ann's bedside so that she could listen if she cared to. It was also for Ann's sake that Matty eventually abandoned the Bible for one of her storybooks, and found this much smoother going, more suitable, as it turned out, for him, too. Matty read to Ann nightly, thereafter. While he read, he held Ann's hand. From time to time, he would gaze up from the page at her sleeping face and do his best to keep from asking himself why this had happened.

Matty O'Leary felt unworthy, and wary, of asking. It was this question above all others, after Heleen's death, that had made him feel responsible. He hadn't the courage for the interrogation now. As Heleen used to—as if there were no hard and fast truths at all. It was an unsettling way for a Catholic to live. Matty recalled how, at night, Heleen's imagination was apt to run wild. She had awakened him once, in a sweat, and said she had seen the body of Christ being eaten by wolves. A pack of wolves, following the scent of death to the site, had set upon the remains of the crucified. Which, Heleen had claimed, explained the disappearance of Jesus' body. Calling into question the Ascension (for questions were like weeds in how they multiplied). He remembered the insistence in her voice. It sounded like blasphemy to Matty, but he held her tight to stop the trembling. Sensed a fever coming. Her wrists and ankles would be swollen by morning, as certain as the rain outside falling.

As the days went by, Julia stayed at Ann's side, hovering thoughtfully when there wasn't something more pressing to do, like clip Ann's fingernails, which had begun to grow at a rapid rate, or massage the purple soles of her feet. They moved Ann's bed into the kitchen once the weather cooled, slipped a hot stone under the covers. They cooked and ate their meals around her, stored potatoes and turnips under her bed. She wore shoes now to preserve the alignment of her feet. Her glowing skin had become sallow, wrinkled and baggy, except after a feeding, when she puffed up like a toad. Father Riley came on Sundays after Mass and led them in prayer. By Easter her hair had begun to fall out at the slightest touch, so they laced the purple hair ribbon through the buttonholes of her nightgown.

• • •

Six weeks into her slumber, Ann O'Leary rolled onto her side one morning and yawned. Julia gave a shout. Ann opened her eyes. "Sweetest face of a baby," gasped Matty O'Leary. It was no less than a miracle, and everybody who saw Ann paraded through town on Matty's shoulder the next day said so. Despite Julia's protest that she was far too fragile and Moira's that she shouldn't be made into a spectacle, Matty wrapped Ann in a blanket and started out. They headed to the church, with a detour through the pub, Ann's head bobbing with its own weight, a bemused smile on her face. Children came running. The butcher closed up shop and joined the party. Frank Harnett brought his fiddle. Quite a crowd marching down the road on a May afternoon. Father Riley's spaniel was soon barking, and then Father, himself, appeared from behind the church, a rake in his hand, to see what all the fuss was about. "Do you believe it, Father? She's risen," said Matty, stepping through the church gate. He held Ann in his arms before the priest, who blessed her and asked her how she was feeling. "I'm thirsty," Ann responded, miffed because, despite the attention she was getting, they'd neglected to offer her anything at the pub. Water was brought from the stream. She was set down in the church garden, Father Riley's spaniel sniffing curiously. Father went into the church and returned in his robes to say a Mass right there in the bright sunshine.

As good as new, they all said, by the looks of her. Only Ann had been in bed a long time and had grown soft, somehow dimmer. She would have to learn certain things again. It was only natural, Julia said. She lacked the motor control for the simplest move-

ments. She was, in this regard, a baby once more, although not
the baby she had been. Ann had lost her independence, it
seemed, her courage and curiosity along with it. At mealtime,
struggling to make the spoon meet her mouth, she was only too
eager when someone offered to feed her. She went right on wearing the diapers Julia had fashioned for her while she was asleep,
wouldn't even acknowledge the chamber pot. Perhaps most striking was the fact that she crab-walked around the house on her
bum instead of walking. "I can't," she'd say when they encouraged
her to try—this from the same Ann who had walked before she
could crawl. "She isn't herself," Moira remarked and said again
as time went by and Ann still wasn't walking. Julia had quit de-
fending Ann's cautiousness as a good thing, a change for the better.
"So what if she *isn't* herself?" she now retorted, though it hurt her
even to consider it, having taken real pride in the earlier, cleverer
Ann, the one she'd reared. To see Ann laugh and play with her doll,
no one would ever guess the time she had missed, but in an instant
her mood might change. Julia would come upon her staring at the
floor, her eyes crossed as an idiot's, and shake her gently to unlock
her gaze. "What is it, Annie, what's the trouble?" Ann usually responded with a question of her own—"What's this called?"—
pointing to the pinafore her doll was wearing or the buggy in which
it was riding, as if she'd been deep in thought, trying to recall.

Ann's speech was not impaired and she could still express herself quite well, despite a lapse in memory regarding certain words.
"I've changed my mind," she would say, pushing away her plate.

"But you love mashed potato," Julia insisted, watching with
dismay.

"No I don't. I don't anymore," Ann replied matter-of-factly.

But it was frustrating for her. She didn't like how they looked at her with surprise, saying "Annie, where's your lion's heart gone to?" when she was afraid to do things, like walk (she'd fall) or dig potatoes (her hands turned brown) or scatter the chicken feed (all those hens pecking around her ankles).

One Sunday morning on the way home from Mass, Ann informed them that she was changing her name. She was riding along in the pram, her legs dangling out over either side. Matty, who went faithfully to church these days, was pushing, beads of sweat gathering. He'd heard what she'd said, but he was too out of breath to speak.

"But why?" asked Moira, leaving the gooseberry bush behind, trotting to catch up.

"You're already Ann," said Julia warily, shaking her head at Moira's offering.

Matty paused, popped a couple of berries into his mouth. He said, "Ann was your mother's mother's name."

Well that might be, but Ann didn't like the name (claimed she never had); it was too plain. "I want a name that suits me." She held out her hand for more berries. She said, "Agnes maybe."

Moira laughed.

Julia said, "That's Widow Scully's name!"

Matty wiped his face with his handkerchief. "The name Agnes never did appeal to me."

"All right. Then Siobhan," said Ann.

"Siobhan?" Julia guffawed.

"It's too fancy," said Moira.

"I like fancy," retorted Ann.

Matty sighed. "I'm afraid my tongue would never get used to it."

Ann could see they were not an easy crowd to please. Brigid, Dierdre, Kate: They made quick work of her favorite names. In the end she returned to Siobhan, stubbornly folding her arms across her chest, tears in her eyes because she hadn't been asking their opinion in the first place.

"We never said we didn't like the name," Julia said, placating.

"It's a bit different from Ann, though, isn't it?" commented Matty.

"I'm different from Ann," sniffled Ann.

"Siobhan," said Moira, addressing Ann. "Siobhan, aren't you too proud to be riding about in a baby pram?"

Ann didn't respond. They rounded the bend. Matty puffed up the hill, Moira and Julia taking hold at either side of the carriage and pulling. Suddenly Ann piped up. "It's true, I wouldn't mind walking."

And so she took her first steps, three months after she woke, with Moira holding one of her arms, Julia holding the other, and Matty leading the way down the road, amazed at how the carriage glided empty. She teetered but she didn't fall and, thus encouraged, decided that Siobhan was capable of all sorts of things that Ann wasn't. Oh, she still needed coaxing; for instance, if the wind was blowing she didn't like to collect the laundry. It was unnerving the way the sheets billowed up into her face and made her dizzy. She started to totter and went down on her knees where it was safe, waited for Julia to come to the rescue. Julia could see that Ann was far from confident on her feet, but she told herself, gazing pensively at the rustling sheets (and told Ann, too, as she helped her up off the ground), that it was nothing plenty of practice wouldn't remedy.

Julia gave Ann tasks to do that required being on her feet and using her hands simultaneously: dish washing, bread kneading, sweeping. "It's for your own good, Siobhan, really." As long as Julia called her by the proper name, Ann complied. It was nice to have some assistance around the house, and over time Ann's movements did reflect a certain confidence, if not a speck of grace. "I'm off to the henhouse," Julia said one afternoon, gathering up the basket, throwing a shawl about her shoulders. "Would you mind setting the kettle, Siobhan, and we'll coddle a couple of eggs for our supper." She started for the door, calling out as she closed it behind her, "Fire'll need stoking."

Julia did not witness Ann's fall, but she heard the kettle clang against the hearthstone, followed by a denser, heavier sound that brought her running to the house with the egg basket bouncing. It was horrible to behold: kettle water seeping across the floor, the top of the kettle reverberating like a cymbal, and the raised edge of the stone that had facilitated the fall jutting conspicuously into Julia's knees as she kneeled beside Ann's convulsing body. All was quiet in a moment, a cat lapping at the puddle of water under the table. Julia gathered her wits and found Ann's pulse. She rolled her over gingerly and saw at once the bump on her head, dark as a plum. Her eyes were closed, her lips parted; there was blood in her mouth and Julia could see the tooth marks on her tongue. She lifted her carefully, carried her to the bed. And stood there, staring thoughtfully: You too, Siobhan, you've drifted off.

Ann's sleep was different this time, neither peaceful nor deep. Her eyelids were squeezed tight and she clenched her teeth. Her thumbs twitched and her breath raced, at times becoming short and choppy. At night it was particularly unnerving, the whole house awake, listening. As well, she was more difficult to feed now, even with the stomach tube; she vomited frequently. They feared that she'd choke, and learned to turn her over, thump her on the back, and scoop what they could out of her mouth—in fact grew so accustomed to doing it that it was simply a part of the feeding routine. It was Moira who first spoke up: "Are we supposed to do this every time she eats?" There was no reply, not even in her own mind.

Several days later, Ann stopped breathing altogether. As it happened, Matty was right there, a book in his lap. He saw Ann turn blue. His first impulse was to jump up and shake her, which was enough to rouse her heart, apparently. She resumed breathing. But after that he was afraid to leave her side, sat up the whole night and went off to his sheep exhausted. His vigilance was justified, he learned later that evening, slumped at the supper table staring vacantly at his food. She'd stopped breathing twice more, and both times Julia'd brought her round with a good shake, the same as Matty. A victory, in Julia's eyes, if taxing just to sit in wait.

Exhausting was only the half of it. It was demoralizing to live as they did, from one risky episode to the next. A rush of adrenaline when she did stop breathing, time standing still while they attempted to rouse her, and a sigh of relief—Amen!—as the dark blue in her cheeks faded back to gray. But the next hour, that which followed her resuscitation, had to be the longest, most hopeless part of any day. Particularly if there was nothing else waiting—a feeding, a diaper change. Life restored to normal never felt so troubling. They might get up and add more peat to the fire. There was a sack of beans at the bedside, with which Matty occupied himself shelling, delighting in the shiny purple beans, like a handful of jewels (a pity how they faded in the soak). Julia darned socks and sweater elbows. Moira stared out the window, fighting off sleep and profound futility.

The storm rode in on balmy winds, unsuspected as the alfalfa sprouting early. The sky thundered. Cold rain pelted the mountain. The sheep were trapped, grazing in the valley. They were able to rescue only two-thirds, forcing the animals along in the downpour, will against will, reaching the farm just before nightfall. They moved the herd, dehydrated and jittery, into the barn and filled the troughs. Matty wrung his hands at the meager numbers. For a moment he looked sharply at his fingers—gone ghostly white and empty of feeling. Frostbite, he realized, squeezing them grimly between his thighs; no time to bring them back slowly. The sheep weren't drinking. Their shallow breathing hadn't ceased. Matty eyed their heaving bellies and determined it was bloat, brought on by the feast of alfalfa and the stressful journey down off the mountain.

He knew that Moira knew nothing about sticking sheep, but he sterilized the trocar over a lantern just the same and told her to make haste. Holding the wheezing ram between his knees, Matty groped with his numb hands to part the thick fleece. "Now, Moira," he urged, "forcefully!" She stuck the blade beneath the flank, puncturing the swollen rumen. Gasping in horror as she pushed the tube in. The trapped gases hurried out and the sheep belched. Matty moved quickly to the next sheep, pulling it to its feet. Moira shook herself and readied the knife, but as she went to thrust in the blade, the ewe slipped from Matty's hold. Blood spurted out. The ewe let out a dreadful sound and sank to its knees.

"Never mind her," said Matty, groping for another sheep.

Moira swallowed her disgust. "We could do with Julia's help," she said, watching her father struggle.

"She's with Ann," Matty replied.

"We'll lose the flock for Ann," Moira muttered.

Matty held the ewe steady. Moira pierced the animal and it vomited, relieved. But for every sheep Matty held on to that night, another he let go of, cursing, wringing his numb hands. The sheep were gasping for air, collapsing onto the floor of the barn. They flopped over sideways on distended bellies. By morning, the stalls were strewn with bloated carcasses. The stench was overwhelming. Half the flock had perished. There was the likelihood of rotting fleece to consider, and ewes aborting under duress. Tax gatherers knocking at the door. To Matty, it didn't make much difference that it was Irish tax now, instead of English. The farm would be bankrupt—not that it hadn't ever been before, but Matty had been younger, with a wife and plenty of pride. He hardly remembered it.

Da, we can't keep on like this," Moira said to him as she crouched on her haunches in front of the fire, a cup of tea cradled in her hands.

"We have no choice," he replied.

"This wouldn't have happened if we hadn't let the flock wander unattended so long," she persisted.

Matty was silent, staring intently in the direction of Ann's bed. "Storm rose up out of nowhere," he said finally, dismissing it. He turned to the open window. Moira's and his own soiled clothing flapped heavily in the cold rain. Behind the barn, the dead sheep were piled high. The wind began to blow the rain at a slant. He latched the shutters. He could feel the damp in the soles of his feet, there being no cellar below, only the hard-packed earth for floor, one threadbare rug in front of the fire, which Heleen had woven years ago, gone gray from the soot now. Sometimes after hard rain they would find snails under the rug. According to Heleen, snails were good luck. Weeds, which they also found, sprouting in the cracks in the walls and beneath the windowsills, such as the one he noticed now, were not lucky at all. Matty took hold of the scraggly stalk and pulled, but it slipped through his stiff fingers as sure as everything else.

Father Riley came that night, came and prayed with them, and stayed on afterwards for a cup of tea and to offer his counsel, wrestling as usual with his words. How to explain to a family, a parish, an entire population that had lost so much already—in famine, in the war fought for England, and in their own strife for freedom—that their suffering was not without meaning? The link between God's benevolence and the Irish seeming so abstract at moments such as this that it would take a poet's understanding. And living hand to mouth left people no time for reflection. He looked around the table at their somber faces. "Perhaps God exists, in part"—Father Riley sighed—"so that, in cases of illness or death which we can neither remedy nor prevent, we do not hold ourselves responsible." He wondered if he was making any sense. He glanced over at the bed. Ann was a bag of bones, with a bruise on the side of her head as hard as a stone. He shook his head for the tragedy. "Life is dear," he said.

"But she doesn't have a life!" Moira burst out. "Just look at her, Father. She can't even breathe by herself."

Julia was quick to correct. "Sometimes she needs help breathing."

Moira shook her head, groping. Her tongue felt thick. "It isn't fair to her," she pleaded.

"But it hasn't anything to do with what is fair," Father Riley replied. "Or at least not as far as we can comprehend." He paused. "She's in God's hands."

"God's hands?" Moira held up her own hands. "Father, *these* are the hands that rouse her every time her breath fails."

"It's hardly an extraordinary measure you're taking," Julia spoke up. "You're just tired of the effort Ann's life requires. Admit it, Moira."

"I am tired!" shouted Moira. "And so are you."

Julia denied it.

"We're all tired," Matty interjected.

"Shall Ann die for it?" Julia shouted.

Father Riley removed his spectacles, unhooking one ear, then the other. He spoke sympathetically. He knew of several in the community who might be able to help with Ann's care. Widows, he said, husbands lost at the Somme. But it was beside the point, and they all knew it. Father Riley fell silent. Julia brought his hat and coat. He stood in the doorway with Matty talking in low tones about the weather (which was, finally, relenting). Faith was always a struggle, said Father Riley, and Matty nodded grimly, hands deep in his trouser pockets, tired of hearing it, frankly.

Moira stood at the well, the ladle to her lips, her first drink of the morning. She glanced over her shoulder—a pair of ravens on the barn roof—but her eyes were drawn to the foothills beyond, glowing golden in the dawn. The mountain beckoned. She carried the water to the house, but instead of going in she set the buckets inside the door where Julia would see them, eventually, without straying too far from Ann's bed. She turned and hurried back down the path, past the barn, to the pasture. She climbed the fence and, clutching the hem of her dress in her fist, waded through the wet grass, stepping high over a glistening spiderweb.

It was exhilarating—to be outside, to be free of the sick house (she'd been up, sitting wait with Ann half the night). Her stomach was howling, awakened by the water she had drunk. She did not consider where she was going. She was just running. Into the sun, it seemed, the way she moved up the incline, casting wild shadows, the whole mountainside bathed in light. She wiped her forehead with her sleeve, a gesture that collapsed the year on top of itself suddenly, returning her to that day, unsuspecting, and she gripped the rock, panting, recalling the unusual heat.

She walked on quiet feet through the meadow beneath the ridge, noting the daisies nodding their heads. She shivered with the breeze against her wet legs, the soles of her feet prickling. She half expected to feel the ground vibrating. Her senses were heightened to such a degree that reliving the stampede seemed her only possibility. She stood stock-still with her eyes closed and her jaw clenched, the flyaway strands from her braid pestering her cheeks. Wishing, of course, though it made little sense really, herself in Ann's place. There would have been no tragedy, she was sure of that; she would have run to safety, knew the distance between herself and an old apple tree without even looking. A deer fly buzzed about Moira's head. She swatted it. She felt the warmth of the sun at her back and kept walking.

On the ridge, she found a boulder on which to sit; didn't recall it being there a year ago, but she'd hardly been noticing the scenery. With her elbows on her knees and her chin in her hands, Moira peered down over the side of the ridge to the grass below, which appeared yellow, drier than usual. They would have long since moved the sheep to something lusher. Nowadays, they hardly ever even grazed the herd at higher ground, it being time-consuming and the situation so dire at home. She could not be sure of the exact place where she'd seen the wolves; it had been so long ago and so much had been said since then about lies and tricks of the imagination that her self-confidence had suffered. Even then, the day after it happened, when she and her father had returned to collect the herd there'd been no proof of it. Other than the one ewe missing. But the rest of the herd hadn't run very far, which Matty said he would have expected given the scent of a predator; a good scare worked like endurance. Matty had walked in circles studying the ground, scratching his whiskers. He muttered something about tinkers' thievery. For there was not a single track or drop of blood to be found—though it could have rained on the mountain, disturbing evidence. It often did without the valley ever knowing it.

Moira flipped her braid back over her shoulder. By and by the wind blew it back to her, and, as well, thoughts of her mother, who'd taught Moira to braid her own hair when she was five years old, saying a good taut braid is a sign to others that you're able to take care of yourself. Heleen had kept a box of ribbon in the sewing basket and she let Moira choose for herself. The velvet was off-limits to Moira then because it attracted bears, by which Heleen meant boys (she called Matty "Da-bear," feeling playful). This left only solids or stripes, since polka dots reminded Moira too much of candy and would make her hungry worn around in

her hair all day. Moira sighed. She hadn't so much as brushed
her hair out all week. The braid was weary as could be, though
still far from unraveled, her mother having taught her well. And
further, she couldn't help thinking, her eyes clouding over, that
Heleen O'Leary was someone Ann had never known and now
there was little hope that Ann would ever be able to do her hair
for herself, let alone tie a bow.

It was the echo of the church bell that brought Moira to her
feet suddenly. Wiping her eyes, she started down, reckoning how
she'd descended the ridge the first time, heart pumping pure fear.
She had seen Julia kneeling as if in prayer and Ann's auburn curls
in the green grass. A year later, she was no longer afraid. She felt
oddly decisive passing back through the meadow. She stopped to
pick a few daisies, as she was in the habit of bringing flowers
home. They brightened the bedside and helped to mask the
smell. Julia would no doubt find fault in daisies, a morbid choice
she'd say, irritated primarily by Moira's disappearance this morning, a Sunday for goodness' sakes, the afternoon Latin Mass now
the only choice remaining.

She was surprised to find Julia crying. Moira quickly glanced
at the bed. Ann had just finished regurgitating her morning feeding and Julia had yet to clean it. "I couldn't find the water," she
complained, and Moira apologized for not bringing in the bucket,
though she could see that wasn't the half of it. Tears streaked
Julia's cheeks. She was wringing the washcloth so tight it was
unsettling. "It's just that . . ." she faltered, her eyes darting away
from Moira's shamefully. "I'm tired. You're right." Her shoulders
curled in, weeping now. Moira muttered something about how it
didn't much help that Da had gone off to Mass and left Julia to
fend for herself. Though, she added—since it was his turn to go,

his and Julia's both—he must have assumed she'd be right home. "I'm sorry," said Moira, reaching out for the washcloth. "Go on, collect yourself. Breath of fresh air. It's a fine day." As she stepped up to take the washcloth (Julia's hands didn't seem capable of surrendering it), something gave way inside and she felt tears at the back of her throat. She took a quick deep breath, which was how she often managed difficult moments, but her inhalation caught Julia's attention. There was no returning. Moira flung her arms around her sister. They hugged each other a long silent time, without any thought of letting go, as if it were that much easier than standing alone.

Two days later, near dawn. Moira was dozing off when Ann's rate of breath suddenly changed, sounding an alarm that reverberated throughout Moira's entire body. She was awake and alert at once, adrenaline coursing. Ann had not had an episode in several days. Her lips moved, ushering the air out, staccato. Moira glanced in the direction of the bedroom, still dark, as the window faced west. Ann's chest jerked up and down and Moira's fingers quivered, moist and itchy, of a mind of their own, for she should be busy now shaking Ann's shoulders, slapping her feet should that fail. Instead, Moira waited. Watching the soft skin beneath Ann's eyes go blue in the shape of crescent moons, standing by as the breath began to wear her down and her puffing cheeks hollowed out. It was a lifetime, wasn't it though—and she felt hateful for her impatience as well as her resolve. The devil himself. She groped impulsively for Ann's hand, but after a moment let it go. She turned her eyes to the light of dawn outside the window, listening keenly to the breath racing out. All at once it slowed and she reached out and felt for a pulse at Ann's throat—quiet, imperceptible, ceasing altogether now. In the strange stillness that immediately followed, Moira imagined her own heart stopped, frozen, garishly hung with icicles. She climbed into the bed beside Ann for some warmth, and kissed her forehead. She was asleep before the cock crowed.

For years to come Julia would wonder about Ann's death. Not a single brown egg to put her fears to rest that morning. She shook her head, counting the eggs. Did Moira ever do *anything* accidentally? The way Matty had claimed when he gave Julia the news. He had come into the bedroom while she was dressing, told her she needn't hurry. Ann was gone, passed on earlier this morning. Julia had turned to him, mouth agape. The room awash in sunlight. "It was an accident," said Matty. "Moira fell asleep." He cleared his throat. "Perhaps it was a blessing. She looks peaceful." Julia burst into tears. Ann had never in her life been peaceful. And what was more, Moira was not one to doze off unintentionally, not once in all these tired nights. She was too intense, too careful, to be taken unaware like that. Julia could not get past this. Moira had strong, deliberate opinions. She knew exactly what she did and didn't care about. The yolk, but not the white, for instance. She would just as soon leave the white of an egg behind, and often did (their mother could no longer protest), which was remarkable given how Moira otherwise licked away all traces of food; her bowl came away from the table sparkling.

"Murderer!" Julia breathed, startling the hens to their feet. She walked back to the house and set the eggs to boil. Sat clutching her teacup, the tears streaming down her cheeks. It was a fatal mistake to have conceded to Moira her own fatigue. Julia could not point a finger, nor level an accusation, without first thinking of their embrace the other day—and feeling, in part, culpable. To say nothing of betrayed. Her tongue stung for acting too hastily. She blew the tea to cool it. Julia could have gone on exhausted! Ann's needs defining every second of every moment and her own self-sacrifice eternally compelling.

She felt utterly lost. Just look around at the filth, the utter disarray of the house. Was this what she had to show for herself? She was loathe to picture the faces of the women who would come to clean for the wake. She took three bowls from the shelf, but she could not open her mouth to call her father and sister to the table. She felt she hated them both. Matty, for the excuses he made. And Moira right down to the dirt under her fingernails. She clanged a spoon against the hearthstone to make the breakfast known.

They washed and dressed Ann for the coffin. The sheets thrown back revealed her tiny shriveled body. Moira thought of feathers, of Heleen O'Leary sitting on the step plucking the Christmas goose. Moira would scramble to catch the feathers fluttering ahead of her every step. Later she would reach her hand inside the quilt before it was sewn closed and marvel at how soft and breathy it felt.

"What's a goose without its wings?" Heleen might say in an altogether different setting, explaining the cause and effect of something. Why she would not be baking a tea cake, shaking the empty sugar can emphatically. The way Moira wanted to shake Julia right now, forcing her understanding. *Would you look at Ann? She's made of air. It wasn't wrong of me.*

There were sores from lying so long in one place and a bald spot at the back of Ann's head. She had lain asleep twice as long the first time, but the erosion had not been as rapid. Then again they had not had to worry about choking and had changed her position routinely. Moira lifted each of Ann's arms so that Julia could rub lavender water underneath. Ann's limbs were already beginning to set. The blue pinafore had buttons and would not have to be pulled over her head like the red, but Julia insisted that red was Ann's favorite color. It wasn't worth arguing. They stuffed Ann's stiff, wooden arms through the sleeves. Dispensed with the woolen leggings only at Matty's insistence—they'd managed to roll the tights up over her knees and would have struggled all the way to her waist (there was no mistaking the resolve on Julia's face). "Leave her be, now," barked Matty, sick watching. He covered Ann's legs over with a blanket.

They waited for the coffin to arrive. Diffident, in silence. The kettle sweating, refilled. A chipmunk scurried along the window ledge and into a hole in the wall of the house. Julia turned to Moira, her eyes bright with pain and disbelief, for she had been Ann's mother and now that Ann was lost to her, so was Heleen O'Leary. "How could you have fallen asleep?" Moira went numb under her sister's gaze, humility stinging her cheeks. For it was vivid as the morning to her, suddenly, why her father had lied. She glanced at Matty but he looked away. "I'm sorry," Moira said and hung her head in shame. The truth like a stone wall dividing them.

Matty had tried, at first, to revive Ann, but Moira had awakened and pulled him away, telling him it was no use. Ann was gone for good. He had looked askance, his eyes searching Moira's face, before he realized: She'd let her sister die.

"I had to," Moira had pleaded.

He had turned away, dazed.

"I had to," she'd insisted. Then she had become angry, accusing, "*You* were too afraid."

"It was fear for a reason," Matty had replied, the courage in her confounding him. He had gazed down at Ann, uttering a silent prayer for her. She looked no different than she had the past several weeks, the life long since gone out of her, it was so. It was the relief he felt that would always trouble him.

Matty lied to Julia because he could otherwise be of no help to either of them. He knew his limits. He wanted only to be left alone. He had felt this acutely, ever since the funeral, which he endured like Sunday Mass, a litany of farm chores reverberating in his head. He even skipped out on the wake, which was something unheard of. The entire village turned out for it, as there was a baked ham, sweet breads, and pies, to say nothing of freely flowing drink. The crowds, the attention spoiled Matty's appetite. He couldn't bear it, and withdrew to the barn, walked among the new lambs counting. He raked the muck from the stalls, taking heart in the work, the stalls having been first on his list that morning. He was laying down new hay when Father Riley came looking for him, full of concern for the loner he was; desire for solitude at a time like this ought to be checked, Father said. "Remember what it led to after Heleen. Learn from the past, Matty." Matty shuddered. Oh, Father, if you only knew. . .Setting down the rake, extinguishing the lantern, latching the barn door behind him.

It was an unusually clear evening, the heavens shining, said Father Riley, who had some knowledge of the configurations, and paused beside the hen house to point out Ursa Major, Cassiopeia, and the Seven Sisters (though only five were visible). Wasn't it amazing, thought Matty, having never before considered the sky in quite this way, and he wondered to himself could it be the same set of stars for everybody, across the ocean, for instance. Just then Father sighed, saying the sky was what the world had in common, and how it gladdened his heart to know it. At that, the hairs on Matty's neck stood on end, as it proved true the claims about priests reading minds. He was thankful for the stirring of the hens, which was reason not to tarry, as well the strain it was on his neck after bearing Ann's coffin.

Several months had passed since Ann was buried. They were sitting with a flask of tea between them on a hillside that overlooked the bay. The scraggly flock grazed around them. "Ireland is beautiful country, but you cannot eat the scenery," declared Matty. He had been gathering his words all morning. "America will stand you a better chance in the long run."

Moira glanced at him. "America?"

"By boat," Matty said, rubbing a hand over his stubbly chin. "In a year I'll have enough set aside for your and Julia's passage."

Moira could not believe her ears. (Her father had never cared to save for anything.)

Matty brought the flask to his lips, eyed her up and down while he swallowed. "Seventeen years, are you? Ought to find yourself a good husband in America, fellow with a bit of know-how."

She was eighteen. She laughed with outrage. "I've no mind for marriage!"

"Soon enough, you will."

She shook her head, confused. "Da, I want to work sheep."

"Won't do to have you hanging about," Matty said, snapping the flask closed.

She could fall on her knees pleading, but he would be put off by such a display. "Please, Da. I don't want to go," she said helplessly.

Getting to his feet, Matty whistled for the dogs. He turned to face her, but paused midway. Reckoning a lingering anger toward her. "I'll take this flock to the grave with me," he said, and thwacked his cane against a rock. His rounded shoulders, the hump in his back, shirt collar brown with sweat: He strode off. Climbed the rocky incline surely as an old goat and, at the top, called out to her. "Sheep won't wait, Moira!"

In the autumn of 1928, Moira and Julia paid a final visit to the graves, the two of them kneeling in the early morning gloom in front of the unmarked stones. Matty stood behind them. There were several gangly rosebushes in this corner of the cemetery, in desperate need of pruning. And although Ann would hardly care about such a thing, Moira felt somehow she owed her mother an apology. The cemetery was an intrinsically lonely place. Moira hoped that Ann's company was a welcome thing to Heleen. Ann was a sweet girl, really, once you were accustomed to her. That is, if you were patient—because Ann didn't like to be rushed and she was slower now than ever. She hoped her mother wouldn't mistake Ann's behavior for insolence when, if anything, it was stubbornness, and hardly Ann's fault once you considered she was always being bossed around by her sisters, and sisters weren't mothers even when they tried hard to be.

Soon Matty said it was time to go, so they climbed back into the cart, and pulled the blanket up over their damp knees.

"Giddyap now," Matty called out. The horse started off straight away. A smile touched Matty's face. He hardly needed the reins, and he remarked that Macaffrey's horse must still remember his voice from all the time they'd once spent looking for ice cream. No point in mentioning that the horse plied this same route to Bantry with the mail sack every week; Moira could only think that her father's good mood was due to her and Julia leaving.

The houses along the road were just waking, thick smoke puffing up from the chimneys. Except for McDermotts, where the lights were all turned up and the fire had been going steady for some time; the midwife's bicycle was parked outside. Kitty O'Rourke opened the shutters to see them passing and waved. They came upon Tom Healy's milk cart. Tommy drew up alongside, bottles softly tinkling, and said so long, pressing a coin into Moira's and Julia's hands. In the old days, after the famine, when it was every-one and their sister leaving for America, there were parties— "American wakes" they came to be called—where people would gather to wish you well and meaningfully slip you money. But it was too hard on the pocket with someone new leaving every week. And just as well, Moira felt, as going off to her death was hard enough without the party.

The sun was burning off the clouds by the time they reached the bay, but they'd been alone with their thoughts for such a long while now that it seemed strange to speak, if only to praise a fine day. Julia put a hat on her head and pretended not to notice Moira staring. She'd sewn a strip of polka-dotted ribbon on the hat for a band; as well, she was wearing Heleen O'Leary's salmon pink gloves on her hands, having come across both the hat and gloves in the trunk while packing. She considered them birthday presents to herself, if anyone was asking.

They paused at roadside to water the horse and then again to eat the supper Julia had packed. The sun went down and the stars came out and Matty said she's practically asleep on her feet, speaking of the horse. He pulled off the road, hopped down, unlatched the cart. The horse gave a soft snort. Her head bobbed up and Matty held her nose and stroked it. They spent the night in the meadow, lying side by side in the back of the cart, suffering the squeeze for the warmth (one of the two blankets having gone to the horse). They could hear the horse busily eating from the pail. All else was quiet, still, except when they gasped in unison at the sight of a shooting star.

The second day was cloudy, drizzling by late afternoon. The horse's pace turned anxious, ever since Bantry. At dusk, they rested the horse in an orchard; the apples took her mind off the unfamiliar road and they pushed on, reaching Cork just after midnight in a downpour. They paid a man to park the cart in a stable, paid him again for the privilege of sleeping there, since it wasn't an inn and he had no reservations about turning them out. The stable was dry, warm, but not near as familiar as a meadow, and the night inched by restlessly. Just before dawn, the street outside began to come alive and there was no longer any use in pretending to be asleep. Matty hitched the cart and they headed for the harbor, following along behind the pushcarts and tinker caravans. Moira and Julia had never in their lives seen so much activity. There was a different smell to the air and hordes of people; there were fruit and vegetable vendors, barrels and barrels of fish everywhere. Of course, it was the sight of the big ship that was truly daunting.

"No sad farewells," was the only thing Matty O'Leary could think to say as he carried Heleen's hope chest up the gangway for them. There was little time before the ship set sail and terrible confusion up and down the pier. It was all very distracting. A ship steward took their tickets and stamped their tuberculosis certificates. Passengers only, he said, barring Matty's entry. Matty shrugged, looking helpless. Julia stepped forward and clutched him, because he'd forgotten to give them the address of his brother in Boston. He dug around in his pocket until he found it, laughing nervously for having to be reminded. He handed Julia the slip of paper and she carefully tucked it away. Then he kissed her forehead, so unexpected that Julia was moved to put her arms around him. Moira's heart leaped watching. She met her father's gaze, sensed herself softening, but her feet stayed put. She was not giving in and since he wasn't either (he was holding up the line—he'd left the horse too long already), he could only turn and walk away.

So it was that in the waning days of the great Irish exodus, Moira and Julia departed. Moira was nineteen and Julia just turned eighteen—still young enough to travel on an excursion fare of sixty-five pounds each. As the ship pulled away from the shore, they were swept up in the excitement, pressed against the rails, waving. Julia's hat blew off and Moira caught it. Suddenly they were both laughing. It was a huge relief, a sister's company, at such a moment.

By day, they roamed about the deck talking with the other passengers. Those who already had family in America seemed to know an awful lot about the canneries, garment factories, and road-construction companies willing to hire new immigrants.

Americans, it was said, liked hard workers with short last names. "Drop the 'O' in the water," people encouraged. "Do well in America to have a name with a little less Irish in it." For the first few days it rained. It was impossible to see beyond the mist—thick, gray, concealing as a blanket. It curled their hair, softened their skin, eerily wrapped itself around each passing moment, cloaking the memory. The people turned up their collars and joked that, with mist such as this, perhaps the boat had never left Ireland. But the captain posted the ship's progress daily on the door to the steerage, and someone else carved the moons into the stairwell. Julia was seasick much of the time, but Moira felt fine. There was plenty to eat if you didn't mind the lines. Parlor games were organized on clement days—cards and jackstones, which was played with a hard rubber ball and a handful of metal pieces, quite like a game Moira and Matty played in the fields except that they used pebbles and a stone, tossing the stone in the air since it could hardly be expected to bounce.

At night they were confined to the bowels of the boat, where it was suffocatingly crowded. The ocean's every move was felt, and the air stank of urine, sweat, and vomit. It was near impossible to sleep what with strangers on either side, to say nothing of the noise—the boat groaning, babies crying, and several men who liked to sing and smoke too, even though it was forbidden in the steerage. Amidst the tumult of the night, they caught snatches of someone whistling. They each clung intently to the tune. It was familiar, a song of their mother's, Julia knew, but it made Moira think of Matty. She had come upon him whistling in the fields from time to time, wouldn't have known he could carry a tune otherwise.

It was early one morning, light streaming in, their first sunny day, that Moira lifted her head and turned to see the young man in the berth across the way who, amidst all the boat's turbulence, was busy drawing—and whistling, though he stopped as soon as he realized he'd waken her.

At daybreak on the third of October, 1928, the boat entered Boston Harbor and everyone scrambled up to the deck for a glimpse of America. Some shouted and cheered. Julia and Moira clung to each other. "What will we do?" Julia whispered, gazing nervously out at the nearing shore. Moira's heart was racing too. She unwrapped the chocolate bar she'd saved for this occasion, broke it in two. "Here," she said to Julia, who cheered instantly. It was a dear thing to be eating chocolate in the morning.

As they stood in line inside the quarantine station waiting stoically for eye and scalp examinations, the young man with the sketchbook tapped Moira on the shoulder and handed her the portrait he'd done of her. Whatever could he be drawing? she remembered wondering, what with rats running over the bed piles, people sleeping fitfully and vomiting.

"What's your name?" he wanted to know.

"Moira Rose O'Leary," she told him, shyly taking the drawing from him.

"It looks just like you," Julia remarked.

But Moira was horrified by the portrait, how tired she appeared, how afraid. "I don't want this," she said after a moment, handing it back.

"Of course you do," said Julia, mortified, restraining her sister's arm. "Thank you."

The young man was blushing, but he walked away whistling.

II

Unity

(1928–1947)

As it turned out, 7A Foster Street where Francis O'Leary once resided was gone altogether, condemned after the last influenza outbreak. They had spoken with the neighbor two doors down, whose name was Mary Kelly, one of the few Irish remaining on the street (the neighborhood was now Negro, she'd told them, shrugging). She shouldn't remember Francis O'Leary but for the weeping after his youngest was killed falling through the window. The family moved out soon after. If she remembered correctly, the missus had a sister in Montana—but then, didn't everybody? It was Mary Kelly who had directed Moira and Julia to the boardinghouse. A perfectly decent place, she'd claimed; they wouldn't have to hide under their hats coming and going.

Water stains soiled the plaster. The paint was peeling. The

mattresses had holes and the sink smelled fierce. They sat in stunned silence, resting back-to-back on their mother's hope chest in the center of their rented room. Julia didn't dare speak. If she spoke, she'd cry and it would be her third time today and Moira had already said enough was enough, firmly, there was no returning. Julia would not have been able to bear the sight of Matty anyway. They'd have been better off trusting the hawkers outside the currency exchange (thick as honey bees around them as they had huddled marveling at their American dollars) for a place to spend the night! Moira got up and stood at the window. Julia's eyes followed and soon they were both absorbed in the busy view below. A dead work horse had been left to rot in the road. Automobiles whizzed past the stiff gray animal. There were several pushcarts on the corner selling fruit and cut flowers. Before long, shopkeepers came out to roll in their awnings. A lamplighter was making his way down the avenue.

The employment agency was a mile from the boardinghouse, no more than a stone's throw to them except that they were lugging along their mother's hope chest, wary of leaving it behind in the room, both for fear of theft (signs were posted everywhere relieving management of responsibility) and the mice that had gnawed a hole in the lid overnight. Julia's breath heaved and Moira's feet throbbed inside the lace-up boots from the Little Sisters of Charity. They turned deaf ears to the buses rumbling past since they were pinching pennies.

As long as Moira and Julia insisted on being employed as a team, which the clerk claimed didn't make sense, their skills being so different, their choices were limited. Very few houses were still employing domestic servants, live-in help having become a luxury since the Depression. As well, the job meant giving up a certain amount of freedom, which most girls nowadays weren't interested in doing.

These were anxious days of bread and jam and nothing but their fingers to spread it. They walked through the market hall with their eyes popping out, and argued over whether they could afford the apples, which stall had the most appealing vegetables, and why anyone in their right mind would buy a rotten yellow cucumber. Moira said the cucumbers must be feed for the pigs and goats, and Julia, laughing, said she hadn't noticed any farms amidst the brick and cobblestone—more likely the cucumbers were for pickling.

The cucumbers were bananas, they soon found out. Their new employer, Mrs. Joseph Hadley, liked hers sliced on her breakfast cereal, breakfast cereal being one of the few ready-made foods of which she wasn't skeptical. She disapproved of canned goods and baker's loaves. She also eschewed such up-to-date conveniences as the vacuum cleaner, wringer washer, and the gas stove, which was just as well, since she might otherwise have done with one house girl instead of two. Mrs. Hadley was a widow twice over, with three grown daughters. Her first husband had made his fortune in furs, the second had been a banker. By her own admission, she preferred widowhood to marriage.

As they stood before her in the servants' entry, Mrs. Hadley looked Moira and Julia up and down carefully. On Monday and Wednesday they were to do the washing and ironing and polish the silver. On Tuesday and Thursday they would dust, sweep, and scrub the floors and front staircase. Friday was reserved for window washing and rug beating, Saturday for cleaning out the

fireplaces and the coal stove. They were off on Sunday and free
to do as they pleased, unless there was a household emergency—
bats flapping about in the stairwell or the cook taking ill, in which
case Mrs. Hadley would need their help. On such occasions,
Mrs. Hadley said, she'd refrain from ringing them until after
they'd returned from church. Mrs. Hadley had been employing
Irish girls for years and had become accustomed to their religious
zealotry. Generally speaking, she approved of it, as she believed
it kept them chaste longer and thus longer in her service.

The cook led the way up the narrow servant staircase. The
footman brought up the rear with Heleen O'Leary's hope chest,
banging it from step to step. Liza Farmer was the cook's name,
but they were to call her Cook. Only Mrs. Hadley ever referred
to her by name. She had been a part of the Hadley household
for several years now, and she could vouch for it being a first-
rate place of employment. Mrs. Hadley was particular, but not
fussy. When she said a three-minute egg she meant it, but, on
the other hand, she wasn't one to interfere in the organization of
the pantry.

Breaking in the new girls wasn't the cook's job customarily, but
Mrs. Hadley was unusual in that she didn't keep a head servant,
other than Doyle the butler and Cook, herself, whose jobs required considerable expertise. All the other servants were on
equal footing—which caused more problems than it solved,
frankly, but if Cook were them (and she wasn't, thankfully) she
wouldn't hold her breath waiting for the situation to change.
There wasn't a mistress in the world more set in her ways.

Cook unlocked the door. It was a corner room with a slanted
ceiling and a window overlooking the street. The room was plainly

appointed with two narrow beds already made up and a set of painted wooden shelves between them. An old oak wardrobe stood against the far wall, and beside it a stout dresser with six drawers, on top of which sat a porcelain pitcher and basin. The lavatory was at the end of the hallway, Cook explained, and was shared by all the female servants, so it was necessary to go about one's business expeditiously. Baths were permitted once a week. Breakfast was at six, lunch at one or one-thirty depending, and dinner some time after the Hadleys finished theirs and the table had been cleared. Servants at the Hadley house took their meals together, seated at the long table in the kitchen. They would no doubt find the meals nutritious and plentiful, said Cook. Roasted chicken, poached fish, fresh fruit and vegetables. Mrs. Hadley didn't skimp on the help. She gave Cook free rein with the ordering and even encouraged her to serve roast beef once a week as it was critical to the blood nowadays.

Cook handed over the room key. She was preparing to go. "Mrs. Hadley will want you fitted for uniforms first thing in the morning."

Moira roused herself. "By chance is there a morsel left over from dinner tonight?"

Cook raised an eyebrow. "Biscuits and a bit of the chowder perhaps."

"My sister and I, we haven't had a proper meal in days," Moira explained.

Cook said she would send up a tray in the dumb waiter and showed them where they could retrieve it, at the head of the staircase. But just so that they knew, it was an irregular request, and they were best advised to keep the dishes in their room until morning and then exercise discretion returning them. Mrs. Hadley didn't approve of servants eating at all hours, let alone outside the dining area.

The door closed behind her. Moira glanced brightly over at her sister. Julia returned the smile; *she* would have gone to bed starving rather than ask for anything to eat. Moira was shameless. But wasn't it a comfort to know that food was soon coming?

The first time Julia turned on the bathroom faucet in the Hadley house and saw the water come rushing down, she gave a shout. What to do about the waste in the bowl was a mystery until she noticed the chain dangling down (at the boardinghouse they had flushed with a bucket of water, the same as back home). She looked on wide-eyed, beguiled, the back of her hand pressed to her mouth. Julia and Moira were both forever trying to blow the electric lights out. Even their uniforms, which were unremarkable—plain blue, with tucks at the chest that squared off the bosom unbecomingly, Julia felt—possessed a certain novelty in that they fastened with zippers. Granted, the novelty quickly wore off; the zipper was always catching and, being at the back of the dress, made life fairly miserable. Moira repeatedly tore her uniform yanking the zipper free and then it was five minutes' harried sewing, the clock ticking audibly, because tardiness was something Mrs. Hadley did not tolerate.

They were schooled in how to set and wait table by the butler, Mr. Doyle. It was Julia who, in her first attempt, achieved a perfect place setting, giving Doyle reason to smile (his chipped front teeth marring an otherwise impeccable appearance). Julia showed a natural inclination for the tasks of the table, declared Doyle, smile fading as he glanced over at her sister, hair straying from her cap, unable to tell the wineglass from the water glass. Or the fish fork from the salad fork, butter plate from dessert plate. Moira would benefit from learning her right from her left, Doyle said. Details. Everything just so. And many times over, depending on the number of guests—at the very least four, as Mrs. Hadley didn't like the look of an empty table, even if she was dining by herself. For the life of her, Moira could not seem to remember the particulars: flowers to be removed from table and set on back buffet once guests were seated; grape scissors in a velvet drawstring bag, unsheathed and laid out before the fruit course; glasses, wine and water, scrupulously refilled; conversation ("chitchat," Doyle called it) if and only if, Mrs. Hadley solicited it.

"Smells heavenly!" Moira would chirp as she brought out the food, or, "Cook's outdone herself this evening, ma'am." She always spoke loudly, which Mrs. Hadley, who was a bit hard of hearing, appreciated. "Well," Mrs. Hadley would say, eyes trailing the platter of glazed ham while, with her fingertips, she stroked the handle of her fork, "Liza certainly deserves praise." Mrs. Hadley loved her supper all right. Her cheeks turned pink as she ate. The folds of her chin jiggled as she ushered forth a satisfied little snort from the back of her throat. Moira stood wait beside the buffet, her mind wandering off, remembering her mother's pig. It had been a gift to Heleen from Matty, following a prosperous spring. Too smart for the barn, said Heleen, and let the piglet run loose in the house while Matty was out. She fed the pig swedes and potato peels, taught him to fetch and come when called. The pig dozed with the kittens on the hearthstone. But by spring the next year, the pig had become unwieldy, demanding. Biting the knob off the door to be let in. Sending her pig off to be slaughtered was, like losing a child, a mixed blessing, Heleen said, her back to the window as Matty ushered his livestock down the road.

The best thing about working for Mrs. Hadley was that Moira no longer needed to wonder about her next meal. Except to try to guess the dish that belonged to the savory smell wafting through the house by five o'clock each afternoon. Her head heavy with the sweet kitchen haze as she swept and mopped the stairway. One day she came across a tray of delicate cakes in the butler's pantry. She hovered adoringly, absently wiping the drool away. "Don't even consider it," she heard someone say. Wheeling around, she found Cook standing in the doorway holding a tube of cake frosting. "Mrs. Hadley counts," Cook informed her. Moira's moist, itchy hands fell at her sides. She mumbled that she was innocent and moved out of the way.

Several days later while she and Julia were cleaning one of the guest bedrooms, they discovered a dollar bill on the floor beneath the bureau. Moira hissed at Julia not to touch it. Perhaps it was another trap. But if it wasn't a trap, they couldn't just leave it. Mrs. Hadley would think they hadn't swept the room thoroughly, Julia pointed out. They decided to set the bill on top of the bureau, overtly pinned beneath the clock.

"She's suspicious of us," Julia said, becoming angry. "It's because you've turned away from the church."

"It doesn't mark me untrustworthy," Moira said defensively. But she had seen the apprehension on Mrs. Hadley's face that very first Sunday. Mrs. Hadley had waltzed into the servants' kitchen in her dressing gown. She had stopped short upon seeing Moira at the table, eating her breakfast. Rather crossly she'd said that she was under the impression that Catholics fasted before church, taking nothing but tea until afterwards.

"You're quite correct," Moira replied.

"Are you ill, then?" Mrs. Hadley asked.

"Oh no, ma'am. I'm fine. But I've made up my mind to leave the church." It was then that Moira had noticed the small glass pitcher Mrs. Hadley was carrying and gathered that she had come in to the servants' kitchen to snitch some cream for her coffee.

"Oh? I see," Mrs. Hadley'd said uneasily. "Well then, Moira, since you have the time this morning, be so kind as to clean out the coal stove for me. My evening entertaining got in the way of it yesterday, and it really shouldn't go another day."

It was the dirtiest work in the house. The ashes had to be raked out and the stove and fire chamber thoroughly scoured. "A proper penance," Julia said, when she came home and saw Moira, apron covered in soot, shoveling on the fresh coal. Moira eyed her coolly. "Since when are hats and gloves permitted at Mass?" she wanted to know. Julia replied that all the ladies wore them. "My own are hardly fashionable. Trimming the brim might help." Holding the hat in one hand, she gave it a twirl. "It's a lovely church," she went on. "Very festive. An organ in the balcony, though you'd think the music were coming right out of the sky the effect is so extraordinary. After the service, tea and coffee were served in the basement. Everyone was chatting it up. I met several people, including the priest, Father O'Neil, who went over the schedule of services with me." She crossed her arms, regarding Moira. "I wrote down the confessional hours for you." Moira opened the drafts and stirred the coals.

. . .

Somewhere out there in the middle of the Atlantic, along with the 'O's in front of names and worthless Irish coins, Moira must have let go her faith. One of those times she leaned over the railing, her hair blowing across her eyes, and felt the salt wind slap her cheeks. She had hoarded dinner rolls on the boat. Julia had told her she ought to be ashamed of herself. But Moira had never understood her sister's willpower and reserve. Moira simply took one look at the rolls and smelled her opportunity, as sure as fat frying. Turned her pockets inside out, later, and watched the crumbs blow away. Empty—free, if she was willing to see it that way.

It felt to Moira that her faith was always on the tip of her tongue. Elusive, easier forgotten. Like the recitation of the rosary at Ann's bedside (choking her fingers with the string of beads to keep from noticing her stomach rumbling). Or the rule to fast before partaking in Communion; regardless of what she'd just eaten (a stale crust or bruised apple out of the pig's trough), she kneeled, mouth open, helpless as a nestling.

"But who will I ride with on the trolley?" Julia had whined that one Sunday.

"All the good Catholics, naturally," Moira had said bitterly. She'd rolled over in bed, tried to go back to sleep, but once her sister closed the door (Moira could hear her careful footsteps on the stairs), the room felt so quiet, so hollowed out she could have cried, or changed her mind—except that she was far too stubborn. Like a potato in the ground after a hard rain. Pull until you were blue, she wasn't coming.

Her disillusionment with religion she likened to a pebble gone sour in her mouth. A pebble staved off hunger for a short while, but then she would spit it out on the ground and go and steal an egg from the henhouse. Crouch behind the barn sucking up the yolk, using her teeth to free it, the white being sour as a runny nose and just as much a waste of time when you were hungry. She threw the eggshell over the fence and went to the well to rinse her smarting hands, pecked raw by the hens. One day she heard her mother calling her to the table, Come see. Heleen was baking bread. She had cracked open an egg and found it had no yolk in it. A marvel, an oddity. Nature was not beyond exceptions to the rule, said Heleen. And it was silly because that egg had nothing to do with her or the ones she'd stolen from the hens, but still Moira had felt guilty.

It was winter, 1930, when Julia came down with what everyone but she thought was the flu. Her symptoms—low fever, swollen glands, and tender, aching joints that caused her to limp—persisted beyond the three days she was permitted to stay in bed, so Mrs. Hadley decided that Julia should be relieved of her Monday and Wednesday duties in the dank basement washrooms and sent to work upstairs in the sewing room. The sewing room was warm and dry, and Julia found the colorful rolls of fabric and ribbons uplifting. She could abide Sheila Ross's lack of organization if she had to. Sheila Ross was Mrs. Hadley's personal seamstress. She worked at night (by day, she worked in a coat factory), so Julia and she overlapped only that last week before Mrs. Hadley's annual Christmas party. There was so much to do that Julia was compelled to sew through the afternoon and on into the night, leaving Moira to polish the silver by herself.

Julia had never used a sewing machine before and was duly impressed. (Between tasks, she soaked her fingers in her tea to bring back feeling.) She also had never worked from a commercial pattern book. "I'd be lost without the pattern," Sheila Ross was always saying, but Julia felt differently. The pattern was a crutch. It limited creativity. She turned her nose up. For Mrs. Hadley's evening gown, she designed the bodice and sleeves herself, ignoring Sheila's warning that Mrs. Hadley always had a certain look in mind and did not like being surprised. "But she's too wide and hasn't the shoulders for the style she's chosen," Julia insisted. "This design is much more becoming."

Mrs. Hadley was delighted as she stood for her fitting. Her ample size had always discouraged her from dwelling on herself in the mirror, but the effect of this particular gown was outstanding. "It suits me," she couldn't help commenting.

Julia's lips were holding pins, but across the room, Sheila Ross spoke up. "It's Julia's work, ma'am. Her own creation. She didn't use the pattern."

"Is that so?" said Mrs. Hadley, meeting Julia's eyes in the mirror. "Very impressive. Of course, I ought to have been consulted."

"Yes, ma'am," Julia stammered, spitting pins into her hand.

The Christmas party came and went, a big success, and Julia received a bonus for the extra work she'd put in. She hoped to buy herself a new hat and matching pair of gloves (the weather was dreadfully cold), but after an exhausting trip shopping, swollen ankles and a headache were all she had to show for it. She came to the conclusion that she could just as well (and for a fraction of the cost) purchase the suede and the lining and do the sewing herself. "So singularly striking were her results," Mrs. Hadley liked to confide to her friends. Straightaway she had requested replicas for herself. And once winter was over, there would be Easter bonnets to consider. Mrs. Hadley commissioned several.

The warmer weather improved Julia's flagging health. The limp was gone from her walk (she had grown so accustomed to favoring a leg that she would always feel more confident taking stairs one at a time). The absence of a fever restored energy and clarity, effecting a nearly euphoric sensation in her, for instance, if she had the window open in the sewing room, a moist breeze was blowing the pussy willows, and she could hear birds chattering. She was employed full time as seamstress now, replacing Sheila Ross, who took the news in stride (Sheila was engaged to be married, which meant that her days at Mrs. Hadley's were already numbered). Julia began riding the trolley downtown for the purpose of purchasing material. She wore her hat and gloves every time she went out, despite the fact that it was sixty degrees outside, and she took care not to remove them in the store, except when judging the texture of fabric. Julia fancied herself the buyer for her own company. No one besides the store clerk had to know that the account wasn't in her name, and she didn't mind that he knew. Timothy Brower was drunk on the job most of the time, but Julia was flattered that he cut long yards for her and sometimes slipped extra buttons into her parcel.

American buttons, Julia discovered, did not compare to Irish. They were overpriced and generally lacking in variety; American button manufacturers did not seem to appreciate quality. In a letter to her father, Julia made a request for buttons, adding a few extra dollars to the sum she and Moira normally sent. That was how it began: buttons crossing the sea inside of envelopes. Though Matty had learned to read, he was never much with pencil and paper. From the occasional note that he wrote, it was difficult to glean any news of home (other than the desperate weather and the number of new lambs in April). The buttons

Matty sent told more. Either extremely colorful and fancy (ornaments really, and she'd be hard pressed to imagine outfits for them), in which case Julia gathered her father'd been drinking, or else they were somber-toned, unoriginal, even ugly, and she could only assume he was feeling sorry for himself. Fortunately, there were exceptions to both rules—buttons so perfect that she imagined the shop clerk must have helped her father choose: octagonal-shaped glass, silver-plated engraved with leaves, shiny brass, and two dozen of the most delicate pearl buttons she could not stop thinking about. She envisioned a wedding dress, the opalescent pearls wandering down and into the sweeping waves of the train. Thinking whimsically of Timothy Brower with his brandy breath and girlish hands. He was attentive at least, and this was one satisfaction she had not designed and sewn herself.

Timothy Brower stood clutching his hat and a bouquet of carnations in the back entry. He had had some luck at the racetrack earlier in the day and was in a romantic frame of mind.

"He's asking for your sister," Cook said. "I'll ring the sewing room."

But Moira said, "Wait," turning off the water, drying her hands on her skirt. She could smell the liquor from where she was standing. She thought instantly of Matty, at whom her mother, six months pregnant with Ann, had hurled the teapot when it was learned he'd drunk the week's earnings. (Another mouth soon to feed, tax gatherer threatening, and as for the leaves floating around in their teacups from that day forward, they had their Da to thank for that, as well!) Moira stepped into the vestibule. "You've nerve to come calling on my sister stinking of the pub."

"I've flowers for her," stammered Timothy Brower.

Moira wheeled around. She went to ring the sewing room. She met Julia in the stairwell. "It's Timothy Brower," she whispered. "Red-nosed and reeling. Shall I send him off for you?"

"He's come calling?" asked Julia. She smoothed her skirt, fussed with her hair.

Moira looked appalled. "Tell me you're not pleased."

Julia did not meet Moira's eyes.

Moira grasped Julia by the shoulders. "He's a bloody drunk. He's nothing but trouble to you."

Julia associated carnations with funerals, since they were always for sale outside the cemeteries. Nevertheless, she was touched by the bouquet in Timothy Brower's hands. There was a little silver tin of butterscotch for her, too. The seal had been broken on it and she surmised from his slightly bulging cheek that he had tried to disguise the liquor on his breath. She fumbled for something to say to him. She could hear Cook's roasting pan entering the oven. Moira had stationed herself at the table, folding dinner napkins. Julia shook herself. "You're very kind, Tim Brower, but I won't mislead you. I can't accept your offerings." Timothy Brower's face fell. He quietly belched.

Julia could crumble. She leaned against the sewing-room door, panting. She had virtually flown up the stairs. Julia stared blankly at the heaps of brocaded material on the sewing table; curtains for the parlor, she reminded herself. Then came a knock and Julia swiftly turned the key in the lock. She squeezed her eyes shut on her tears. It was to her credit, Moira said through the door, she'd acted smartly. For goodness' sakes, he was hardly worthy of her. "You'd be better off entering the cloister than marrying Timothy Brower." But she'd said the same thing a year ago when

Julia agreed to go for a walk with Doyle. (Doyle? He was old enough to be her uncle! Besides which, he was greedy—or hadn't Julia noticed how he always helped himself to the last slice of roast beef on the table?)

Julia listened numbly to Moira's footsteps retreating down the hall. What with the nuns at primary school looking so fondly on her—attempting to protect her from the school-yard teasing and making her believe that the sloping aspect of her head was God's way of marking her so that He would recognize her straightaway come Judgment Day—it would have been surprising if Julia had *not* given thought to the sisterhood. In Ireland, it was one of the only routes a poor girl with intellectual interests could journey. Heleen O'Leary once said that she wished she had entered the convent herself, but of course it was not unusual for a married woman to have regrets. It was the charity, the devotion, and piety of the cloistered life that intrigued Julia, but whenever she set out to imagine such a life for herself, she would get distracted by the clothes: the habit and robe, black as coal, indiscriminately draped over the thin, fat, short, and tall. A silver or gold crucifix adorning her bosom, a handkerchief tucked rudely inside her sleeve for lack of any place else—but certainly not a handkerchief such as the embroidered linen one in her hand, sewn from a scrap Mrs. Hadley would otherwise have had her use to restuff a couch cushion.

Julia blew her nose. She tidied herself in front of the dressing mirror. Ireland was long ago. And it was true what people said: America was ripe for the picking. If not a nun, then what—who—might she become? Certainly, a girl as gifted as she would not be content to remain in the service of Mrs. Joseph Hadley forever. Julia didn't know how Moira kept from complaining. Moira performed the same laborious tasks day in and day out and, except in a strictly physical sense (Moira had always been athletic), reaped little satisfaction from it. Even the gleam of the just-polished silver was lost on Moira. She paid no attention to detail and seemed content with mediocrity, which, perhaps, explained why she wasn't preoccupied the way Julia was with the future. Honestly, Moira went about each day as if there were no tomorrow! All in all, it sickened Julia to think how, in spite of her own superiority, she so often succumbed to her sister's influence.

It had been almost four years since they'd come over on the boat, but Moira took one look at the sketchbook in his hand and remembered him. He was offering his seat. "Moira Rose O'Leary, won't you sit down?"

She shook her head, No thank you. The streetcar was crowded, and she would gladly have saved the fare and walked with Mrs. Hadley's groceries if it weren't for Julia, who'd said she'd faint before she'd go another step. Just then the streetcar lurched and several potatoes jumped from her shopping bag and rolled down the aisle. The young man retrieved them for her. She thanked him.

"Who is it?" Julia whispered in her ear.

"It's that fellow from the boat! The artist." Moira whispered back.

Julia paused. "After all this time, he remembers you?"

"Hush," said Moira, peering out the window. "I remember him, too." Clandestinely, of course; for instance, when she heard Julia's bathwater running, she would raise the lid on the hope chest to unearth the book in which Julia had preserved the portrait he'd drawn of her.

"Aren't you going to say hello, Moira?" Julia asked. She regarded the man curiously. A good-tempered, intelligent face. His hair was dark, curly, showing gray at the temples. He was wearing work clothes, canvas overalls, and by the soiled looks of them she gathered he was on his way home.

"Are you a bit more fatigued than your sister, perhaps?" he asked Julia.

In fact, her feet were throbbing. "Thank you. I wouldn't mind sitting a spell."

He stood up, taking hold of the same bar that Moira held. Moira met his gaze for an instant. She turned again to the window. Her breath was fogging the glass. For an Irishman, he was tall. She dared herself to look back up at him. He took this opportunity to introduce himself.

Michael Sheehan was nearly a whole foot taller than Moira, and ten years older. He was fortunate to have secured, upon arriving in Boston, a position as sternman on a large commercial fishing boat. He worked six days a week and reserved the seventh for church. But, he told Moira as the bus stood in traffic, he was an early riser—he'd be pleased if she would meet him in the mornings.

Before the city awoke, even before the fishing boats loaded for departure, they hurried down to the docks to meet him—Moira and Julia both. "It isn't right, you going alone," Julia had said, fussing to tie a silk scarf around her neck. She had sensed Moira's dismay and hastily thrust at her the scarf, which was delicately patterned with spring flowers. "Here. The blue in it suits you."

It was too cold to stand around so they walked, along the harbor, through the empty fish market, past the locked-up push-carts, the rows of garbage cans and rummaging cats. When the bakery opened, they bought jelly doughnuts and huddled at the counter, warming their feet. They were not a talkative couple, Julia noted, too shy or simply unaccustomed to socializing, but now and then Michael Sheehan asked Moira something and she managed a curt reply.

As the day warmed, talking became easier, and they began to know each other. He was from Bantry, one of five children. He'd followed his brother over. They both worked out of the harbor on other men's boats but were saving for a boat of their own. He said he liked America—the little he'd seen of it—but he longed to get out of the city, go up north, where he'd heard there was wonderful country. Moira agreed, saying she'd heard the same, and wouldn't it be nice someday. A pointed silence followed and Julia was certain they were both blushing, although it might have been the wind in their cheeks.

Michael Sheehan said that what he liked about America was how people were free to think and do as they pleased as long as they weren't pestering anybody. Moira reminded him of his words when he learned she did not go to church. He had never met an Irish girl who did not attend Mass regularly and was visibly surprised. He wanted to know what she believed in, if not God. Moira noted a smug expression on her sister's face. Julia had been waiting for this moment, hadn't she? Moira felt cornered.

"It isn't that I would deny Him," she said carefully, breathing a sigh. "But if He does exist, He does so without the slightest notion of me."

"It is troubling at times," Michael agreed.

"But it doesn't warrant abandoning faith," Julia piped in defensively.

Moira glared at her. "Faith abandoned *me*."

"When?" Michael wondered. "Was there a moment at which you knew it to be?"

Moira could feel Julia bristling beside her. She shrugged. She couldn't say. Gazing up at the sky. Wasn't it getting late, besides?

As they climbed the steep hill back to the Hadley house that morning, the silence grew too palpable until Julia, paused along the brick wall at Cherry Street (they often stopped here for her to catch her breath), burst out mockingly, "Your faith? Well let's see now, we know it must have been gone by the time you let Ann die."

Moira turned to her. "You would rather Michael have been affronted than interested, isn't it so?"

Julia made no reply.

At 14 Wilson Place, the outside lamps were still burning. They slipped inside the gate and walked up the drive to the servants' entry. The kitchen light was on. They could smell coffee. Cook said good morning, setting a basket of bread out on the table. "How was the fisherman this morning?"

"We'll never do as a pair," said Moira, reaching for a roll.

"That's a change of tune," Cook remarked, tying her apron strings.

"Yes, well, I've been fooling myself. I'd just as soon break it off next time."

Julia gasped.

Moira eyed her coolly. She tore open her roll. "We aren't compatible."

"You make each other laugh," Julia said hopefully.

"That always helps," added Cook.

Moira was quiet, buttering her roll. She smiled, wistful, glancing over at Julia. "Did you notice he has a gold tooth?"

Julia pressed a finger indicatively to her left cheek. "It catches the sunlight when he laughs."

Of course Julia had noticed! *She* paid attention to details. His favorite flower: irises (wasn't it uncanny how she'd loaned Moira that scarf—as if she'd always known). Shoe size: 42 (just right for a man of his height). Preferred brand of pipe tobacco: Prince Albert (such a heady, heavenly smell). His nostrils flared when he was angry; this she'd witnessed when a pushcart vendor had tried to shortchange them. The index finger of his left hand did not bend, the tendon having been severed by a fishhook. In the breast pocket of his overcoat, he carried charcoal pencils, and the reassuring way he patted the side of his coat from time to time told her he kept his sketchbook in the inside pocket. Judging from the charcoal stains on his shirtsleeves, he was fond of drawing the sunrise.

Michael Sheehan was earnest, somber, with his pensive jaw, musing lips. Intelligent, hardworking, hopeful: a near-perfect man, she felt, except for the fact that he was a good bit older. But he looked to be in good health, so it wasn't something to worry about. Every time Moira expressed the slightest doubt, it seemed, Julia hastened to find something reassuring to say. Yet Moira was so undeserving! She never cared the way she should about anyone.

One morning, Michael Sheehan reached for Moira's hand and Julia, struggling to compose herself, turned her gaze coolly to the sea as they kissed. It was a relief when she took ill again that winter and hadn't the energy to witness their folly.

They were night and day, the two of them, but he'd gotten so he couldn't imagine it otherwise. In 1934, Michael asked Moira to marry him. He was asking, he said, several things, and she should deliberate before giving her reply. He had been up to Portland, Maine, to look at a boat. A decent boat, meant for lobstering. His brother James was ready to buy, and so was Michael. Portland was still the city, but once they saved enough they could move out to the country. He had a dream of one day building his own house.

Moira interrupted him. "My sister. Perhaps she'll come to Portland with us?"

"She was with us for the courting." Michael sighed. "She can visit on the train. It isn't that far away." He cupped Moira's face in his hands. "We'll be newly wedded, after all."

"I only mention it because you talk of saving money," Moira said, lowering her eyes. "Julia doesn't spend a penny."

Her hands tingled, holding his. At such moments how transformed Moira felt. Her hands, a pair of hummingbirds. So that, later that same morning, it was odd to see her hands for what they really were: calloused, overworked. She was busily mopping the staircase. If there were someone else Moira trusted (she'd considered telling Cook about the engagement but Cook was too tight with Mrs. Hadley), Julia's opinion wouldn't matter so much. Moira thought fleetingly of writing to Matty. But a shepherd had a loner's soul; she could hardly expect him to be a good judge of people. As long as the marriage did not interfere with the monthly cash remittances she sent him, she imagined she'd have his blessing. From a note that Matty had included in the last parcel of buttons he sent to Julia, they had learned that he had bought himself a horse. Twilight he was calling her, and it made Moira happy to picture him in the saddle.

Julia had once said that Michael brought out the best in Moira, the way chamois brings out the shine in an apple. He had apple-red lips, didn't he though, softer than chamois. Sleepy eyelids and thick straight brows. The color of his eyes made Moira think of fir trees. And she was terrified. She sloshed the mop head in the bucket and dragged it back and forth across the same step yet again, dreading finishing, as if that would be her undoing.

"I wonder, does he know you well enough to marry you?" Julia asked upon hearing the news, and Moira knew just what she was questioning.

"I've kept no secrets," she replied, her color rising, for she had told Michael about Ann. The truth. It was not an accident. But Julia mustn't know. She remembered the astonished look in his eyes. He had held her in his arms but said nothing, and she'd thought better of asking if in her shoes, he'd have done the same thing.

It was the tradition in America for the wedding dress to be white as snow. Julia emptied her button jar out on the bed one evening and bit her lip as Moira chose the pearls. Fitting her fidgety sister for the dress one evening, Julia caught sight of herself in the mirror. The illness had retreated, leaving an unusual skin rash in its wake. Julia was reminded suddenly of her mother, who had been similarly wise and tolerant of the unwise world around her.

Heleen O'Leary had attributed her own patchy complexion to a giant butterfly resting on her nose, wings stretched out across her cheeks.

The wedding took place at Saint Andrew's Church on the twenty-first of May. Cook, Jordie Woods the coachman, and Mr. Hummer the gardener, attended. There were several friends of Michael's present. His brother James stood up for him. Julia was the maid of honor. Moira had not been inside a church in some time, and it gave her the chills. But the ceremony was over soon enough. In fact the whole day raced by. There was a champagne toast in the public garden and a photograph taken of the happy couple, both of which Michael's brother insisted on paying for. But isn't James the big spender, Julia commented, and Moira whispered back that he was just trying to make it up to Michael. In the ladies' room at the train station, where she changed into traveling clothes, Moira explained how it should have been the three of them—Moira, Michael, and James—boarding the train to Portland. Julia was surprised to hear it. She wondered why James had changed his mind. Moira shrugged. He was happy where he was at the moment, making plenty of money, and was loathe to leave it behind for the risk of captaining. Of course, the purchase of the lobster boat was already final and Michael didn't want out of the deal, even if he had to go it alone. Julia said no, she wouldn't think so, feeling perfectly insignificant zippering Moira's dress.

She stood on the platform with James, waving off the train. A warm wind rushed in as the train pulled away, and she held on to her hat and blinked tears. Choked on the air, filling up her throat. She turned, desperate to go. She declined James's offer to pay her taxi home. (She thought him a fool not to have joined them.) She would rather walk, thank you.

Their first morning as husband and wife, Michael left the bed early, it being a Sunday, and Moira lay there, staring at the bloodstain they'd left on the sheet. She gazed down at herself, at the sun on her bony legs, and thought momentarily of shepherding. She scrutinized her thighs, her calves, their potential for running. She sighed. If her own mother could follow her heart, then she should as well. What an unlikely pair Matty and Heleen had made. They'd met at a fair in Kildare. She was Heleen Sullivan then, watching from the sidelines, and he was the auburn-headed boy from the peninsula clipping the fleece from the sheep in one effortless piece. The fleece fell away magically and the surprising, slender ewe inside jumped to its feet. Afterwards, when the winner wrapped the fleece around himself, as was the custom, Heleen noticed his smile, his crafty bright eyes, and told herself, don't be a fool, he's a wolf in sheep's clothes.

Moira climbed out of bed and quickly stripped the mattress. He'd left her plenty of water for the kettle. She emptied the water into a tin washbasin and submerged the soiled sheet. The water was suitably cold and, with a good scrubbing, she rinsed the blood away. She wrung the sheet, carried it to the window, and pinned it to the clothesline. Turning the crank, she sent it out into the sunshine. It was a beautiful day. Laundry was strung between the brick tenement buildings as far as the eye could see, lending a festive look to the alley. Still she couldn't help feeling she'd never get used to this life. Although Boston was a much larger city than Portland, Maine, at Mrs. Hadley's house she'd been removed from the smog and the noise. There was less autonomy, certainly, but there were also trees out every window and a flower garden at the back of the house. The food had been plentiful, and Cook never served the same thing twice in one week. The work was arduous at times and certain tasks she liked more than others (she would *not* miss dusting the chandeliers), but all in all she could not have complained.

When she told Mrs. Hadley that she was getting married, it seemed to come as no surprise, and Moira gathered that Cook had kept her apprised of the courtship. On Moira's last day of work, Mrs. Hadley presented her with a dozen coin-silver spoons as a wedding gift. She jested that she would remember Moira fondly as the girl who faithfully cleaned out the coal stove every Sunday. She was also the girl who took the stairs on all fours when in a hurry, rather unsightly, but Mrs. Hadley had gotten used to it. Quite frankly, Mrs. Hadley regretted having to let Moira go. She knew full well she'd never find another girl with the same energy, who could do the work of two, as Moira had done ever since Julia moved to the sewing room.

"We'll certainly miss you, Moira Rose."

Moira sighed. "In a way, ma'am, I'm sorry to be leaving. A good position isn't easy to come by."

Mrs. Hadley smiled. "Yes, well. I imagine soon you'll be starting a family."

"Oh no, ma'am. I've no intentions of that sort," Moira replied.

Mrs. Hadley raised an eyebrow. "You're taking the necessary precautions, are you?"

Moira hesitated. "Precautions?" and then it dawned on her. "Why yes, ma'am. Indeed. Whatever is necessary."

Having grown up on a farm, Moira knew the ways of the birds and the bees perfectly. But she hadn't imagined that it was possible to prevent what happened naturally, short of keeping a weak ram separate from the ewes at breeding time. Or, in the case of a prolific cat, shutting her up in the house all day, turning a deaf ear to her wistful cries. The first time they'd attempted this, the tom had found his way in through the chimney. Done his business before anyone noticed him. The next time, they were more careful. A month later, the cat's belly swelled. Julia said it was too soon, but still the cat set about nesting inside Heleen's wardrobe the way she always did, but this time for kittens that never came. Julia called it a false pregnancy and said that it just went to show the strength of instincts which shouldn't be denied.

Moira went to show Julia the spoons from Mrs. Hadley. She found her in the sewing room. She said, "I'm wondering, Julia, is there some kind of pregnancy precaution I should know of?"

Julia raised an eyebrow. "The Church is against it." She paused. "Not that you would care about that, but he might."

"Please," Moira begged.

Julia eyed her critically. "Well of course there are *steps* one can take."

Moira was instructed to take her temperature regularly and count the calendar days. It wasn't a foolproof method, Julia warned, but if she was careful and abstained from sex as soon as the mercury rose, she could control her fertility without offending anybody. Julia went on to detail the early symptoms of pregnancy. But Moira interrupted, "None of that concerns me."

Julia looked startled. Then she said, "Well not right away maybe. That's sensible enough."

"Yes," said Moira as she gathered up the spoons, wondering

how she'd ever find room in her suitcase. What with the canister of tea, sugar cubes, and the candle and matches Julia had insisted on her packing. You never knew when you were going to need them.

Michael had arranged for the apartment in advance. He'd carried her across the threshold and straight to the bed—not to be forward, he said, but it was the only comfortable place to sit. She replied that forward was fine by her, in fact it seemed the only way to begin. Pretty soon it was dark outside and that was when they realized that there were no lightbulbs in any of the sockets.

Candlelight was kinder than daylight, Moira realized, roaming around the apartment while she waited for the bedsheet to dry. The kitchen was the size of a closet—shelves, a stove and sink, no icebox. The bathroom and toilet were down the hall. (She made a mental note to purchase a chamber pot.) The only furniture in the apartment, besides the bed and a lopsided bureau in the bedroom, was a small table and three chairs, which occupied a second adjoining room. She noticed that Michael had left his sketchbook open on the table. She had wondered what he'd been doing, up so early before Mass. He had drawn the view through the bedroom doorway from where he was sitting: *That* was the bedpost and *there* were her bare shoulders, her hair unraveled, the back of her head. Moira was incensed! She tore the page from the binding and ripped it to shreds.

How was she going to survive this? She went and got dressed. She took the dry sheet down from the line and made the bed back up in the way she'd learned to at Mrs. Hadley's, so that it looked as if it had never been slept in. She was sitting at the table when he came in. "I'll have no more pictures of me," was the first thing she said, on her feet suddenly, her jaw set. "Even as your wife, Michael, I'm entitled to a bit of privacy."

Michael looked baffled. Then he noticed the pieces of paper scattered about the table. He came closer and recognized his charcoal lines. His face flushed red. She watched him go about picking up the paper shreds. He balled them in his fist. He walked over to the window and tossed the shreds and she heard the flap of wings, pigeons mistakenly pursuing. All of a sudden she felt terrible. She'd hurt him, their marriage just hours old.

"I shouldn't have torn it. I acted too quickly," she said, pausing. "It unsettled me. I can't bear to see myself that way."

"What way?" he asked, turning from the window to face her.

She averted her eyes. "The way *you* see me."

He said nothing. He went into the bedroom.

"Have you had your tea yet?" she called out. She bit her fingernail. He was still wearing his coat. She watched him go into the kitchen and panicked, imagining him leaving through the rear door. She raced in after him, crying, "Wait!" But he was only filling the kettle. Standing at the sink. She breathed deep. "Take off your coat at least."

He set the kettle down and slowly unbuttoned his coat, all the while watching her. She stepped close and rolled up his shirtsleeves for him. First the right and then the left.

A Maine fishing community, Michael Sheehan soon learned, was a knot tied tight. It didn't matter if you captained your own boat; if you were "from away," there were rites of passage. Lobster traps sabotaged, a perpetually broken water pump, essential parts "out of stock" at the marina store. Michael weathered the treatment resolutely, teaching Moira the boat when there were no reliable sternmen for hire. It was her idea, made perfect sense, she said; otherwise, she was just sitting at home reading the cookbook Julia had sent.

Her first week in Portland, Moira had made inquiries at several employment agencies, armed with a letter of reference from Mrs. Hadley. But domestic service was out of fashion except for the very rich, of which there were few in Portland, and, in such cases, servants were expected to live in. Moira had found some work through a woman on the first floor who ran a little business taking in laundry. The woman farmed out the washing to several other women in the building—which explained why there was never any hot water when it came time to bathe and why the clotheslines were always full, even early on a Sunday. For someone such as Moira who was used to doing the washing, ironing, and silver polishing all in the same day, it wasn't enough to keep her busy. "Teach me to fish," she pleaded.

So Moira became the only woman putting to sea out of the Portland harbor. She was agile, strong. A natural, said Michael, and if folks were looking at her funny, well, she'd just have to look the other way. She did so gladly. Moira was disdainful of numerous Yankee ways—particularly the aloof attitude toward strangers—and was not interested in gaining acceptance.

In two years' time, Michael and Moira doubled the number of traps they managed, from fifty to one hundred. They caught their own bait, for which they sewed their own nets, and were proud of their self-sufficiency. At times, far out at sea, theirs the only boat for miles around and the vastness of the ocean so pronounced, it felt as though they were the only living souls on earth. They could go a whole day without uttering a word, moving about the boat with such perfect coordination that, to some degree, they were oblivious to each other's presence. One gaffed the buoy, hooked the line on the winch, and hauled up the trap. The other measured and pegged the catch. After several strings of traps, they switched off.

Once they were headed home and didn't have the anticipation of the catch to distract them, their silence would give way to discussion. It was usually Michael's doing. He enjoyed serious conversation, and he was unusual for a fisherman in that he found the ocean a romantic place. There were certain topics they never tired of: the tides, the weather, the future of lobstering, designing the perfect trap. With the motor running low, bow headed dead into chop, he told her that he had faith in the sea. He had a way of confiding his thoughts that made her feel extraordinary. But it frightened her, too, to hear him talk. She had never met anyone (other than Julia, perhaps) who thought as much about the future. He didn't just want his house in the country, he wanted children in it. Moira told him they couldn't afford a family, not right away; every month, at the right time, she reminded him and, still, he was hurt by it.

Biology is destiny," insisted Julia. "You certainly can't deny him forever. If you're married, which you are, and you're acting as a good Catholic, which one of you is, thankfully, children happen naturally."

Moira sighed. "I've been a mother once already."

They were strolling in a hilltop park overlooking the Portland waterfront. A large naval ship was preparing to dock, tugs sidling up to it. They sat down on a bench to watch. "Moira Rose," Julia said, "you're afraid."

Moira looked at her. "Wouldn't you be?"

Julia took out the apple she was saving for the return train trip and bit in to it. She thought about Moira and about herself and how true it was that their mother's death still united them. "Yes," she conceded, "but for different reasons." It was the physical toll of motherhood she feared, whereas Moira was wary of self-sacrifice. She handed off the apple to her sister. Moira made quick work of it, tossing out the core. A seagull swooped down. Julia sighed, glancing at her wristwatch. The watch was brand-new. Julia had plenty of money to spend on herself these days. What with Moira gone, she didn't like going to the movies and although she sometimes craved an eclair from the Royal Pastry Shop, it was a long way to travel alone. Julia's social life consisted of going to church, though most of the people her age in the parish were paired off and marrying.

Every other Sunday, after Mass, Julia rode the train to Portland to spend the day at Moira's—that is, unless there was work pressing. Julia fashioned hats for several of Mrs. Hadley's closest friends and although it was true, as Moira said, that the extra work was more trouble than it was worth, Julia never could say no to anybody. Besides, Julia thought it prudent to be too busy to visit sometimes, even if it meant another lonely week ahead. It reinforced the idea that when she came to Portland she was doing Moira a favor.

She had better be getting to the station. They walked out of the park and down the street. Moira was awfully quiet and Julia finally asked her if she and Michael had been quarreling over starting a family. It would explain for Julia why he had been down at the docks mending traps on a Sunday (and subsequently why their checkers rematch had to be postponed until next time).

But Moira shook her head. "We scarcely fight. He doesn't like to." She paused. "I wish you didn't live quite so far. It's a comfort to me, your understanding."

"I'll be back in two weeks," Julia replied, unproductively. She felt taken aback. It simply wasn't true about her understanding.

They arrived at the station and were quickly swept up in the hustle and bustle. A whistle blew. Julia checked her watch (the clock on the departure board was always, unforgivably, off). They hurried down the track to second class, embraced hastily, and, with a lift-up from Moira, Julia climbed aboard. Once settled in her seat, nothing left to eat besides a stick of jerky and nothing but knitting to occupy her, she regretted not having replied more challengingly: "Actually, Moira, you've always been a puzzle to me."

She peered out at Moira's face. In two weeks it would be May, and that meant warmer weather, even in Maine. Her red gabardine blazer came to mind, her navy pillbox hat with red piping. The coach shifted forward as the wheels began to turn. Julia concentrated on her outfit for next time and kept from feeling forlorn—which was always tempting what with the sun going down and the train moving her slowly away.

As it so happened, two weeks later Julia's winter coat and a pair of galoshes made the most sensible traveling clothes. She waited in the parlor from five minutes before six to twenty minutes past for Moira to telephone as she always did the evening before. It was possible, Mrs. Hadley said, that telephone lines were down and her sister was having difficulty getting through. She could rest assured that if the weather was bad in Boston, it was worse in Portland. Julia went upstairs to bed feeling dejected. Wouldn't Moira be sorry if she decided not to visit tomorrow? Julia had packed her measuring tape in order to measure their apartment windows for a set of curtains. She really didn't know how the two of them had gone this long with the entire neighborhood capable of looking in. Julia envisioned Moira and Michael through the window. Would there be a pot of tea on the table? What on earth would they be talking about? It was difficult for her to imagine a context that didn't involve herself. For all she knew, the window was black. She was struck by this possibility. But, for goodness' sakes, where else would they be other than at home—at this hour, in this weather?

They had been headed for harbor Saturday afternoon as usual when a gale blew up on them. A breaker hit the boat from behind, dousing them in water. The sea was churning wildly, the boat lurching from side to side. Snow was soon pouring out of the sky. They could not see the entrance to the harbor. For an hour they tried to find it. But the closer in they went, the rougher it was.

"I'm going to turn her around!" Michael shouted.

"And head back out?" asked Moira.

"We'll be lost on those rocks otherwise."

Moira's heart sank. "Turn her around."

As expected, it was somewhat calmer five or six miles out. They tripled the anchor line and got down to business, preparing the boat for the wait. They kept the motor idling low, turned the heater down. By dusk, great seas began coming over the boat, filling it with water. They pumped it out by hand. No sooner would they empty it than another wave would come, breaking mercilessly over the sides, filling the boat right up again. They pumped and pumped and pumped. Darkness enveloped them and they kept on pumping, doggedly, into the night.

There was nothing to do but sit there on the ocean, work the pump, and weather it. No lull and no choice. A hundred times that night Moira had pumped for as long as she possibly could, her fingers throbbing, her back and shoulders burning. Another wave thundered over them. She stopped anticipating the seas. She stopped hoping for relief. Pulled her hat down over her ears, bent her head in to the motion. She pumped with all her might and then he spelled her.

At four o'clock in the morning the wind shifted. They could feel it on their faces. The snow stopped falling. The wind was coming in from the west and clearing up the air. Michael Sheehan gazed out into the morning light and spotted land. He called to her. She looked where he was pointing: three gray hills where the mist had parted. "Storm's over," he said. She nodded bleakly. She went to pull in the anchor.

The boat was covered with ice frozen thick over the sides. Both bow and stern were shining slick, and icicles hung from the canopy. As they entered the harbor, people saw them coming and rushed down to help. They were ushered inside, offered coffee and blankets.

"Is there someone we should telephone for you?" asked a Coast Guard official.

Moira said with a start, "My sister. Yes. Thank you," suddenly coming to.

In Boston, rain had turned to sleet overnight. The roads were glazed with ice and the buses weren't running. Julia was late for

Mass, ducking in just before the Gospel, one of a handful whose devotion was harder than the weather. She would have to forgo coffee and doughnuts downstairs so that she could get to the train station in time.

She trudged through the sloppy streets holding on to her umbrella with both hands until the wind turned it inside out, the frame snapped, and she let go of it. She was wet, shivering. The lights were on inside the train station, but it was ghostly quiet, with only pigeons cooing. She rang the bell at the ticket window, and after a moment a man stepped out. She eyed his loose shirttails. The man informed her that all trains had been delayed. The rails were iced over. He put a toothpick in his mouth. With a bit of luck, she might get out this afternoon.

Julia turned away. She was chilled through to the bone. She would catch cold. And lose pay recovering. She peered grimly out the window. She noticed a taxi parked on the opposite street. Its lights were off, but she could make out a driver inside, the soft glow of a pipe. She dashed out of the train station. The driver saw her coming and shook his head at her—not in service—but she wouldn't take no for an answer. She pounded on the glass until he unlocked the door. She jumped in, pulled the door closed behind her. The wind was muffled. It was warm and cozy. Then she sneezed.

"God Bless," the driver said.

Julia met his eyes in the rearview mirror. "I haven't the heart to walk all the way home." She swallowed back the lump in her throat.

He asked her for the address, stowing his pipe in the ashtray. The taxi ventured along cautiously. Julia took out her handkerchief, but it was too wet to be of use; she applied it, instead, to wiping the glass as it fogged.

"Were you going somewhere or coming from somewhere?" the driver asked her.

She sighed. "Going."

"Visiting someone special?"

She nodded. She wiped her eyes with the back of her hand.

"A sweetheart," the driver said knowingly.

Her tongue went thick. She said quietly, "He lives in Portland."

"Surely you'll see him again?"

"Yes. It's just that I've been waiting weeks as it is."

He smiled, reaching for his pipe. "What's he do, your fellow?"

"He's a fisherman. His own captain," she said.

The pipe between his teeth, he said, "Hard work. Hope he doesn't ever go out in weather like this." He held a lit match to the bowl, glancing back at her. "Do you mind?"

She shook her head. "Is it Prince Andrew?"

"Red Rover," he said, holding up his pouch of tobacco.

When Julia arrived home, Mrs. Hadley climbed the stairs to tell her personally that there had been a phone call from the Coast Guard in Portland. There was no cause for alarm. Moira and her husband were both safe, although it *had* been a close call. "That sister of yours!" Mrs. Hadley said in amazement.

Several days later, Julia received a letter in the mail. Moira had enclosed a clipping from the Portland paper detailing the story of their survival. Two other boats had been lost out of that harbor the same afternoon and never returned.

Everyone had known the Irish were a tough pair, but this incident earned Michael and Moira a certain sober respect. The day they returned to the harbor to clean out the boat and assess the necessary repairs, they were treated as if they had just brought in a record-breaking catch. Every fisherman in the harbor stopped by the boat to pay his regards.

"Thick as fog, wasn't it though? And then with the snows," said Ronny Peterson, shaking his head. "What, you compass your way in finally?"

"Just weathered it," said Michael. "Storm broke at sunrise."

"Some boat," said Long Bennard, his bait boy standing beside him and grunting his agreement.

"Took a beating," said Michael, "but she'll live all right."

"Strange custom," Moira remarked, watching Long Bennard and his bait boy walk away.

"They think we're lucky," Michael said.

"So suddenly we're worth talking to?"

Michael shrugged. "Fishermen, Moira, they admire luck."

She thought about this for a moment. "We weren't so lucky."

Their first day out on the water again she was jittery, distracted. There had to be some way to tell a storm from a distance, she said, cranking the winch. Michael admitted that sometimes he could smell it. Snowfall. But only from closer in. Moira felt irritated. They had been only two miles offshore to begin with. Michael hauled the trap over the side. It was full from days of neglect: starfish, a knot of sea urchins, only three lobsters and one too small to keep. He emptied it out on the floor of the boat. She pegged the two good lobsters and dropped them in the tank.

"It was too big a storm to miss, is all," she finally said.

"Morning weather station didn't anticipate it," replied Michael.

"Farmer's almanac called for rain," she mused. "Late rains this year."

Michael sighed. "The wind shifts, Moira."

"That's no answer."

"It's what saved us next morning," he said, resetting the trap. "Answer to my prayers." He dropped the trap in the water and watched it descend.

She was incredulous. "You find your faith enhanced by this?"

He gazed steadily across the boat at her. "I do. Yes."

For her twenty-fifth birthday, Michael made Moira a kite. A paper diamond with a lightweight wood frame and a ribbon tail. One side he painted with waves and a boat being tossed about, the other with a tall, far-reaching tree. When it rolled in the sky, showing off both sides, she couldn't help calling it the most beautiful thing. She stood inside his arms with her back leaned into him, and together they held the string, which was not unlike a fishing line the way it was tugging.

The kite tail eventually snagged on the branch of a tree. The tree was holding on tight and it was clear that if they pulled any harder they'd break the string. Moira said come give a boost, she'd climb up and retrieve it. Michael thought it was too dangerous, hardly worth it, but she was adamant. Kicking off her shoes and socks, she stepped one foot into his clasped hands and he hoisted her. Up she climbed, the bow she'd tied in her hair loose, blowing. He glanced down at her strewn shoes, which were more often than not untied. She could tie a knot to hold a boat in a storm, but she couldn't tie a proper bow. Because, she'd told him, she never learned how, her mother having died before her first pair of shoes.

She shook the branch until it let go of the kite. The kite went swooping down. Michael, cheering, ran after it. The park was empty but for them. The sun setting. She started climbing down. As her braid swung forward, she noticed the dangling ribbon. Pulled it out, pausing to watch it float down to him. She chided him for looking up her skirt. He said it was quite impossible not to. When she dropped from the tree, he caught her. Pressed her up against the trunk and kissed her. She opened her mouth to let him in.

Then, she was late. She went back to the calendar. She lay awake at night. In the moon high above the buildings, she glimpsed her mother's face. Then, one day while at work, she started to bleed. Through the salt and fish she could smell it. She went directly to her bath when she got home. She slowly stripped off her pants. Stuffed the soiled clothing into the garbage can. She let the faucet roar. Stepping carefully into the water, she sat back, her braid coiling itself around her neck, and worked the sliver of soap between her legs.

The rich, dark color of it, the dank stench. In her mind's eye, she was twelve years old again. And the blood was her mother's. How the smell had suffocated her, but she was scolded for opening the shutters. The draft a menace to a newborn. Ann was days old and Heleen was still bleeding. The midwife returned. There were no doors inside the house, so an old blanket was hung back up across the bedroom entry like it had been when the baby was coming. With Matty madly pacing, the blanket swinging and Moira and Julia able to see in. Except that now their mother wasn't screaming out in pain, she was perfectly silent. It was Ann who was crying because she wanted to be fed. They were instructed to console her until the midwife finished working, but Ann screamed mercilessly. She knew the difference between her mother's nipple and her sister's pinky, never mind what the midwife had said, passing the baby out through the blanket—*find her something to suck on*—as if it were all the same.

They had not been able to keep up with the bloody laundry. Heleen soaked through every rag in the house, and became angry when the rags came in off the clothesline stained. "Now everybody and his mother knows I'm dying." She called Moira and Julia to her bedside and explained about using cold water to get out blood. The sooner it soaked, the better. It was just something every girl learned growing up. Because once a month the heat would come. She would have put off telling them until later, but what if later turned out to be never, then they'd be as ignorant as she had been. She didn't want to confuse them, she said. The monthly blood was perfectly normal. What she was experiencing was something else altogether. Try a clear, babbling brook so small you straddled it to drink, as compared to, say, the ocean on its darkest day. Even if the source was the same. She looked at their frightened faces and promised that it wasn't nearly as scary when it was your own blood flowing.

Moira stayed in the tub until the water turned color. She fit a pair of underpants with several layers of menstrual pads, put on her long johns, and padded quickly down the hall back to the apartment. Michael was cooking oatmeal and she could also smell hot cocoa, and this was her favorite supper, one he always fixed for her when she was menstruating, so she figured she didn't need to say anything about a miscarriage, only thank you when he brought out the food.

. . .

In 1939, they became United States citizens. It had meant several Sundays of sitting around the table studying the booklets Julia had sent for from the immigration office, a good excuse for Julia to visit on consecutive weekends and to match wits with Michael on the subject of United States history. Moira and Michael took the day off to travel to Boston to take the test, and Julia was granted leave from Mrs. Hadley's. Several weeks later, they each received an official invitation to be sworn in as a United States citizen. Michael and Moira rode the early train in to Boston for the ceremony, and Julia met them at the station. They sat in the park and ate doughnuts as they had in the old days when they'd first met. Julia was too nervous to eat, and threw most of her doughnut to the pigeons. She realized, for the first time, that she'd long ago stopped thinking of Ireland as her home.

At City Hall, they filed into a courtroom and took their places among the large number gathered. The actual swearing in was over in a few minutes, then there was a reading off of the names present, followed by a speech about what it meant to be a good citizen. Afterwards, everyone applauded and shook hands with each other, and it really did feel remarkable to be united with all these different nations by virtue of being American, which was the very claim the study booklet had made.

They received their citizenship papers by mail a month later.

The following autumn, Moira and Michael noticed construction crews on the islands in Casco Bay. They rode the boat in closer to watch them pouring cement. Moira remarked that she couldn't imagine who would want to live in such dreary, colorless buildings. The United States Marines, Michael replied. They were bunkers.

Moira looked in amazement at the surrounding waters, and laughed despite herself.

"Krauts? Right here?"

"U-boats," suggested Michael.

When the United States finally entered the war in 1942, new citizens were called to service along with everyone else. Michael's assignment came in the mail on a Saturday. Julia learned the news from Moira when she arrived on the train the following day. They made their way back to the apartment building in silence. In the hallway of the ground floor of the building they came across an old couch. A disgruntled, heavyset woman in a bathrobe, struggling to get past the couch on her way to the bathroom, informed them that 1B had moved out and left the couch. It looked to be in good condition, said Moira. She would just run up and summon Michael's help. Julia protested that it wasn't worth the trouble—the cushions were crawling with mites, no doubt. Really, Michael had more important things on his mind right now. They spent the better half of the morning wrestling the couch up the four flights. When they got it into the apartment, they flounced down on it, exhausted. Sunlight filled the room. It was a hot, summer's day, a day Julia would remember for how her life was then changed. They were going to lease the boat and the traps while Michael was away so that Moira could pay the rent without dipping into savings. Moira would try for a job at one of the canneries. She was hoping that Julia would consider moving to Portland. Julia could do much better for herself than service Mrs. Hadley. There were tailors in town who would jump at the chance to hire someone with her talent, Michael put in. They were both looking at her in earnest. Julia

didn't know what to say—Moira was now clutching her sleeve—
other than of course she'd keep her company. Moira sighed with
relief. "I knew you wouldn't deny me." Julia got up to close the
curtains on the heat, remarking irrelevantly that she had chosen
the heavy, opaque material for its versatility.

It was a dangerous time to love him, but tomorrow he was leaving.
His shoulders, the breadth and length of his back, the soft flesh
of his bottom. Please. She was kissing him for the last time. The
inside of his mouth was suffocating. She broke her lips away for
his nose, his cheeks, tasting the ocean on his eyelids. She held
his face in her hands the way he often did hers and looked far
into his eyes, thinking to herself how she was less afraid now of
what she saw and of what her own reflection showed, and it
struck her that they were as many as eight years married.

He turned her over. She stared at their shadow cast by the
candle. He straightened up, gripping her hips, and became a towering tree. She closed her eyes, swayed in the breeze. An apple,
a nut could fall. Knock her on the head. She was old enough to
know how some accidents happened: with desire finally. She felt
her breasts nodding furiously and clutched the bedsheet.

Michael departed for Spartanburg, South Carolina, for infantry
basic training, the following day. Moira saw him off at the station
but could not distinguish his hand from the many waving from
the windows. She watched until the hands turned into birds'
wings. Then she consulted the arrival board. She made her way
over to the right track and sat down to wait for the nine o'clock
from Boston.

Julia made a slipcover for the couch, fixed the stopper in the tub, restuffed the bed pillows, and soaked the fish out of Michael Sheehan's clothes. She behaved as if the place had always been hers, which was comforting to Moira, who resisted her own domestic instincts. Living with her sister, Julia no longer felt the need to carry her money on her person, pinned inside pockets sewn into her underclothes. She added her savings to the soda tin that Moira and Michael kept beneath the kitchen floorboard. She slept on the couch, disdaining the offer to share the bed and just as well, she felt, poking her head in to give a shout mornings, since Moira was always sprawled across it, face in the pillow, arms outstretched, welcoming no one.

Moira was hired on as an assembly-line worker at the baked-bean factory. She held cans in place and pulled down the arm of a machine that imprinted the company logo, P & B SWEET AND SPICY, in ten-second intervals. It was thankless monotony and she still had to awake at dawn each morning. Julia took it upon herself to cook oatmeal and brew tea. Moira was out of the door and headed for the bus stop by five-thirty. Julia usually went back to bed. Within two weeks of her arrival in Portland, she had taken ill. She was familiar with her condition now: the inflamed joints, fingers that turned blue at the slightest use. It was only as depressing as the cold weather. At least, here in the apartment, she could nurse herself in private. She pestered the druggist around the corner for herbs he had never heard of, which she used in making poultices, steaming up the kitchen window, her nostrils tingling with the smell. For the first time, she began to record her symptoms (nausea, cold sores, slight hair loss), charting their curious comings and goings in a notebook. It was helpful to have the time to devote to her illness, but it was also frustrating. She searched her mother's old books for answers, despairing,

eventually, of her lack of resources and tiring of the leaves clinging to her skin after a bath. It cheered her up to look at Michael
Sheehan's sketchbooks. She also enjoyed knitting him socks.
Socks were the only things he asked for in his letters, socks and
a reply from his wife.

But I don't write letters," protested Moira.

Julia was the one who wrote the monthly letter home to Ireland, though she signed it from both of them. "Well, it's time you
started," Julia said, setting a piece of paper down in front of her
and offering a pen.

Moira shook her head. "I've nothing to say."

"You have *no* news whatsoever?"

Moira looked away.

"Don't you think he should know that you were pregnant?"
asked Julia.

"It would only upset him." She pushed the paper and pen
away. "It's the fourth time."

Julia was surprised. She said quietly, "I see."

"But he only knows about two," Moira confessed. She remembered clearly the eve of his departure, how she had wanted a part
of him safe within her, and still she had miscarried. She said, "I
wouldn't want him to give up on me." They sat for a moment
drinking their tea. Then Julia reached for the pen. She glanced
tentatively at Moira. *Dear Michael,* she wrote at the top of the
page. *I trust you remain safe and sound since your last letter. Julia
and I are both in good health.* She paused. It was true enough;
the miscarriage had been quick and, according to Moira (crouching over the washbasin all night), not painful. Though Moira's
threshold for pain was unnaturally high. Julia sighed resignedly.

We were pleased to learn that you had been recruited by the specialized training unit. You are too modest when you say that the army must be desperate for engineers since they are willing to employ fishermen in this capacity.

"Ask him what a proximity fuse is," Moira said, reading over Julia's shoulder.

"It's a device for exploding shells," Julia replied, and went on writing. *My work continues to provide for us, but fails to stimulate or challenge. Julia seems especially bored and is eager to be back on her feet again.*

"Stop complaining," said Moira. "Finish it off already."

Julia looked up. "Shall I sign your name for you?"

Moira paused. "Who else's?"

The reply came two weeks later. Julia tucked it into her pocket. She went round the corner and bought cream and a package of biscuits for tea. Moira came up from the basement washroom with a mound of wet laundry and hung it to dry indoors, because the bedsheets were stained despite her cold water and scrubbing.

Julia sat warming her hands between the pot and the cozy. She had placed the letter on Moira's plate. When the last item of laundry was fastened to the clothesline, she said, "Moira, come. Tea's waiting."

Upon noticing the letter, Moira asked "From Michael?"

"I think so," Julia casually replied, pouring tea into the cups.

Moira tore open the envelope. She read the letter out loud. He had been moved to Raleigh, North Carolina, where he was assisting in new research, attempting to determine the optimal detonation height of shells to achieve maximum casualties among ground troops in foxholes. *I'm hard pressed to see the relationship between my recent engineering training and the monotonous hours I now spend with a posthole digger in a sandlot digging up fired shells.*

Moira paused, glancing up. "He sounds unhappy."

"Of course he's unhappy," Julia said impatiently. "He's a peace-loving man, but he believes in the struggle of good against evil."

"He misses me," said Moira, and read on for further proof.

Julia blushed hearing Michael's longing. He called the days a desert between them.

"So sentimental!" Moira exclaimed.

There was a postscript. Julia's sore fingers tingled suddenly at the mention of her name. *Tell Julia that the socks fit perfectly and keep me warm and dry on a long rainy day. You sister really is very handy. She should have no trouble at all finding employment once her health returns.* Julia reached for the warmth of her teacup. "It's too personal," she found herself saying. "You needn't share his letters."

She came with a good reference, although it was barely legible (Mrs. Hadley was by now quite elderly). But Julia insisted that her work spoke for itself. To be sure, the hats and garments she displayed were exceptional. Moira's wedding gown stole the show. Mr. Lieberman, the proprietor of the shop, eyed Julia over his spectacles. He pointed out the scrap bins and incited her to sew something on the spot. The bell over the door jingled announcing a customer, and Mr. Lieberman turned his back on Julia. She sifted through the scrapbin, at last uncovering several yards of muslin delaine. The fabric was dyed a luxurious magenta color and she couldn't help but feel encouraged by it. It was fabric suitable for a lady's dress, she decided, and gamely set to work. Zip-backed, with a V-neck, shaped bodice, and sweeping calf-length skirt.

"I'd prefer it to have buttons, of course," she said to Mr. Lieberman, who had come to peer over her shoulder.

"Buttons," Mr. Lieberman murmured, nodding his head with guarded approval. "Yah, I see what you mean."

Julia could not contain herself. She looked eagerly about the house for Moira, but it was early still. She set the kettle and unwrapped the sticky buns she had bought in celebration. She stood at the window, waiting on the whistle. In the building opposite, a woman was hanging out clothes. Julia had never understood the point of colored bath towels; the dye made them so much less absorbent. She sat down at the table. She went ahead and ate a sticky bun. Considered turning on the radio, but didn't think she could bear another discouraging report of the war in Europe right now.

Dear Michael,

At last Julia has taken your good advice! Her new employer, Mr. Lieberman, is a German Jew, emigrated after the Great War, fortunately. He runs an efficient business, providing custom design and tailoring for a small but discerning clientele. Julia's exceptional skills were not lost on Mr. Lieberman and she is grateful to you for encouraging her to stand up and be noticed. It pleases her to know that you think so highly of her, since she feels similarly about you.

She wrote quickly, urgently, pausing only to down more tea and pick the walnuts off the sticky bun she had been saving for Moira. *Radio news broadcasts do not make us confident that we will see you anytime soon. We do hope that you will always be within reach of the United States Post Office. God bless you, Michael.* She knew she was taking a risk with that last line, but she left it intact, and signed her sister's name.

Six months before the Normandy invasion, Michael Sheehan's program was terminated and he was transported to England to prepare for D day. When a letter arrived for Moira from the United States Army, Julia tore it open without pause. Her eyes raced over the page. Michael's brother James had been killed. An errant shell in a training mission. Efforts were being made to inform immediate family members in Bantry, Ireland. Julia slumped down on the couch, one hand pressed to her heart. She sat this way a long time, barely noticing the pair of pigeons that flapped down onto the window ledge to eat the crumbs that rained down out of someone's tablecloth.

The news of James made the arrival of the mail each day dreadful. Yet, the only other letter of importance that found its way into the mailbox during that time was one from Matty O'Leary. Since the postmark was smudged and the letter wasn't dated, there was no way for Moira to tell how long it had been in transit. The letter was written in long hand on several small sheets of very thin paper, penned by Father Thomas Glynn, who didn't dot his *i*'s and who'd become the parish priest five years ago, after Father Riley's stroke. There had been a fire, said Father Glynn, a lantern in the barn left burning.

It had been Matty's habit to stop off at the barn before going in-side after returning home from the pub. First he would banish the dogs from the barn so that he could open up the stalls and usher out the sheep. Stand there with the animals milling around him, palms turned out to their scratchy fleece. It was the barking of the dogs that woke him late that night. He had forgotten to return the dogs to the barn. No telling what all the fuss was. Then he heard his horse and it occurred to him that he'd left her out too, tied to the clothesline post. As soon as he was upright, he smelled the smoke. He ran to the window and threw open the shutters. The light was dazzling. Matty raced out of the house. He jumped onto his spooked horse, and galloped off strenuously. Pulling the reins up short on the edge of town, Matty looked back over his shoulder. The silo had caught, all the feed would be lost; he could already smell the fodder.

Father Glynn said nothing in the letter about Matty having been drunk, but it was understood. He was calling on Moira and Julia to support their father in this crisis. Moira stared at the apples in the bowl on the table. She had been going to eat an apple upon arriving home. Peel and salt it before biting in—the way Michael ate his fruit—because nowadays she felt she had forgotten everything: coarse calico curls, clammy-soled feet, a moon for every fingernail. Once, when Michael insisted she *must* believe in something, Moira had said she believed in Nature. Nature, as in the plants and animals. Because it did not depend on her in any way for its existence. Moira turned and opened the oven hatch. She stuffed in Father Glynn's letter. It was impulsive of her, but she didn't regret it. The flock perished! There would have been new lambs. She listened to the ash whisper up the stovepipe. She and Julia were often discussing the monthly money they sent home—how it perpetuated Matty's dependence, how he never said so much as thank you. Her eyes filled with tears. She took a butter knife from the drawer and pried up the floorboard for the soda tin, swearing he didn't deserve it.

Michael Sheehan sustained a piece of American shrapnel in his left leg, just below the knee, on the shore at Normandy. The chaotic scramble up the beach had been, for him, unprecedented. After months of controlled research and experimentation, he had run with the wave into the fire, so entirely against his sense of logic, his will, that by the time the shell exploded in front of him and he dropped, choking on sand, heat jolting up his calf, he was grateful. He had awoken in a Red Cross hospital in Dover, better off than most, and was shipped home within the month. He was not interested in talking about the Purple Heart Moira found at the bottom of his bag. It meant nothing. He had been out of the fight in minutes.

Michael Sheehan came home changed. Taciturn, silent almost. He couldn't bear the radio. Neither the news broadcasts nor the Boston Symphony, which they'd listened to for years, every Saturday afternoon on the transistor, returning to harbor. He slept fitfully and complained about Moira's habit of grinding her teeth in her sleep. She suggested he plug up his ears with cotton balls, and then regretted it because he was leaving the cotton balls in all day.

He persuaded Moira to buy him a cane. He refused to rest his leg and ended up with an infection. They had to muscle him back to bed. Julia cleaned and irrigated the wound. Moira forced cups of infused hops and goldenseal down him. The sedative in the tea made him talkative. Moira and Julia sat on either side of the bed listening sheepishly. Like a bottle uncorked, exploding. In his whole life, he'd never felt farther from God. The only thing that had kept him going in the foxholes was hope of a child some day. He groped for Julia's hand, mistaking it for Moira's. Julia patted the hand, her color rising. Moira stared. "He's quieting down," she said pointedly, meeting Julia's eyes. "You needn't stay."

Julia smoothed her skirt. She collected the empty teacup, and went quickly out of the room. Moira got up and closed the door behind her. She climbed into the bed and held him beneath the quilt. He was rapidly fading, and so she spoke in whispers of her own desire for a baby, for his sake, which was the only way she could consider it and still she hoped it was reassuring. Michael rolled over heavily. She rested her head beside his on the pillow. He had grown a beard after returning home. She stroked the whiskers with her fingers. She lay there a long time. The street light came on. The house was silent. Her stomach was howling. She pulled back the covers and crept out of the bedroom and into the kitchen. On her tiptoes, reaching into the cupboard, she paused—alert, listening. Her husband, her sister; they were both snoring.

In the spring of 1944, they emptied out the soda tin. A good portion of the money was Julia's, but Julia herself insisted Michael take it. Whatever else was money for? "I'll pay you back," he said. "With interest," she teased. The addition of the soda-tin money to the GI loan Michael received would secure his bid at the land auction. Moira held up crossed fingers for him to kiss. Julia looked on, smiling. An ointment made of mint leaf and comfrey had sealed the wound in his leg. Julia had sworn to herself she wouldn't leave a limp. He was tall and strong as a tree now. The door closed quietly behind him. Julia returned to her knitting, Moira to sweeping the kitchen.

"Should he win the bid," Julia mused, "what will he do then?"

"Clear the land some, first, I presume," Moira answered. "Then build a house."

Julia looked up. "A house?"

"The way he always talks about. Up north."

"But we're already *up north*."

"In the country!" laughed Moira.

"The country," Julia murmured, heart sinking. She didn't see how anybody, after escaping the farm, would desire a return to it. A wave of melancholy washed over her. She tried to tell herself that she need not include herself in their plans to move. She had her own ways and means. She earned a good wage. Mr. Lieberman paid overtime and never begrudged her a customer's tip. She enjoyed the challenge of properly outfitting people, especially when it was not an easy task: square hips, no bust, daddy longlegs. If she knew the customer well, she might even add a surprise pocket on the inside lining or an extra silver clip at the hip. The thought of leaving all this for the remote reaches of Maine—where surely no one had any need to be well outfitted, let alone any inkling of the latest fashions—didn't agree with her at all. She looked down at her knitting. A lump rose in her throat. She'd stay right where she was, thank you. In fact, she'd probably enjoy having the apartment all to herself. It would be much easier than sharing, especially since she ended up doing all the serious housekeeping anyway. Moira was good for a few swept floors every Saturday, but don't dare look in the corners afterward!

That afternoon at the market, Julia made disparaging remarks about the produce Moira and Michael would find up north. She shook her head at the tomato Moira held in her hand. The price was too dear. Anyway, Moira and Michael ought to get used to doing without tomatoes. The frost would kill them on the vine long before they ripened.

"Wait a minute," Moira said, stopping short in the middle of the market hall. "What about you, Julia? Won't you be buried right along with us under ten foot snows?"

Julia hesitated. "Well, I don't know that *I'm* coming."

"Nonsense," said Moira. "Of course you're coming."

Julia blushed. "The idea takes a certain amount of getting used to." But she *would* adjust, *of course* she would, no matter what kind of alternative plans she concocted for herself. It was a fact of her life by now that Moira's will prevailed. She watched Moira pay for a head of cabbage, jangling the coins confidently in her palm before handing them over. Every inch of her sure of itself.

Julia sighed. She was loyal to a fault, she concluded, and, for the most part, loyalty was an excellent quality (in all fairness, she shouldn't have to feel badly about herself right now). Her loyalty reflected a tenacious, earnest heart, which, admittedly, was vulnerable to the whims and influence of certain, selfish people. They walked home from the market in silence, the shopping bags rustling out of proportion. Julia made a pot of tea and sat down with the newspaper, but she was too troubled to keep to her reading. Moira was pacing back and forth, just like their father used to. The afternoon wore on. Julia could have screamed, except that she was already employing the silent treatment. Eventually they heard Michael's boots on the stairs. Julia set down the paper. She held her breath. Michael burst into the room. He had a magnificent way of filling the space. Julia gazed unabashedly at his beaming face. He had won the bid. The land was theirs. Moira flew into his arms. Julia busied herself, pouring a cup of tea for him, fending off tears. "Congratulations," she managed, glancing at him, but she couldn't bear to join them at the table. She returned to her place on the couch, hid behind the newspaper eavesdropping.

Ten pristine acres on the outskirts of the town of Unity, some thirty miles up the coast. A forested hillside where a house could perch, watching the ocean. A foundation and chimney built of stones carted up from the shoreline. A shingled cape with a porch, just the right size for a family. *Our* family, he said, after Moira begged pardon. He had made a few quick sketches.

"It isn't a great big house," she commented.

"Big enough," he said, defensive.

Later, when Moira went to bring in the laundry and Michael

was in the kitchen cleaning a fish for supper, Julia stole a look at the sketches which he'd left out on the table. The proposed space was all neatly labeled. The variously angled units carefully nestled around the chimney. Every door, every closet, every inch planned for. She could not begrudge him her respect. That evening at bedtime, the door was ajar, and Julia saw him kneel beside the bed with his head in his hands. The sheer physical energy that building a house demanded would perhaps be enough to bring him to his knees at the end of the day. He was making peace with the Lord again after the war, and she wished him the best, knowing what a necessity it was, no less than the windows on a house.

With what little money they had left over after the year in which the house was built, Michael managed to buy a used pick-up truck. They packed the back of the truck with their possessions, hooked on a rented trailer to carry the boat, and drove up to Unity in the summer of 1946.

Michael's status as a war veteran commanded tolerance among the fishermen in Unity. He could have hired on crew, except that Moira wouldn't hear of it. She'd learned to haul traps with the best of them. But when her sea legs failed her and she was sick each time they went out that fall, she thought perhaps she was going to keep this pregnancy. She confided in Julia that her period was now three weeks late. Julia agreed it was a good sign. They could only pray. But hadn't the whole village prayed for Heleen O'Leary? Moira shuddered inside.

At eighteen weeks, she felt movement, minnows under the skin. She decided it was time to tell Michael. He kissed her hopefully. Later she found him sitting by the fire, sketchbook open on his lap, drawing her boots drying. He was whistling. She lingered in the doorway, one hand pressed absently to her belly.

Although her morning sickness was gone, Michael didn't want her lobstering and had gone ahead and hired a sternman. Moira kept busy mending traps, canning vegetables, and making blackberry jam. She developed an enormous appetite, cravings for baked beans and sweet potato pie. Taking interest in her changing body, the added weight of curves and full bosom, the luster of her hair after a bath. She surprised herself by enjoying her husband's notice too, sitting on top of him in full view as she was coming.

Since it was to be their first garden in Maine, there were all sorts of decisions to be made, and pleasing everyone was not easy. Michael Sheehan wanted peppers, chard, and turnips—swedes they had called them in Ireland. Julia wanted beans and flowers and space set aside for herbs. They each had a different opinion as to the arrangement of the beds. Moira finally threw her hands up. At that moment, she felt a gush of water down her legs. She looked at them, stricken. Breathe, urged Julia. Michael would call the doctor, he'd bring the truck. Moira shook her head, walking away from them. She closed herself off in the bathroom, grunting more or less reassuringly whenever they knocked. Hours later, when her labor reached its peak, she flung open the door. They came running. Julia with a cup of bitter, blue cohosh tea for her to drink. Michael with sheets and a steaming kettle. They scrubbed up to their elbows in scalding water. Moira, crouched on the bathroom floor, looking up with bloodshot eyes, asked them what she should think of and they told her, for all its strength, the ocean.

The baby, a girl, was pushed out facefirst, dark-eyed as the night outside, umbilical cord snaking round her. Michael clipped the cord like a weed and tossed it into the ocean after, when he walked down to the shore too full of wonder to sleep.

III

At Sea

(1947–1966)

S HE WAS NAMED Kathleen, after Michael's mother, but they were already calling her Kate. She was twelve weeks old before Moira agreed to have her baptized. She might have held out longer but for the milk fever, which sapped her of the strength she had regained after the delivery, so that she hardly trusted herself to carry the baby. She lay in bed feeling insecure and out of sorts with the entire world, Kate beside her swaddled tight in the bed they'd fashioned for her out of a dresser drawer. Her wrinkled, ancient face sleeping tight. Moira intently watching, slipping a finger inside the pink cotton nightie to feel for certain the movement of the heart beneath the rib cage. She was often struck by how urgently the baby's heart beat—recalling her sister Ann's rapid, dying breath—and felt Kate's fragility and helplessness deeply. She was unfit, she told Michael, too sick to argue over original sin. Every time she looked at Kate she felt her own instability, as walls caving in. How could it compare to Michael's dedication and certainty? Then one night Kate cried inconsolably. "Your Mama's here, Kate," Moira coaxed. "Mama's right here." Her tiny body stiffened and she threw her head back, protesting all the harder the nearness of her mother's breast. Michael walked the baby up and down. He was as panicked as Moira was and she felt oddly ashamed for it and wanted to, but could not look away.

"It's just gas," Julia said, reassuringly. "It'll pass."

But by the time it passed, Moira had all but bargained her own soul. As she sat to nurse the quieted baby, relief washing painfully over her as the milk ran down, she said to Michael, "I've come 'round to the baptism." She was expecting a few questions, a comment as to her change of heart. He was lying across the foot of the bed, exhausted, and only sighed in reply.

Even before the telegram from the Coast Guard arrived, they had heard about the shipwreck. All of the local papers carried the story. An ocean liner had gone off course and run aground along the coast of Nova Scotia. More than half the passengers perished. To their amazement, Moira and Julia learned that their father was among the passengers, and had survived the wreck. The telegram said he was scheduled to arrive in Portland on Friday morning, by boat from Halifax. It was the first they had heard that he was coming. "In time for his granddaughter's christening," Michael said cheerfully. Moira and Julia looked at one another in disbelief. On Friday, Michael and Julia drove to Portland to meet Matty at the boat terminal while Moira stayed at home with

Kate, waiting anxiously. Moira had by now recovered from the fever (although she continued to wrap the infected breast in cabbage leaves at night) and could manage the baby on her own more or less confidently. This morning, she bathed Kate and dressed her in a clean gown. She carried her out onto the porch and sat down in the rocking chair. From here she had a view of the road and of the flower beds at the front of the house, which were in sorrowful disarray. She looked critically about the yard at the long grass overrun with dandelions. Her heart began to sink. A moment later, it leapt at the sound of a truck in low gear, climbing. Moira stood up, bearing the baby and bursting with pride. She stumbled down the porch steps and across the lawn, her face wrought with confusion. Matty was not in the truck. He had never arrived, Michael told her. They had waited until the last passenger filed down the gangway. Moira looked askance at Julia, who shrugged and slammed the truck door shut.

Baby Kathleen screamed as the priest at Saint John's-by-the-Sea in Free Harbor poured the holy water over her big bald head. Julia, Kate's godmother, and Skinny Roberts, her godfather, also Michael's sternman, both grinned. As for Moira, her breasts were heaving. The ceremony ended and she took Kate out of Julia's arms and hurried out of the church.

"It was freezing cold—it was ice water!"

Michael followed her down the steps. "No one's blaming the child for crying."

"Original sin," Julia commented gaily when she caught up to them. "It isn't so easily washed away." She straightened the train of the christening gown she'd made. "Kate's in the Lord's house finally."

"She'd have done just as well to stay at home!" Moira all but shouted.

"Don't impose your godforsaken will on this baby, Moira," Julia said crisply.

"Yoo-hoo!" called Skinny Roberts, brandishing the camera. They looked askance at him and he snapped the picture.

"Fine," said Moira, handing the baby to Michael. "The next christening you'll attend without me."

"The 'next christening'?" He raised an eyebrow. "I look forward to it, Moira."

He was sitting on the front steps, fanning himself with his hat. As the truck pulled in, he stood and awkwardly smoothed back his hair. He was smiling, showing his straight teeth. The only other time Moira could remember seeing her father in a suit jacket was at her mother's funeral. Julia was the first one out of the truck, then Moira with the baby. Michael walked around to help. He shut the door behind them. There was only the lawn dividing them from their father, but, for Moira, each step was years. Julia was already kissing Matty's cheek, saying, "Da, you haven't changed a day." Moira bit her lip; that was *just* it—except that his hair was white as snow now, but thick and unruly as ever. Julia complimented his jacket, calling it "dapper," and Matty laughed and said don't forget the shoes, lifting up his pant legs to show them off. "I've blisters on both my heels by now."

The sound of her father's voice set Moira's legs trembling and, for an instant, she felt as she had when she was sick, weak enough to drop the baby. Michael appeared at her side. He said quietly, "Shall I carry the baby?" She held Kate out to him, blinking back tears. Michael ushered her forward, so that finally she was standing in front of her father.

"You're late," was all she could think of to say.

Matty laughed. "Lucky I'm not dead on the doorstep!"

They sat in chairs on the porch and drained a pitcher of iced tea, listening with rapt attention while Matty recounted for them his survival—he had been bound to the mast of the ship with rope by a crew member. It sure felt sweet to have his feet firmly on the ground again. The ocean-liner executives could buy him all the new clothes they wanted to, said Matty, but they were mad if they thought he was ever getting on a boat again. So they had his apologies for arriving late. He had taken a bus to Augusta, another bus over to Unity. He walked from the bus station, asking directions along the way. Even met a couple of horses from the farm down the way, nosing up to inquire while he leaned on the fence in the shade. Did he mention that he'd sold his own horse following the fire? There wasn't anything left for him in Ireland. Besides the bottle, which went without saying since it had caused the trouble in the first place. A crying shame because it had been a good season for him and the lambs were all sweet innocence.

"I've bid it all good-bye," said Matty.

Moira and Julia looked surprised. "You've no plans of returning, Da?" Julia asked.

"Here to stay," replied Matty.

Moira said rashly, "But we've only three bedrooms, Da."

"A palace!" laughed Matty, but he added tersely, "I'm not asking to share your roof." He was going to travel, have a look around before he settled. Atlanta, Georgia, maybe. On the boat, he'd met a fellow from Atlanta whose brother owned a shoe factory. He reached out his arms, beckoning for the baby. Sweet Kathleen. But didn't she look like an O'Leary!

"Shall I take a photograph?" Michael asked, getting out the camera though no one replied. Matty handed off the baby while he put his jacket back on. He stood stiffly serious for the picture, Kate cradled awkwardly in his arms.

He hadn't so much as a toothbrush with him, his baggage having been lost in the wreck. He had carried his money and papers in a pouch at his belt, thank goodness. The pouch was soaked through, but at the bank in Halifax he'd been shown special treatment. Michael drove Matty in to town to buy a few things he needed. Matty was intrigued by a postcard of a lobster that he saw on the rack in the drugstore, so Michael swung by the lobster pound on the way home in order for him to meet one in person. They talked about fishing and a little bit about Moira, since Matty'd heard she'd worked right beside him on the boat. Before the baby, said Michael, she certainly had—the only woman around lobstering. Long day, too, but she never seemed to mind. Oh no, agreed Matty, as strong as they came.

On Sunday he went to church in Free Harbor with Julia and Michael. Gave Moira a hand in the garden after returning from Mass. He remarked that it had been a quick service and she eyed him tentatively and said she gathered Julia had told him she'd become a lapsed Catholic. He shook his head; as a matter of fact Julia hadn't. He just assumed that Moira had stayed at home for the baby.

"Well then, you may as well know." A hand on her hip, she gazed over at him. "I'm no longer practicing. I don't believe in

God, you see." He was silent and she went back to her hoeing, feeling vaguely ashamed.

Then he said, "It comes as no surprise to me." He was wearing an old pair of Michael's jeans, the cuffs rolled up several times. He was crouched, pulling up weeds. He didn't look up as he said, "You've always been bolder than me."

She heard the baby crying, the screen door swinging. Michael bringing Kate. She took off her gardening gloves. Sat in the grass to nurse. Matty took a break, too, lying on his back beside her, his hat shading his face. "Sandy soil," he remarked. "Similar to home. Ought to try potatoes."

"Maybe next year," Moira replied.

He sighed. "The baby will be toddling around a year from now."

"I'll have to harness her," Moira quipped, and Matty chuckled beneath the hat. She shifted the baby to the other side, reclining gingerly on the grass. The sun felt warm and lovely. Matty rested a hand on her shoulder.

After four days in Maine, two of which it rained and he was cooped up in the house all day without a drop to drink, Matty decided he was leaving—couldn't abide the northern climate, he said jokingly, hadn't left Ireland for nothing. Moira offered to accompany him on the bus as far as Portland. She had errands.

She suggested Matty take the window seat. He showed no particular interest in the scenery, though, perked up only at the sight of a bright blue convertible passing them on the highway. He'd mentioned Georgia, but he'd also talked about California and Arizona, turning the pages of the pocket atlas Michael had bought for him at the gas station. It became clear that Matty hadn't an itinerary. Moira began to worry and feel responsible. She could remember thinking as he walked off the gangway all those years ago, What in the world will he do with himself? But it was his own fault, his doing, after all. She sat up straighter, pointing out the window, Portland ahead.

The connecting bus to New York was already in the station. Matty handed his ticket to the driver and turned to embrace Moira. Her nose flattened against his shoulder. The bus sent out a spume of blue smoke as it lumbered away.

She could do with a cup of tea just now. She crossed the street and went into a diner. Sat absently stirring her cup. In her mind's eye, stood Heleen O'Leary, one hand on her swollen belly. Heleen had known better than to make Matty choose between his solitude and his family. She said nothing when he came in late or when he wouldn't come in at all, got as far as the barn and no farther. She would see the light from the lantern and know he was out there, knock and leave a basket with bread and hard-boiled eggs in it. It meant a carefree night of sleep for herself; alone in the bed, she wouldn't bother to button her nightgown.

The waitress brought the bill. Moira paid, then went to use the ladies' room. She had spent the morning expressing her milk into a baby bottle just in case the bus broke down. But she was full to bursting anyhow. Took the liberty of unbuttoning her shirt and washing herself.

She walked past the shipyard and ferry terminals. She walked through the commerce section, past the nautical map store Michael hoped she might have time to stop in and the herbarium Julia sometimes ordered from. Pausing at a phone booth to check an address in the book. She passed the department store with its large front windows displaying toys and a gallant-looking pram.

Eventually, she found the building she was looking for. The doctor's office was on the second floor.

When Michael and Julia asked her about a pram, Moira told them there was no use spending money on something that wasn't likely to last a year on the dirt roads in Unity. She'd carry Kathleen around on her back in that basket with the straps they used for bringing in firewood.

The doctor had told Moira that some men didn't even notice the diaphragm, so she was a little taken aback when Michael Sheehan got up on his elbows and looked at her, stricken. "Something's in there!"

She hesitated a moment. "It's a device."

"I beg your pardon?"

"It's called a diaphragm. It prevents pregnancy."

"Does it come out?" he asked.

She smiled. "Yes, it comes out."

"Take it out," he said.

"Not until afterward," Moira said firmly.

He rolled away from her.

"What's so wrong with it?" she asked him.

"It obstructs life."

"Just the possibility of life," said Moira.

He was silent a long time. "I want more children."

She sat up in bed. "Kate is just a baby!" She shook her head. All that time spent in the bathroom beforehand. "It comes out, I said. It's not permanent."

Skinny Roberts had wanted off the boat ever since he'd found out what they were earning driving deliveries over at the packing plant. If Moira was ever going to put to sea again, now was her chance. So Julia became Kate's primary caretaker. The move to Unity had meant the end of her career, and she had little else to occupy her. There was not a single dress shop in the whole town and although she had advertised her skills on the community board in the post office, it had led only to a trickle of tailoring jobs, mostly for bachelors and widowers, people who couldn't do their own buttons and hems.

At two years, Kate had silky, milkweed hair and soft blue eyes. She was tough and tireless. Once, when the gate was down, she went into Julia's room and found her rosary beads dangling over the bedpost. Bit by bit Kate managed to stuff the whole string of beads into her mouth. Julia discovered her waddling about swollen-cheeked, the silver cross dangling down. She told her no. Kate squealed and ran off. Julia gave chase. Kate raced gleefully through the kitchen into the mudroom and burrowed in behind the fish pails. Julia could not reach her there. She laughed at her aunt's frustration. When Julia worked an arm in, Kate shrieked and scooted back even farther. Exasperated, Julia lunged forward. The fish pails toppled and, startled, Kate sucked her breath in. Julia saw the silver cross disappearing, she saw the surprise on Kate's face. Cheeks deflating, turning blue. Julia stuck her fingers down Kate's throat, felt for the crucifix, and pulled. Kate gagged and out came the rosary, glistening with saliva. Julia set Kate down on the mudroom floor, where she sat for a long time, listening curiously to her own breathing.

At the end of the day, when they heard the truck pull into the driveway, Julia opened the door and Kate went racing out, down the steps and across the lawn to her parents as fast as her little legs could travel. Julia looked on with a mix of resentment and hurt pride, which turned to pity for Kate as the dinner hour arrived and she tried repeatedly to reach under her mother's shirt and was shooed away.

Michael saw to Kate's bath after supper. It was a favorite time of Julia's, hearing him whistling and Kate splashing while she and Moira washed the dishes. He had more luck reading to Kate than Julia did, certainly. Kate sat in his lap in her flannel pajamas, fresh-faced from her bath, sucking her thumb, watching with interest her father's stiff, unbending index finger as it turned the pages.

They always shared a late pot of tea after Kate went to sleep. In winter, the teapot stayed in its cozy and they sat around the woodstove mending nets with the radio going. Sometimes Michael and Julia played checkers or chess. In warmer weather, they moved out onto the porch. Moira took her teacup with her while she watered the garden. Julia and Michael discussed politics. They had both supported Truman in the election, but Julia continued to light a candle every Sunday for FDR, with whom, as an invalid, she'd identified strongly. They spent hours talking about the technical achievement of the Berlin Airlift. Or else they might indulge in a trivia game they'd created called Bible Wits. They were both enthusiastic competitors. Julia kept score in a notebook and it was always a melancholy day when she stowed the notebook away with her summer clothes and lilac sachets all because Moira couldn't bear to be within earshot of the game and claimed that, if they played inside, their hooting and hollering would wake Kate.

Julia's chronic illness flared several times a year. It could come on overnight and stay several weeks. She applied compresses to her swollen joints and took nothing but cranberry tea in the mornings to combat her nausea. While Kate napped, Julia lay on the couch studying her afflicted knees and wrists, and the purple rash on her feet, eventually coming to believe that her symptoms were simply evidence of the real battle, the invisible one, raging within. When Moira asked her how she was feeling, Julia said, "I'm dying. Quite systematically." It was happening on a cellular level, she explained. Michael suggested she see a doctor. "So as I can surrender entirely?" Julia refused. She would prefer to figure it out for herself, except that she lacked the resources. They suggested the library.

"I'm too sick to be going back and forth to the library every day," Julia said impatiently.

"Tell us what books you need," said Michael. "We'd be happy to bring them home for you."

"Bring them home?" asked Julia. "How?"

"It's a library!" Moira shouted.

"You'd never be able to locate the books I need," Julia stammered. "I'll go myself one of these days."

She knew about the card catalog and about keeping her voice down. She even knew about the archive rooms, where old newspapers and periodicals were housed. The actual purpose of the library had somehow escaped her, though. She had no idea that one could take books out. Perhaps it was just that she couldn't have imagined a public program this gracious; America rarely lived up to its benevolent image. To be sure, after rummaging around in the stacks all afternoon, she did find that the borrowing system was too good to be true. Only two of the five books that she had chosen could actually be taken out. The others were reference books, prohibited from circulation.

She hated having had to leave behind the journals of medical research with that supercilious little librarian. Hadn't she a right to a few answers? She waited for her ride on the library steps.

Michael Sheehan pushed the truck door open for her. "Find what you need?" he asked her.

She climbed in. "More or less." She gazed out the window, hugging her bag of books. "What happens," she asked Michael, "if I don't bring the books back when I'm supposed to?"

"Then there's a fine to pay."

"They've certainly thought of everything!" Julia said crisply.

Julia's desire for a diagnosis heated up as she passed the weeks reading books of cellular biology, pathology, homeopathic science, and the history of diseases in America. She circled the reference stacks, intent, nostrils flaring. *Loss of appetite, low fever, multiple allergies, scaly rash, aching joints, sun sensitivity.* Symptoms identical to her own! She glanced furtively over her shoulder. Certainly she should be allowed to savor this extraordinary discovery. She turned the book over, gazing thoughtfully at the cover. She walked swiftly to the window, shoved it up a few inches, and slid the book out. It dropped onto the snow-covered bushes below.

In the truck that day she was chatty. But she did not give herself away. The book safely secured in her bag. She removed it after dinner, the first meal she'd eaten in weeks with any gusto, and read well past her customary bedtime. She was stirred to tears in her reading and yet noted with some satisfaction that the tears did not come. It wasn't, precisely, that she was dying, but rather that she was killing herself. Her body's defenders, incited to malapropos behavior, were attacking the very organism of which they were a part. Her theft had been entirely worth it;

lupus was one of the most difficult illnesses to diagnose. It broke her heart to read how thousands suffered from it in ignorance. The malfunctioning of her moisture glands keeping her tears at bay.

Julia thought apprehensively of the day she would have to return that remarkable book to the library. But of course there was no due date on it. She could return it whenever she liked. No one in town had any desire for such a specialized text anyway. She was rescuing it from obscurity. All right, she was also stealing, but God never punished the little boy who pilfered a loaf of bread for his starving family. God knew an act of heroism when He saw one. Setting her bookmark, she reached for the light.

The knowledge of a diagnosis was deeply satisfying. Although her manner of care remained virtually unchanged—Julia was already doing more to treat herself than most authors on the subject thought possible—she became more vigorous and forthright in these efforts, assured now of a definite end. Albeit a never-ending end, lupus was not curable, but it was, in fact, comprehensible, containable in this sense. She spent every spare moment at the library, often special-ordering reading material from Portland and Boston. Developed a distinct distaste for librarians in the process—the smarter-than-thou attitude, the self-important, soft-soled shoes. She relished pointing out improperly classified titles in the catalog and gamely interrupted the quiet with a nice long slurp at the water fountain.

"I think I'll close this window," said the librarian.

Julia nearly jumped out of her skin. That was another thing about librarians: They were always sneaking up on her. Particularly this little man who patrolled the reference shelves. A nervous sort, with an unbecoming comb-over to hide his shiny head.

"I'd prefer the window kept open," she responded. "I'm allergic to book dust."

He looked skeptical.

She took out her handkerchief and blew into it.

Julia visited the children's room before leaving, as she always did, randomly selecting a few books to bring up to the checkout counter. Then she raced out into the summer downpour and around the side of the building. She reached her hand down behind the bush, found the books she had dropped from the window, and began stuffing them into her bag with the others.

"Stop, thief!"

Julia looked up and saw the librarian from the reference room peering down from the window. It would be undignified to run. So she stood her ground, clutching the goods to her under her umbrella. She refused to talk to him when he emerged from the building demanding an explanation.

"You know you've broken the law. I've called the sheriff."

Fifteen minutes later, she was ushered through the small crowd of onlookers into a patrol car and driven off, lights flashing.

Since she objected to paying the fifty-dollar fine, the sheriff said he would have to put her in a holding cell. "I'm sorry, Miss O'Leary, but it's a serious offense, pilfering public property."

"You don't have to tell *me* that," Julia said haughtily. "I'm a citizen of this country. I know the rules."

She was allowed a phone call, then the sheriff's deputy unlocked the cell and showed her in. Julia seated herself on the metal cot against the wall. Despite her fatigue, she wasn't inclined to lie down, as both mattress and pillow were unspeakably soiled. She occupied herself by reading the graffiti on the walls.

Mostly vile curses and sex talk, although she did come across a few declarations of love and even a quote from Scripture: *The Lord is my shepherd, I shall not want.* To be sure, thought Julia. All kinds had to do their time.

She told Michael Sheehan when he arrived at the station that he was wasting his energy. She didn't want him to pay the fine for her. "I'm not interested in serving the system's purse." She cast him an annoyed look. "You of all people ought to know better than to try and persuade me."

Michael scratched his beard, perplexed. "Sheriff says he'll keep you here all night otherwise."

"All night?" Julia asked faintly.

"He can't let you go without paying for the crime somehow."

"The crime!" shouted Julia. "Where are those reference books now? Buried in the herd! That's the only crime *I* know anything about."

He was compelled to leave her there, sitting upright on the cot, hands folded in her lap because it was 9:00 P.M., lights-out if she wasn't going anywhere, sheriff said.

The darkness was cold and unsettling, but at least it afforded her a bit of privacy when using the toilet in the corner. She balled up her raincoat, fit it behind her head for a pillow, and listened to her stomach growl. A bowl of gruel, she had thought, maybe, a cup of weak tea. The sheriff apparently would like to starve her out of her convictions. Little did he know, though, about who she was, where she came from. When she was as a girl in Ardgroom her constant hunger had been comforted by prayer. "The Lord is my shepherd," Julia sighed, shutting her eyes since it was dark regardless.

. . .

The first thing Julia did when she got out of jail was knit herself a sweater.

"A sweater?" Moira laughed. "In the middle of July?"

"It's a memento," Julia replied. "Prison is cold no matter the season."

She put the skeins of wool she'd bought at Winkel's summer sale and a pair of needles into the beach bag along with her bathing cap and followed Moira down the path through the woods to the shore. Michael had gone on ahead with Kate. He was helping her build a sand castle. So sweet and patient the way he filled the sand pail up again as Kate smashed the turrets with her shovel. Julia sat down on the beach blanket. Kate trotted over and asked could she bury Julia's feet in the sand. Julia kicked off her flip-flops. The sand felt cool on her hot toes. Then Kate wanted to swim. Moira said she'd take her in. They walked down to the edge, the waves swirling up their ankles. Kate balked. She dug in her heels. Suit yourself, Moira finally said, and plunged in. Kate watched her mother swim away, her body rising with the swell of the waves, kicking up a shimmering spray. Kate splashed about in the shallow water. Crouching down in the quiet, jumping up off the balls of her feet when the wave came. She could barely see her mother now. So much glittery ocean.

"Mama's swimming a long way!" Kate looked eagerly up the beach at Julia and her father.

Her father waved. "Come in for a sandwich, Kate?"

Kate shook her head. She climbed onto a boulder and sat shivering. Absently picked at the lichen. Eyes searching the surging horizon. Her heart leaped suddenly. She caught sight of her mother, swimming in.

The following evening, Michael was reading Kate bedtime stories and Julia found herself listening. A horse with wings, a lucky pebble, a magic kettle. She smiled wistfully at Michael when he emerged from Kate's room. She noticed he was wearing a pair of the argyle socks she had knit for him when he was in the Army.

"Care for a spot of tea?" he asked her.

"I wouldn't mind," she replied.

He brought the tray in and Julia was pleased to see that there were only two cups set out on it. He knew without asking how she took hers: one lump, no milk in the evening. He passed a cup and saucer to her and their hands touched for an instant. He sat down on the couch and picked up his sketchbook. It delighted Julia when she realized it was the balls of yarn at her feet that he was drawing; she was pleased with herself for having left all the yarn out in what apparently was an aesthetically appealing way. He was a clever talent, Julia felt, and yet he lacked the self-consciousness or vanity that often accompanied artists. She began to wonder, as the moments silently passed, if her racing pulse hadn't something to do with the sweater she was knitting. Ever since she'd started it, she'd felt herself yearning for Michael. She decided that if she didn't finish the sweater this evening, she would abandon the project altogether.

Moira came in from watering the garden. She sat down on the couch beside Michael and begged a piece of his pipe. Julia listened as they discussed what sort of present to get Kate for her third birthday. She wanted a bike, but she was too little to manage one. It would only lead to tears and frustration. Kate couldn't stand it when she didn't do something well. Just like her mother behind the wheel of an automobile, said Michael. And Moira said, So?, then, softer, Maybe so. She stretched out her leg to show Michael a scar she had from falling off her father's bicycle as a child. He bent to kiss the spot and she laughed, smiling winningly. Moira had always had good teeth.

Handsome men liked handsome women; that was all there was to it. With a decisive rock of the chair, Julia crossed her legs, upsetting the still life. She took back what she'd surmised earlier about Michael. His intellectual side had simply never reconciled his vanity, let alone his attraction to Moira. Her fine bones, her fair hair. Moira had all the confidence in the world—believed herself to be in complete control actually, which was why, of course, she had so glibly left her faith behind. It struck Julia, suddenly, that she was blessed to be homely; the graceless middle child, Julia's looks at least did not interfere with her character. She was, in this sense, pure. She paused. She held her work up to the light.

"It's lovely," remarked Michael.

Julia blushed despite herself.

Recently Julia had received a packet of buttons in the mail from Matty, like old times. Sturdy, silver-plated buttons: ideal for a cardigan, come to think of it. She didn't know what had moved him, unless it was the money she'd wired him last Christmas. He was in Seattle, arrested on a drunk-and-disorderly charge. He was calling to ask them to send money, and Moira hung up on him. "Come now," Julia said to her. "It's Christmas. We can't up and abandon him." "*He* abandoned us!" Moira replied. Matty had simply never meant as much to Julia, and she had few reservations about dialing up Western Union. Occasionally she wished she felt differently about Matty, but it was easier not to expect too much of him. She cherished the buttons he sent, as they were the most he had ever given her. It was a sacrifice parting with her buttons; she might spend an hour sifting through the jar before selecting. And whenever, by chance, a button on her clothing disappeared (the wringer washer was often to blame for this), she was overwhelmed by the indignity. It sounded foolish but, my goodness, she meant it. Buttons held her in.

Sadly, the cardigan with the silver buttons was misplaced in the hamper one day and Moira, who never sorted out anything, laundered it in hot water with the towels and sheets. The sweater shrank to less than half its original size. It was a long time before Julia swallowed her rage. She gave the sweater to Kate. Kate loved the cardigan with the silver buttons. Her robin's egg, her lake, her warm blueberry. Then one afternoon she came in from playing with a button missing. Julia chased her around the table. "Where's the button?" she demanded. "I don't know. It must have fallen off while I was playing," said Kate. Julia boiled over. She caught Kate by the collar and slapped her. Kate burst into tears. "Undeserving girl," Julia said, angrily. "I ought to be the one crying." She composed herself. Taking down the button jar, she unearthed a large plastic button she had removed from something store-bought a long time ago. She glanced scornfully at Kate and sat down to sew the plastic button onto the cardigan.

Since her sister's manner of child rearing lacked conviction, to say the least, Julia took it upon herself to teach Kate certain things—table manners, sharing, responsibility—and when Kate made mistakes or was slow to learn, Julia reacted with all the indignation of a woman who wished she had better things to do.

Sometimes, as in the case of the missing button, she struck out with her hands. It didn't happen often, and when it did she regretted it. She went to give her sliding sewing glasses a nudge and noticed Kate flinch. She slowly lowered her hand. Turned away from the table to gaze out the window. The first dark always made Julia feel gloomy. What kept her in her sister's house? Poor health, a well-stocked sewing box, a careless child to tell her life to? She could see a rabbit hopping across the grass outside. If she had her slingshot handy, she'd nail it between the eyes. Skin it and fix a savory stew. It bothered her, really, how she could always find something to do.

Helen was different from Kate in every way: weighing nearly twice as much, with a head of curly jet black hair and her father's green eyes, she was born without a fuss just a few hours into the new year, 1950. Watching Julia wash and wrap the baby in towels, Moira reminded herself that this one was for Kate. Kate, well into her third year, doted upon, quite the temper; she was in desperate need of a sibling. Julia carried the baby out of the room and paper birds came soaring down to greet her. Upstairs, Michael had been showing Kate how to fold the paper while she waited impatiently for a sister.

It was Julia who first raised the subject of religious education for the girls. Saint Francis Catholic Church was erected in Unity in 1953. As yet, there were no parochial schools but Julia had seen a notice in the church bulletin for the start of catechism classes in the fall. Kate would soon be old enough to make her First Communion, Julia pointed out one Sunday afternoon. They were grilling fish in the backyard while the girls raced back and forth through the sprinkler in their bathing suits. Goodness, time flew, said Michael, glancing at Moira. She was shucking corn, her back to them, bristling perceptibly as they launched into a discussion of the virtues and importance of a Catholic upbringing. She gathered that this conversation was for her benefit, which immediately put her on the defensive. She felt an undertone of self-righteousness in everything Julia and Michael said. She sighed loudly in exasperation and yet they carried on, important as air. As if God were the inspiration for all of human goodness and morality—and the surprise on their faces when she questioned it.

"Surely, Moira, it is God who makes a person stop and think," Michael said to her.

"God doesn't give me pause," said Moira, swiping the air and catching a mosquito in her hand.

"You're unique," Julia said flatly.

"Why couldn't our morality have come about just the same as the opposable thumb did?" suggested Moira. "Perhaps good behavior was simply a matter of necessity and survival. Cooperation with the pack, in other words."

"You've confused moral behavior with opportunism," said Julia. She added harshly, "Not surprisingly."

Moira's cheeks blazed. She did not know how to respond and was glad of the corn to occupy her. She tore off the husks with frustration. Long ago she had concluded that there was something she was missing—as basic as mathematical aptitude or the ability to carry a tune—that allowed other people their belief. But it wasn't as if it had been easy to count herself out. Particularly since Julia and Michael's shared faith constituted a certain intimacy, which unnerved her as much as it bewildered her. She glanced carefully over at the two of them. She had to wonder if her lack of faith stood in the way of Michael loving her fully.

Thick fog on the sea for weeks, long, cold days lobstering, and not a spot of warmth between them. He was stooped over the bait box, elbow deep in stinking redfish. She sipped black tea from the Thermos, and struggled with herself to surrender. He felt the girls ought to be free to decide the matter of religion for themselves. But they were children, hardly free. It was foolish of him to think otherwise. Especially, she said, since Julia and he were always parading their beliefs in front of Kate and Helen. Her remark offended him. He called her stubborn and narrow-minded and slammed the lid on the bait box. He stared grimly out at the water, refusing to meet her eyes. Yet he could never be as bitter or angry as she, and she felt powerful and hateful knowing it.

On Sunday, Moira awoke thinking of Heleen O'Leary. Her mother had a habit of coming to mind for her whenever she felt confused. There was a familiar, irritable look on Heleen O'Leary's face today, a look she wore when she was doing the baking. The sweat gathered above her pursed lips and her brow furrowed deeply so that her eyebrows met and appeared grown together over her nose. With the mixing bowl propped on her swollen belly, she beat the batter to silk. Wasn't it odd how Heleen's aversion to bread baking seemed to have influenced Moira? Whenever Moira donned an apron, she felt like she was doing penance.

The wind was blowing hard against the house. Moira climbed out of bed and put on her slippers and robe. She felt the draft at the window. They would have frost soon. Tiptoeing out past Michael, she went downstairs to the kitchen and sat with elbows on the table, chin in hands, staring thoughtfully into her tea. Heleen O'Leary had been superstitious and accustomed to letting happenstance guide her—and she defended this behavior as an extension of her faith. Heleen felt entitled to this point of view. She referred to her daughters as her "lucky strokes." And into the bannock batter she would add a fava bean for them, declaring the one whose slice it ended up in queen for a day, which meant that she could leave off fetching the water, or some such chore, without a scolding. Given the choice whether or not to raise her daughters with religion, Heleen would have laughed scornfully. After all, what was the harm in believing? Heleen's numerous failed pregnancies were far outside her understanding. There was, seemingly, no rhyme or reason to life's essence. The outcome of a pregnancy had virtually nothing to do with her, which was why, when good fortune finally dawned and there in her arms was a red and wrinkled infant bawling, Heleen's instinct was to thank someone else besides herself. God came easily to mind.

The floor creaked. Moira glanced up. Her eyes fell upon Kate in her pajamas and Helen, shuffling in behind her, with a wild mop of hair and still sucking her thumb.

"What's for breakfast?" asked Kate.

Moira shook her head. "Nothing, until after church." She met the surprise in Kate's eyes with a sharp look. "You girls are going to church with your father today," she told them, in a measured voice. "Now you'd best go and get dressed. Woolen tights under your dresses, mind you. Clean teeth and combed hair." She pushed back her chair. "You're meant to look your best before the Lord," she said, escorting them.

They were dressed, their scalps tingling from the hair brushing. Moira ushered them into the living room to sit and wait on the couch. Kate complained that she was hungry and Moira explained to her the rule of fasting, although she doubted she was conveying it with sincerity. "It'll be all the sweeter for the wait, Kate," she offered, perfunctorily. It was something her own mother used to say.

Michael came down the stairs just as Julia was emerging from her room. Moira announced that the girls would be accompanying them to church.

"Is that so?" said Michael, pausing on the steps.

"You've had a change of heart," concluded Julia.

"That's going a bit far," Moira replied.

Michael smiled at Kate and Helen. "Don't you two look fine."

Kate sulked. "I want my breakfast."

"Afterward," Moira reminded.

Julia patted Kate good-naturedly on the shoulder. "It will be all the sweeter for the wait!"

Kate frowned. "I know that already."

Moira cleared her throat, gesturing at the clock. "Well then, isn't it time the faithful were going?"

She watched out the window as they made their way across the lawn, Michael holding Helen's hand, Julia holding Kate's, and was, for a moment, overcome with longing. As the truck drove off, she willed herself to turn away. She breathed in the silence surrounding her. Took an apron from the hook and carefully tied it on.

In the recipe file, she came upon a recipe for doughnuts. She found where Julia kept the measuring spoons and cups. She brought out flour, sugar, and lard. She measured and mixed and would not ask herself nor answer, later, when Julia asked her, what, in God's name, had moved her.

"My grumbling belly," she replied, a little defensively.

"Doughnuts!" Kate exclaimed, jumping up and down delighted.

"May I have a doughnut?" asked Helen.

"When they cool," Moira told her, dropping another ring of dough into the sputtering frying pan. She rolled each one dripping hot in cinnamon and powdered sugar. Kate and Helen stood staring. "How was church?" she asked them casually.

"It was so gloomy! It was so dull! I just wanted to fall asleep," Kate declared. She vowed she'd never go to church again and, if she hadn't been so vocal about it, Moira always felt, Helen might have agreed. But Helen had recently discovered the satisfaction in defining herself against her sister. Helen said simply, "I liked it," and skipped gayly out of the kitchen. Kate shrugged. Moira regarded Kate thoughtfully. Then she handed her a doughnut.

By spring, Helen hadn't changed her mind and Moira decided what Helen liked most of all was being with her Daddy, which was not such a bad reason to be going to church, after all. Every Sunday morning, Moira and Kate took a walk or worked in the garden. Of course, the way Kate walked in the woods—crunching leaves and twigs, chattering like a magpie—Moira had little hope of seeing wildlife. Kate was a curious customer, interested in everything, brimming with questions. "What do wolves eat?" she asked her mother. She was making her way down a long list of animals. "Oh, all sorts of things," Moira said to her. "Wolves aren't fussy like you." They sat on a rotted birch log eating the grapes they had brought along in a satchel. A starling alighted on the log. Moira put her finger to her lips and they watched as the bird hopped up close and pecked a grape from the bundle.

Birds, Kate wanted to know, did wolves eat birds? Not so many. Only those that nested on the ground: partridge, grouse—oh, and the little woodcock, too. Do wolves eat people? No, she didn't believe so, except perhaps when there was nothing else—starving, under duress, wouldn't you? Kate shrugged. She didn't know. Yes, of course, said Moira, you would be foolish not to. They kept walking, eventually coming upon a clearing where bear paws sprouted every summer in the shade of two towering red pines. As Moira went about gathering the mushrooms, a hush fell over Kate. She stood beneath the massive trees and gazed upward into the whispering sky of green branches. "A pair of giants," Moira remarked, speaking of the red pines, and Kate thought of her parents, her father because he was tall and her mother because she was formidable.

In the garden that summer there were asparagus, lettuce, bush beans, early peas, carrots, and a whole host of things that needed doing every week. A pot of tea and two cups sat in the grass beside them as they worked. Moira was pleased at how quickly Kate caught on. Certainly, she had her mother's knack for growing things. By the time of the first harvest, a union was forged between them. Moira was pulling up the carrots one Sunday when she uncovered in the dirt the missing silver button from Kate's old cardigan. She picked it up and wiped it on her apron. Kate looked at the tarnished button in her mother's hand.   "Go sew it back on, why don't you," said Moira.

Kate thought for a minute. "What will Julia say?"

"I'll defend you," Moira assured her. Kate raced off toward the house, blond hair streaming, silver button clenched in her fist. Moira looked on, suddenly pensive. Thinking that what was true for plants was probably true for animals. Animals, meaning humans. And why not? Moira was to Kate what Michael was to Helen: the dominant influence. But even so, even if there were predetermined aspects, like the shape of a leaf or an adaptability to change in climate, somewhere within lay the potential self. She had to believe this. Unpredictable, hybrid—regardless.

By 1956, they had traded in the old boat for a new thirty-six-footer with a canopy. Since they kept only a quarter of their traps going through the cold months, in the winter they used the boat for dragging shrimp. Shrimping and winter lobstering were done in deep water, and in a boat such as theirs weather conditions had to be just right or it wasn't worth the venture. They saw no reason to invest in fancy equipment. They threw over a lead line with a tin cup tied to it to find bottom. If the cup came up empty they knew they were hovering over rocks and they moved on. If there was mud or gravel in the cup, they threw their net over and started dragging. They dragged for three or four hours before hauling back, passing the time with their backs to the heater, chewing licorice.

In autumn, when the herring swam shallow, they torched for bait. The business of catching enough bait to last several months was hard work, since it was done at night, after a whole day's fishing, and the catch had to be properly salted and stored afterward. They used an old dory for the job. Moira rowed. Michael crouched in the stern holding a lantern. The herring chased the light. The mass formed just under the water, and grew thicker and thicker. They dipped the net and hauled up—five or six bushels a shot. Headed for harbor at one hundred bushels and spent the rest of the night in the bait shed rolling the fish in salt.

Julia usually met them at the door with a bucket of green soap, and saw that they soaked and scrubbed up to the elbows before coming into the house. But she had her hands full this morning with the two girls and simultaneously stirring oatmeal, turning toast, and pouring cocoa. One ear to the radio local news and one ear to Helen's protest that Kate was hoarding all the crayons. Julia hadn't heard the truck pull in, or the back door opening. If it weren't for the herring stench, she wouldn't have noticed Michael wandering past her. She watched him go into the living room, absently patting the girls on the head as he stepped over them. Julia looked askance. "He doesn't look well," she remarked to Moira.

Moira, shrugging, peered into the oatmeal pot. "A touch of flu."

But he was never one to get sick. Michael and Moira both— hard nuts, a pair of oxen, healthy as sea air. Julia went for the thermometer. His temperature was 104.5 and rising, she reported from the staircase landing. Moira swallowed hard. She went running for the items Julia requested: mustard, lemons, comfrey tea, cheesecloth, a ball jar for distilling. When Kate and Helen asked her why Daddy was sick, Moira told them something shamefully silly: He'd swallowed a silver herring and had a bellyache. The girls were nine and six years old now and knew better; they took it upon themselves to seek an answer from Julia. The fever was fierce, said Julia. She had noted joint inflammation and suspected infection. Was she going to call the doctor? Kate wondered. Only if she felt the need to. Now then, they shouldn't dillydally. School bus would be along presently.

The house fell quiet once the girls went off. Moira walked around restlessly, tidying. Depositing into the toy box Parcheesi chips, stray Lincoln Logs, a miniature wooden tea set, and a stack of tin sand pails dented from having been worn around as shoes. She paused at the window in the girls' bedroom to press to her ear a conch shell. Outside, a pair of cardinals perched on the pinecones the girls had rolled in peanut butter and seed and strung up in the hawthorn.

It was torture to sit and wait, to spend the day at Julia's beck and call. But Moira couldn't bring herself to climb the stairs otherwise. Passing more cheesecloth into Julia's hands, she glanced into the bedroom. He was rolled up in the quilt like a worm in a cocoon.

"How is he?" she asked tentatively.

"No change," Julia replied.

"I could go to the store for groceries," Moira offered, her eyes meeting her sister's. "Unless you need my help here."

"No, I don't," Julia said plainly.

The sun cast a monster-sized shadow of the truck on the road. A flock of Canada geese alighted in a frozen blueberry field. She kept her hand poised atop the steering wheel, since it was the custom in Unity for drivers to wave and she didn't like to be caught unaware. She drove past a ramshackle farmhouse and a pond glassy with new ice. There were sheep clustered under the bare crab-apple trees. She slowed the truck and rolled down the window, clicking her tongue fetchingly. The sheep scuffled off. She never really could look at sheep again without thinking of Ann. Her heart quickened with fear. She gunned the gas and the truck's tires squealed. Just then, she heard something scramble up alongside, and caught the flicker of ears and flash of tail in her side mirror. Surely a farm hound, but she peered anxiously into the rearview mirror. Having given up the chase, the animal stood in a cloud of dust kicked up by the truck. Moira stared. When she returned her attention to the driving, the road was about to T-out. She drove headlong into a field.

She was not hurt. Shaken, only. The rosary beads that hung from the mirror swung wildly. She had had several close calls over the years, including a near collision with a hay baler while Julia was in the passenger's seat, after which Julia had seen fit to outfit the truck with its own set of rosary beads. The distinction between right and left had always required deliberation on Moira's part, and she had seen how the dangling crucifix might be helpful since left was the direction in which Christ's head hung in sorrow and right was the side of his body that bore the thin red mark of a lance wound. But a moment ago, in need, she hadn't thought to look to Christ for guidance.

Raindrops fell on the windshield. She tried to back up, but the truck wheels spun. Eventually a car came along—George Reed on his way home from hauling. He pushed, she gave it gas. The truck sailed up over the bank. She was much obliged. He tipped his cap. Wouldn't want her to be stuck out here. Radio said they were going to see some weather. Folks at the grocery store reiterated the storm prediction. Moira bought an extra quart of milk and loaf of bread. Drove home at a snail's pace, rain turning to sleet already.

The next day, the ocean was draped in cold mist, waves crashing in against boulders slick with ice. Yellow grass and juniper trees cambered in the wind on Diamond Island. Lobster buoys bobbed in the chop. Kate and Helen climbed carefully down the rocks. School that day had been canceled, but by noon it was no longer stormy. Moira, calling the girls stir crazy, had sent them out for a walk. They made their way along the beach, which was littered with debris from the storm—big chunks of driftwood, busted lobster traps, a life jacket, plastic detergent bottles, rope, fishing net—all tangled in the mounds of kelp. As they entered the woods on the other side of the cove, dismembered tree trunks appeared, lost lobster buoys in the snow, an old boat steering wheel in a web of broken branches on the trail. Kate spotted an owl in one of the pitch pines. They reached the head of the clearing, stopping short suddenly. "Look!" gasped Helen. "Yes," Kate breathed, staring in disbelief at the fallen tree. The great stump had been partially uprooted in the fall. The trunk had split down the middle, plummeting to either side, taking numerous birches and aspen with it.

A rich fleshy color, the raw pulp. A pair of woodpeckers flew off at their approach. Sap pores in the bark glistened. Helen pulled off her mitten and scraped up a sample. On the edge of the wind, Kate heard a howl, and looked around. Maybe it was more of a hoot. Earlier she had seen that snowy owl. A shiver raced up her spine. Gusts whistling out of the sky. She stepped up to the tree, reaching her arms around as far as she could, cheek pressed against the cold trunk, and gazed across the clearing at the other red pine.

They stood in their underpants on the hearthstone, heat coming fast to their bodies. Their skin burned with feeling. A dusky glow out the window, the edge of the woods black as charcoal. Moira came into the room. How was the walk, she wanted to know.

They told her about the fallen tree. A gaping hole in the sky. Kate swallowed. Moira said that lightning must have struck the tree. She opened the stove door and shoved a new log in.

"Were you spooked?" she asked the girls.

Kate glanced at Helen.

Moira went on, "A great tree like that? I should certainly hope so."

Later that night found her sitting by the stove with fishing nets and mending needle. She was waiting for Julia to come downstairs. "I'll take the boat out myself tomorrow, weather allowing," Moira announced.

Julia regarded her warily. Michael's fever hadn't budged. Sighing, she slumped into a chair. "Denying he's sick won't make him well, Moira."

"There's no reason for me to stop fishing," Moira insisted.

"You're heartless," Julia said.

"Because I don't revel in someone else's pain and suffering the same as you?" shouted Moira.

By week's end, Julia had determined that it was rheumatic fever—which made it easier for Moira to respond whenever the other fishermen asked her, "Where's your captain?" Michael Sheehan lay in bed, immobile, often delirious, while Moira took the boat out by herself. It was not easy doing the work of two, but she was stoic. Someone had to sit in the captain's chair, harvest the lobster. (Sheep won't wait, her father used to say.) Moira simply couldn't go back there—to the sickbed—not even in her mind; it was so hopeless. She felt betrayed, standing there at the bedside at Julia's urging, and did not think to tell him of the unusually high number of keepers she'd hauled that day or that she attributed it to the new rectangular traps they were using, urchin-proof seemingly. She did not describe for him how the sky was wide open after the wind and snow, even though she had thought of it earlier, turning the boat toward harbor, squinting into the sun. Good weather ought to speak to him.

Your mother will never be prepared in the case of tragedy," Julia told the girls gravely.

"But why?" asked Kate.

Julia sighed. "She can't bear to consider it."

"Why?" Helen echoed.

Julia paused, thoughtfully. She wasn't in the habit of speaking of the past with them. It was enough that she had rallied them around her cause; they were helping her pull the leaves off devil's bit and boxwood plants and talking in whispers so that Michael could sleep. They were allowed upstairs for a visit after school. They had snacks on a blanket on the bedroom floor. Helen kneeled at the head of the bed and said her rosary while Kate combed the fever-loose hair from her father's head. "No matter," Julia said, putting her arms protectively around both of them. "If your ma's not prepared, I will be." Kate wriggled out of her grasp. Lately she was doing that.

Moira went down into the cellar to bring up some pickled vegetables for supper. She felt a draft at the bottom of the basement stairs and realized that the outside door was ajar. As soon as she'd shut it, she smelled the cured sausages that hung from the overhead pipes. She looked up and then stopped short, as there wasn't a sausage in sight. Instead, she found several slick, chewed pieces of string and bits of meat on the sandy floor. And then she saw the animal tracks. She knelt down, tentatively reached out her hand to measure the impression. Out flickered the light suddenly. She was engulfed by the dark. She panicked, knocking over bicycles, a clothes-drying rack. Barged her way back to the stairs. She raced up them and flung open the kitchen door. There was Kate, trying to hoist a large kettle into the sink. "Fever's peaking," she said over her shoulder. Moira nudged her off the stepstool, "I'll do it."

Julia eyed Moira coolly as she carried in the kettle. She set to organizing the assembly line: Kate and Helen were to plunge towels into the water, Moira to wring out the towels and hand them over to Julia. Julia then drew the bed covers off. Moira's jaw dropped open at the sight of Michael's sweat-drenched body. He was trembling uncontrollably. He had grown very pale and very thin, his rib cage shuddering visibly beneath the skin. She stared, absently wringing out the towel, but instead of passing the towel to Julia, she held fast to it. There was an uncharacteristically timid expression on her face as she stepped in front of Julia, saying, "Let me."

Julia watched Moira wrap the wet towel around Michael's arm. "Inch by inch," she instructed her, holding out another towel.

"Like a mummy," Kate suggested.

And Moira thought, yes, preserved, the important person that he was, under layers of wrapping. If they unraveled him years from now, how would they find him? As ever? But she would never have been able to wait while time stood still—growing desperate, defensive, the couch becoming more familiar than her bed. Left to fend for two children and a begrudging sister, there was no telling what she'd do to save herself.

. . .

He's cured," Julia said to her when she tiptoed upstairs the next morning.

Michael was sitting up in bed.

Blinking back tears, her smile quivering, Moira said good morning. She felt conspicuous, relief washing over her. She hastily buttoned up her overalls. She was fixing to leave, go off in the boat and fish her heart out, but he was well enough now to protest.

"Stay," he said to her. "It won't do, you fishing alone."

She sat down beside him on the bed. They held hands. Talked a little lobstering. There was no escape, she realized suddenly, glancing fleetingly across the room for Julia, but Julia had slipped out. Moira sighed. Michael was drinking down a bowl of soup as if he had crossed the desert. She watched his Adam's apple rise and fall.

A wolf?" Michael gazed at her across the boat. "Not this far south. Up north, inland perhaps."

Moira set the trap and dropped it over the side. "Don't try and tell me it was that setter from down the way," she said, turning to face him. "I've had an earful from Julia already, and you both ought to know the dog's too dumb to pop a lock."

He looked at her curiously. "We'll put a new lock on the cellar door."

That was exactly what Julia had said. Moira sighed. It was not the wolf, itself, after all, but that the wolf was possible. She ought to have known the point would be lost on them. She eyed him. He wore a thick wool sweater and hat, just out to test his sea legs after so many days sick. She reached for the Thermos, urged

on him a steaming cup. He couldn't tell her anything about hunt-
ers, the forests cut down. She felt old frustration. "I saw the
tracks, Michael!" Although, when she had returned and screwed
in a new lightbulb, the tracks were no longer evident, obscured
by her own footprints as she had groped fretfully about in the
dark. But wasn't she relieved, somehow? To be without proof or
certainty. To go on living with her usual yearning.

He was standing at the wheel. The boat bounding over the
water, headed for harbor. The spray touched down ice-cold on
their faces. She made her way up the side and ducked under his
steering arm so that she stood at the wheel with him. He said to
her, "It isn't true that you haven't faith, Moira."

Perhaps it was that holidays encouraged reflection, which Moira
found troubling, or that they marked time in a way that seemed
arbitrary to her. She was not one to look back fondly or longingly,
nor was she inclined to envision the future. She was most at ease
in the present, not unlike an animal absorbed exclusively in what
was happening—that osprey she had seen through the monocle
the other day, up and abandoning her nest to dive for whatever
it was that had caught her attention.

She stood at the sink filling the kettle, staring out the window
at the evergreen tree leaning against the porch rails. It was Christmas, 1957. The girls had begged for a tree this year. They'd
scouted out the perfect one and Michael had felled it for them
with a hatchet. He'd bring the tree in when he got home from
church. (He went every day during Advent.) The girls were busy
cutting out gingerbread men. Moira tried to be a good sport at
Christmastime for their sake. She had even done a little holiday
shopping. Michael and Julia had drawn a blank when it came to

buying presents for Kate. Kate didn't like to read and draw the way Helen did. (As if Helen actually needed one more book or box of crayons.) Come to think of it, Moira had said, what *Helen* needed was a pair of mittens she could call her own. So that she wouldn't be coming home with her fingers nearly falling off frost-bitten because she refused to wear her sister's hand-me-downs. And it went to show that Moira *did* know her own daughters. In spite of what Julia was always intimating to the contrary. Julia could button her lip and knit the mittens. Except that Moira went and brought home yellow wool, so Julia had the last word after all, sending her back to exchange the yellow for purple, Helen's favorite color, or hadn't she ever noticed?

Just a few inches of snow on the ground Christmas morning. Santa Claus might not have found his way in the blizzard they were expecting. Michael winked at the girls, directing them to the swollen stockings that hung from the mantel. The living room was soon littered with tissue paper. Then it was time for Mass. The house fell quiet, except for the sound of beads whirling around as Kate practiced with her new hula hoop. Moira went out to collect the newspaper and found a bird's nest on the ground. She brought it inside with her. Arranging in it several of the eggs the girls had hollowed out and colored last Easter. Too beautiful to stow away, everyone had agreed, and the eggs had remained on the hutch in a basket. Moira set the nest in the Christmas tree branches.

She was having her tea, reading the obituaries, when Kate called out that there was a taxi cab in the driveway. Moira rubbed her fist on the window, fogged from the steaming kettle. He was stepping out of the cab, thick white hair blowing in his eyes and jacket flapping. "Matty," she murmured.

. . .

He hadn't money to pay the cab fare. No sir, a round-trip bus ticket and that was all. He would have walked from the bus station, if he'd had the right shoes. He was wearing cowboy boots, standing on the doorstep. Moira let the storm door swing closed on him while she searched her purse. Handing Kate the money, she said it was Bob Marsh at the wheel and to wish him a happy holiday.

"You must be Kathleen," Matty said to her.

Kate smiled. "How did you know?"

"You're the spitting image of your mother."

Kate took a running jump and leaped off the stairs. Matty chuckled, watching her tear across the frozen grass. He turned to Moira. "Will you invite me in? Or have I come the distance for nothing?"

She held open the door for him and then for Kate, back in no time, cheeks red from running. My, was it cold out. Matty said that was the first thing he'd noticed, stepping off the bus in Unity. Still, he was glad to be there, after two whole days traveling. Glad, he said, to have the opportunity to visit with his granddaughter. If she'd be so kind as to help him with his boots, he'd warm his toes by the fire. Kate pulled and pulled. The boot shot off and she flew backwards laughing, landing on her bottom. Matty offered up his other foot to her.

Although he lived in a trailer park, he fancied himself a rancher. Goats. Goats were his hope. More confidence than sheep. No fleece to bother about. He wasn't exactly getting rich off the milk (couldn't even call it a living) but he drank it every morning, steeped it overnight on the radiator when he wanted yogurt, and he swore it was better for you than milk from a cow. He never minded the sour aspect.

Moira didn't ever recall her father being so talkative. She was relieved when the others returned from church and there was Christmas dinner to attend to. It had started to snow. Large fat flakes swirling down outside the window. Julia had joined Matty in extolling the wonders of goat's milk. Helen was reared on it, Julia told him, after her mother weaned her prematurely. And Matty said, so that explained it, referring to Helen's height. He'd made quite a fuss about Helen when she first came in. Somehow, he hadn't realized he had *two* grandchildren. At which remark Julia had looked startled, for she'd always been good about writing Matty the news and, from time to time, she even sent photos. Kate and Helen were as different looking as two sisters could be, claimed Matty, and he'd be hard pressed to say which one was prettier. The girls seemed genuinely charmed by him. He gamely took a turn with the hula hoop, swiveling unabashedly, and when Helen drew him a picture of a horse with her new pastels, he behaved as if she'd given him the world. "Oh, but isn't it a perfect likeness? You're a horse lover, are you? Well then, that's something you and I have in common."

The girls wanted their grandfather to go ice skating with them. The clearing in the woods flooded and froze every winter. Matty didn't look too enthusiastic about heading back out into the cold, but he agreed to go. Snow was falling steadily by now. The wind whistled. The going was slow. The girls were bundled up in snowsuits. Matty carried their ice skates slung over his shoulder.

"Is it much farther, this clearing?" he asked, after a while.

"No," said Kate. "Not really. It shouldn't be."

Matty said that it seemed they had been walking a long time. They could hear the ocean.

In a small voice, Kate said, "Maybe we missed the turn."

"We've come too far, have we?" asked Matty. Dark water suddenly rushed in over their boots. The snow became slush. "Watch yourselves now." He took each girl by the arm. They splashed up a small incline, and peered out through the trees. The rocky coastline had vanished, and the water was overflowing into the forest. Matty steered Kate and Helen back the way they'd come. Eventually Kate spotted one of the tall red pines. "The clearing!" she shouted, and rushed toward it.

"Well now," said Matty, relieved. While the girls laced up their skates, he went and urinated against a tree. The girls skated around and around. Matty stood on the side, shivering, squinting upward into the trees, but the snow was falling so fast through the branches he couldn't see. Then Helen tripped over a tree root and fell facedown on the ice. She was in tears, complaining of the cold. Matty said he'd best be getting them home. The girls put their boots back on. Helen was still sniffling. "Will you have a horseback ride?" Matty asked her. They started off, Helen clinging to his shoulders, Kate to his arm, ice skates swinging.

"Look! There's a dog!" Kate said suddenly.

Matty froze where he stood. Not twenty yards off, camouflaged by the falling snow, it stood with its head turned, watching them. Frosty white muzzle. Yellow eyes glowing.

"Where?" Helen whined. "I can't see!"

Kate stepped toward it. Matty laid a protective hand on her shoulder. They could just make out the silvery haunches, a curved tail, before the animal vanished from view.

. . .

All lit up, smoke spouting out of the chimney, a house never looked so cheerful. Matty knelt down in the snow and Helen slid off. The girls raced up the porch steps. The door swung open— warm light flooding out, Moira in silhouette. They were home. She ushered them in. "Rough seas, I imagine."

"Aye," Matty said.

In the vestibule, Kate and Helen busily kicked off boots.

"We saw a big dog in the woods," Kate reported.

"But I didn't see it," bemoaned Helen.

Moira looked askance at them. She turned to Matty.

"Blinding snow," he said, pushing past. He needed a drink. They were having eggnog. "No," he said, "a real drink." Michael produced a bottle of Scotch whiskey. He took the glass, stood staring into the fire.

Moira pressed him. "What was it you saw out there, Da?"

He tipped back his glass, glancing uneasily at her. "Couldn't say for certain."

He was sauced before long, pacing back and forth in front of the fire with the whiskey bottle, a pained expression on his face, which Julia took for self-pity and so avoided lifting her eyes from the coffee table and the new jigsaw puzzle Michael had given her. She was truly amazed when Matty stopped short and, reaching over her shoulder, fit a significant piece of the puzzle together. All afternoon she'd been stumped by that corner.

Matty fell asleep in front of the fire after eating his fill of Christmas dinner. Moira draped a blanket over him. His eyes fluttered open for a moment. "The wolves have followed you across the ocean, have they?" She paused, studying his face. Soon he was snoring. She moved his wet boots nearer the fire.

It eased the pain, Julia had discovered, to contemplate something white. Trumpeter swans moving across the cloudy sky. So far below, in her tidy bedroom, she could barely hear their wild honking. With the arrival of the wet spring weather, Julia's legs had swelled up so painfully that she had taken to bed, to ponder silently her plaster ceiling. She abandoned her reverie at the sound of the back door opening, the stamping of Michael's boots in the mudroom. Michael made and applied Julia's hyssop poultices every afternoon. Perhaps he felt beholden to her after she had nursed him through rheumatic fever, but she would rather believe he looked forward to their time together, the same as she. Kennedy had been elected, the Irish Catholic president, and there was much on the political front for them to talk about, but lately Julia would rather talk about her faith, as she found it gave her strength.

She received the Eucharist at home in her nightgown every Friday from Father Keane, the parish priest. It warmed and nourished her to reenact the sharing of the holy meal under her own roof each week. Michael always partook. And if Helen hadn't plans to go with her sister to the movies or to a baseball game at the grange, she might join them. Then it really was a celebration of community—Father Keane passing a plate with the blessed bread and everyone helping themselves to it. Deep down Julia suspected that Father opted not to administer the Eucharist personally because he was afraid her lupus was catching, nevertheless she found that the gesture had an equalizing effect on her understanding of the sacrifice. Julia had never really liked being served by the priest. The point in the Mass at which he held the Eucharist up for all to see, then broke it down the middle, was hard for her to bear. Ever since she was a child, she had been steeling her gaze lest she be overcome with grief. For, in that moment, she saw her mother and, of course, Ann. She was surrounded by broken bodies, her own most profoundly.

Father Keane was very caring—there was no doubt about it (dependable as a mailman in his weekly house call)—but lacking in edge and intellect. After Communion, Julia was only too eager for him to leave so that she could take up where she had left off with Michael.

"You know, Michael," she said, "the Eucharist has always made me nostalgiac. I've thought of it primarily as an occasion for remembrance. But taking the bread of Christ into my own hand like that, it changes everything. It's nourishing, and hopeful."

Michael nodded his head. "An act of renewal."

"And redemption," she added. She reached impulsively for his hand and gave it a quick squeeze. "My heart is flooded with the pureness of it."

She followed his gaze to the window. Outside, the sun had gone down. The sky was glowing.

Without Michael, it would have been a desperately lonely time for her. She had precious few other visitors. Lucy Lutz, with whom she co-wrote the church bulletin, showed up with typewriter and mimeograph paper once a week; Skinny Roberts might drop by on a Saturday; and the ladies from her quilting bee took turns coming. Moira's idea of providing company consisted of lying across the foot of the bed reading the Sunday paper. The girls rarely made an appearance. They were busy with school, end-of-the-year activities, poking their heads in only to say good night. Kate and Helen were growing up at a rapid rate. At fourteen, Kate was a hopeless case—silly, distracted, irresponsible. Earning a D in geometry. Even Michael had criticized. Growing up in Ireland, not one of them had gone to school past age twelve. Michael was often saying it was his biggest regret. He told Kate that finishing high school was an achievement, and he would be proud, however many Cs it took her to do so, but a D meant she wasn't trying.

Julia had worn Saint Jude out praying for Kate. Thank goodness Helen was nothing like her. Helen was studying to be confirmed in the Catholic Church. She was growing her hair long to resemble Saint Teresa's. Rather zealous of her, but Julia was only encouraging. If she had learned anything in her years of surrogate mothering it was that children were a gamble.

The Memorial Day parade came and went without Julia that year. She lay in bed with the window open, curtains billowing. At least she could hear the bagpipes, Tom Yardley leading the way down Main Street (always something of a shock to see him in a kilt after three hundred and sixty four days of nothing but rubber boots and overalls). In healthier years, Julia had gone mainly to see the veterans, waving her little flag wildly as they marched by, hoping to catch Michael's eye. She'd also been known to indulge once a year in a stick of cotton candy. The Memorial Day parade was the only annual, public celebration in the town of Unity (besides the July Fourth fireworks and clambake, instituted in recent years to encourage tourist trade), starting off promptly at noon. If you blinked, you'd miss it going past you.

Julia was ill straight through the spring and on into summer. She missed the planting of the garden and the reshingling of the roof. She might have missed the family of raccoons beneath the porch floorboards, ousted and transported to a distant locale, except that days later one more turned up in the trap and from her bedroom window she could hear it. She hobbled outside in her nightgown, eased herself down on the ground, and spotted the animal's glistening eyes. She pulled the trap out from under the porch. The raccoon blinked up at her. It reached a delicate black paw through the slats of the cage. Tentatively, Julia offered her finger. The raccoon grabbed hold. She kept her composure. With her free hand, she unlatched the trap. The raccoon scampered off toward the trees.

Julia had hoped the summer might bring her the girls' company, but it was wishful thinking. Kate was working for her parents down at the marina three days a week. She was also learning to drive. Michael had told her that once she got her license, she could start taking the truck to Portland to buy supplies wholesale for him. A little responsibility was turning into a lot, lately. It made Julia anxious, yet she couldn't deny how grown-up Kate seemed, driving out to the Mr. Frostee last week. It was the first time in months Julia had been to town. "Come for an ice cream," Michael had coaxed. He helped her out to the car. She gripped her seat the entire way, but really there was no need. Kate was quite capable, and she took her father's advice seriously. "Coming up on blacktop, now. Steady as she goes, Katy-lady." He was the only one of them who could get away with calling her nicknames. On the way home, they had come across Helen walking back from the Francoeurs' farm. "Get a horse," they had all shouted out the window, a big joke. Kate pulled the truck over and Helen hopped in back, flushed and excited after a whole day of riding.

The horse had entered Helen's life, lumbering purposefully across the road to eat the wild strawberries, when she was walking home from confirmation class one July day. A chestnut-colored mare with a stubborn disposition and an insatiable appetite. Helen coaxed her back to the Francoeur farm with licorice drops and learned from Mrs. Francoeur, who was sitting on the porch step shelling beans and smoking a cigarette, that Tulip jumped the fence every year for the strawberries. Arlene Francoeur had invited Helen to come back for a riding lesson. Suffice it to say that that was the last Julia saw of Helen for the remainder of the summer.

Julia was well enough to resume a few house chores by summer's end, which was how Moira came upon her ironing Michael's undershirts and socks one Saturday. Since when did a fisherman have a need for pressed underclothes, Moira asked, and laughed. Julia couldn't help blushing.

"Since you haven't anything better to do and you're feeling well enough," Moira said, "I could use an extra pair of hands with the jamming."

"I'd rather press clothes," answered Julia.

"Michael's clothes," Moira said knowingly. She turned away. "You spoil him."

Julia heard her go down into the cellar. Ball jars clinking prettily as she returned, carrying them up the staircase. Cupboards opening and closing. Something inside Julia just giving. She collapsed the ironing board and went into the kitchen. The smell of bubbling blackberries already thick and sticky. Moira, at the stove, stirring with a long spoon. Julia tied on an apron.

The first snows arrived early. They always hired Ralph Wentworth to plow their road, but that year he sent out his son Buddy. Buddy Wentworth stood in the kitchen rosy-cheeked and awkward, waiting for Julia to pay him. It was a Wednesday evening,

Kate's night for cooking. Stuffed peppers, usually. Kate and Buddy were talking. They were in the same year at the high school, apparently. Julia glanced out the window to make sure he'd done the entire driveway. "Thank you, ma'am," Buddy said, pocketing the money. She was surprised to see him loitering. As for Kate, she'd been trimming the same green pepper ever since he'd walked in the door. They'd all go hungry at this rate.

Julia cleared her throat. "Mr. Wentworth, a puddle is gathering under you."

"Sorry, ma'am," he stammered, glancing down at his boots.

"Wait," said Kate. "You don't have to leave."

But he was out the door already, gone in a flash. Kate was red-faced, stalking over to the sink to rinse clean the inside of the pepper.

Julia took up her wooden hospital crutches and swung herself out with gusto. She went to draw herself a bath, setting her crutches aside with a sigh. Armpits stinging where she'd broken open blisters. She had acted so delighted when Michael first brought the crutches home and had relished the evening he spent teaching her to use them. The crutches were useful, it was true, but they gave her less excuse to shout for things and less leverage in ordering the girls around. For instance, she wouldn't mind a bit of oatmeal to soften the water, but Kate was sulking now, and she didn't dare ask for it. She slowly undressed, stepped gingerly in. Oh, but it was scalding. She forced herself to sit.

If Mr. Wentworth had gone about asking Kate to the New Year's Eve ball properly, Julia said, she might feel more charitably toward him. Buddy had called up on the telephone, inviting Kate to the dance. "So cowardly!" declared Julia. "One orders groceries over the phone." But what really got Julia's goat was the fact that Kate had bought herself a dress to wear at Winkel's department store. "For goodness' sakes, go and get your money back. Look at the tailoring! You can't possibly wear *that*."

Kate tried to explain. "I didn't think you were feeling well enough to sew."

Julia called for her hat and coat. Hobbling out to the truck on Kate's arm, she ventured into town for the first time since the snows. They purchased three and a half yards of indigo blue velvet at the Calico Cat, and got matching thread and zipper thrown in because Peg Anderson, the proprietor of the shop, was one of Julia's quilters. But Julia wouldn't be using the zipper. She had in mind a wide, gracefully scooping neck and narrow, three-quarter-length sleeves. A skirt that hugged the waist and thighs, and fastened with buttons in a line down the side. Kate was ordered in for a fitting the following week. She pulled on the dress, nudging the material down over her hips, while Julia stood back, measuring tape draped around her neck, pins between her lips.

"You'll have to wear heels, you know."

"High heels?" asked Kate.

"Definitely," said Julia, unable to help herself.

She felt overcome with exhaustion now. She was going to bed directly, and if it wasn't too much to ask, she'd have her uva ursi later, perhaps an ankle dressing. She was thinking of Michael, mainly. She waited all evening. At last he came knocking. She beckoned him in. They had returned to harbor late. She said he needn't apologize, watched him preparing the poultice. He had the most elegant fingers. She closed her eyes in anticipation. Telling herself that the love of God was eternal. To covet was unbecoming. Oh, but it was difficult! Her heart fluttered as he touched her ankle. She let out a gasp.

"Are you in pain?" Michael asked.

"Yes, torturous," she answered. Pressing her hand to her heart. She could feel his handsome, soulful gaze.

"We'll see you on your feet again, eventually," he encouraged.

Julia sighed. "You don't understand, Michael. How could you? I'm afraid I'll expire from the pain!"

"You mustn't do that. What would I do without you, Julia?"

She opened her eyes, gazing up at him.

He smiled at her. "You're a sister to me."

Presently Moira turned up with the tea tray. Julia pushed herself up on the pillows, shaking her head No thank you before the tea was even proferred, ignoring her parched throat. Her hands were trembling and she was wary of spilling. The solicitous way Michael took the tray out of Moira's hands was as much as she could take. She turned her head away. Moira started in with idle conversation. Michael seemed only too eager to join her. For goodness' sakes, Julia would just as soon hear them creaking the floorboards upstairs.

A sister? She couldn't think of a worse fate! Yet, after all, wasn't that primarily what she was? It occurred to Julia that her feelings of love for Michael and resentment for Moira were one and the same. Nothing had changed. The pain of the years came back in a heartbeat. Sisters; it was a mercilessly dependable relationship.

• • •

For Helen's birthday there was eggnog and Moira's shortbread. Helen turned twelve years old at the stroke of midnight. As usual, they folded paper birds, climbed upstairs, and sent them soaring down, heralds of the New Year. Helen opened up her presents. A gold necklace with a crucifix, a horse-grooming brush, and, most precious of all, a leather-bound sketchbook. As vital as real life to an artist, Michael said, handing her an ink pen so that she could write her name in it. Julia poured more eggnog. Michael took out his harmonica. Moira was coaxed into dancing. She stamped her heels, turning in lively circles. The floor vibrated with the pounding. Helen thought fleetingly of Kate weaving across the gym floor in her slinky sapphire dress. She licked the eggnog from her lip, imagining for a moment that she was an only child, singular and unconflicted as a golden egg. She bit into a piece of shortbread. There were never birthday candles. Her mother didn't abide by that tradition. Never, in this respect, was there anything to wish for. Helen gazed downstairs at the folded-up pieces of paper scattered about the living room. It was 1962 now.

While riding Tulip in the woods, collecting whatever treasures the melting snow uncovered—sea glass, beer-bottle caps, mushrooms once it warmed up, and lily of the valley—Helen contemplated the life of Saint Teresa. Teresa of Avila had a calling. She could not deny the rapturous voices in her ears even if she wanted to. Teresa was a teenager when she experienced her first full-fledged ecstatic vision, and from then on there was no protection from herself. A life so passionate, so full of drama and preternatural suffering, was fascinating; a hundred times now,

Helen had read the part about the visions that left Teresa quaking in the convent garden, holding fast to the gate lest she be lifted into the sky, seized by a tremendous fire burning inside, and then mercilessly hurled to the ground an empty vessel. But since biographies of the saints tended to focus on the period of life during which the first steps on the arduous path to sainthood were taken, Helen knew few details of Teresa's childhood. Often she made up things. Roaming through the forest, a Swiss army knife in her pocket, Helen pictured Teresa on her horse in the highlands of Spain. Alert to every upturned twig, every trace of deer and fox and hare, but as yet unconscious of her remarkable fate.

"Whoa," Helen said, pulling up the reins. She peered out through the trees. Kate and Buddy Wentworth stood in the clearing kissing. Helen was riveted. She nearly jolted out of the saddle when Tulip sneezed. Kate looked around anxiously. Helen held her breath. She watched as Kate and Buddy hurried off through the birch trees. She dismounted, heart beating rapidly—and led Tulip into the clearing. She stared at the trampled violets at the base of the tall tree stump. Several years ago, her father had taken a bucksaw to the felled tree. Enough firewood to last a lifetime, he'd said, but again they'd gotten down to the last logs in February.

Helen took out her pocket knife and flipped open the carving blade. Stepping up to the tree stump, she drove it in deep. Both hands were needed to extract the blade. She gripped it tightly and pulled it out. She began to stab the tree furiously. One of her hands slipped and she nicked herself. She pressed the cut to her lips and, working more carefully now, carved a long slender crucifix in the surface of the tree stump.

. . .

In July of 1963, Arlene Francoeur died of cancer and her husband put the farm up for sale. Mr. Francoeur telephoned the house to ask Helen if she'd like to have Tulip. A horse was a big responsibility, her father said, did she think she was ready? She was, yes; she nodded her head for certain. She had prayed to God for her own horse. They could make a stall for it in the shed. And she would paint lobster buoys for her parents in exchange for the cost of Tulip's feed.

So Tulip came to live with them. And very quickly made her presence known. She nosed the screen out of the kitchen window and licked clean the sugar bowl. She ate the raspberries off the bushes before they ripened. She competed with the deer for whatever leaves and vegetables she could reach through the garden fence, and she slurped up maple sap from the buckets on the trees. Tulip was a nuisance, everyone agreed, but quietly. Helen was very sensitive, serious, clearly in love with the horse. She sat in the grass with her sketchbook while the horse stood in the shade of the apple tree, her tail flicking the flies. Her father might come out and join her. Side by side they'd sit, drawing. Moira knew better than to interrupt then. She'd set a couple of glasses of iced tea on the porch railing, let the door swing going in so that they'd notice them.

One night, Moira awoke to hear the horse making a stir in the shed. She climbed out of bed and went to the open window. A warm, wet breeze was stirring the leaves. The horse whinnied uneasily. Moira glanced at the bed, where Michael lay asleep. She padded out of the room. As soon as she stepped outside the house, she could hear Tulip shuffling restlessly. She came closer, shining her flashlight. She could also make out a persistent scratching sound. It came from the back, near the door. She paused and the scratching paused too. Then she heard a scuffle of paws over the woodpile. Logs shifting. Moira hurried around to catch a glimpse. She shone the light, but she was a moment too late.

She talked through the door to calm the horse. "Settle down, old girl. The intruder's gone." Tulip snorted in response. They'd be better off keeping the horse's feed inside the mudroom. Whatever it was had managed to claw a hole in the base of the shed door. "All right, then," she soothed.

The Francoeur land was purchased by the State Park Service in 1964, which meant it would not be threatened by subdivision or commercial development. For the most part, the news came as a relief. Michael and Moira were home when the green truck with the state-flag emblem drove into the driveway. The brown-shirted Park Service manager knocked on the door. He introduced himself. Michael shook his hand. The Park Service manager informed them that as neighboring property owners they would be compelled to comply with rules restricting the use of power equipment and the farming of certain crops prone to insect infestation. The Park Service was also planning a number of nature trails for the property, with the intention of opening it as a year-round park to the local public in two years.

"I'm going to build a wall," Moira said after he'd gone. Michael laughed, but she was quite serious. It would be a stone wall running along the perimeter of the property. She envisioned it girding the land, demarcating boundaries. He said she'd be wasting her time; it wasn't worth the effort.

As Michael and Moira walked into the kitchen, Julia, who'd

been eavesdropping, lifted a corner of her towel, revealing her perspiring face; steam from the pot she was hovered over wafted out. She said she had a book on the subject of stone walls, one of those carried across the sea in Heleen O'Leary's hope chest. She was pleased to be able to make practical use of it. She'd go and fetch it. She got up from the table, poured her steam bath out in the sink.

"If you're planning on using the rocks I blasted," Michael said, "there isn't enough there for the length of wall you're speaking of." He was referring to the pile of rocks from the dynamiting that had been done to lay the foundation for the house. Hard shale and slate, an eyesore out beyond the garden fence, trampled down by snow and heaving frosts and Helen and Kate playing king-of-the-mountain.

Moira laughed. "Have you forgotten the Maine coastline? My back will break before I run out of stones, Michael."

From the bedroom window, Michael looked on as the sorting of rocks from the dynamite pile began. She had not asked for his help. Instead, Kate and Helen had been called in to assist and, together with their mother, and Julia to supervise the placing of stones into various functional piles, they were making quick work of it. He had once had a notion to do something with those rocks himself. He watched Moira dropping the stones into the wheel-barrow, her tireless, dogged motion. She had endless patience for the work she believed in, but little left over for anything else. She was wiping her brow with the back of her hand, her other hand resting on her hip; he knew that stance, that bountiful confidence. She gazed out over the fruits of her labor. He opened to a clean page in his sketchbook and sketched her standing there.

The worst stones, those unwieldy and oddly shaped, would best serve the purpose of footing. She could simply bury the least reasonable protuberance in whatever size hole was necessary to leave the best side exposed. It made sense to use large stones first to avoid having to lift them. The shale and slate out back, easy as wood to split, should be reserved for the upper layers and for chinking in along the way. She concluded that they would need to haul more rocks for the base from the shoreline. Kate and Helen seemed bleak at the prospect of working every Saturday for the rest of their lives. Julia, too, sighed. "Oh my. It is an enormous undertaking, isn't it?"

Moira spent her weekends in the woods now, forgoing supper until the twilight dwindled. She had located the old boundary posts, plotted the first course of the wall using boat cord looped to sticks, grubbing out the underbrush and saplings in her path. She dug out the sod for the wall footing. She hammered stakes into the ground to mark the end corners of the wall and stretched a guide line between them. Extra auxiliary stakes were hammered in on the downgrade and the line stapled to them. Michael hiked out to visit her, following the line, pausing to adjust slack. He would have a Thermos full of iced tea with him, his pipe in his pocket. She took a break then. Crouching on their haunches, a little refreshment. Birds chatty in the surrounding trees.

She was chipping off knobs in the rock or chiseling joints in the ones below to accommodate the wobble. She used the footpath that led down from the house to cart the rocks through the woods. The beach was littered with tools. It was summer now, sun up late, so she worked nearly every night and all day Sunday. Back when the work first started, Julia had come out to sight along the course with the mason's level. She dangled a small pebble on a length of string to check the vertical. The girls, too, curious or bored, used to wander by every once in a while, but their interest fell off in the summer heat. Helen and her horse were busy with 4-H fairs. Kate was at the town beach with Buddy.

Michael followed the sound of her steel-edged spade striking rock. He caught sight of her through the trees, wedging out a rock, tipping it on end, and rolling it down a pair of iron pipes into the wheelbarrow. She carted the rock over to the wall, turned the wheelbarrow around, and went back for another. He saw plainly that the work was never-ending. "Who is your wall keeping out?" he had asked her one night, but she was silent, asleep before her head touched the pillow. He stood watching until the sun sank so low he could see only her silhouette, now and again fireflies.

He came up behind her, setting his hands on her shoulders. "Call it a day, Moira."

Startled, she dropped her hoe pick. There was a clatter against the rocks. "Just a few more," she said, stooping to retrieve the tool.

He said, "It's become a golden calf, your wall."

She laughed, looking up at him. He put his arms around her. She rested her cheek against him. He was wearing only a flannel shirt. She could hear his heart beat. She glimpsed the shimmer of the sea through the trees, and sighed. "I'm set on finishing it before the winter."

He looked at her in astonishment. "It will take a lifetime, a wall of this size."

"Done proper," she replied, "it ought to last even longer. Forever."

"Nothing's permanent," said Michael.

She paused. "What about the ocean? What about the earth under our feet?"

He took her hand. They started walking.

Moira never completed the wall as she'd intended. In August of that year, 1964, they were hauling off Seal Ledge when a sudden, crushing pressure gripped Michael's chest. He let go of the winch and the trap hit the water with a loud slap. He fell forward. The boat lurched. Moira turned to see him sliding over the side. She threw herself across the boat and grabbed hold of his legs. Groping frantically up the length of his trousers, she hooked her hand under his belt and heaved, throwing her weight back. His head came out of the water, then flopped down under again and hit the side of the boat. "No!" she told him, clutching his thighs, and she tried again and again to pull him up, a belt loop tearing, wondering why for the first time in her life she couldn't find the strength she needed. She saw his arm moving under the water, almost as if (she thought eerily later) he were waving to her. Then she noticed the line wrapped around his wrist and suddenly understood it wasn't just him but the full trap she was pulling against. "Oh God, oh God," she cried. "Help me!" Stretching her leg out behind her, she managed with her foot to unhook the radio receiver.

Hurry, get your keys, Kate. There's been an accident," Julia said, setting down the phone.

They raced out to the truck and drove down the hill, arriving at the harbor just as the Coast Guard boat was pulling up to the pier, towing Michael's boat. A crowd of people had gathered.

They pushed through. The stretcher with Michael's body was lifted off the boat.

"Looks like a heart attack," the Coast Guard official was saying.

"He had a rheumatic heart," Julia managed. "Left by the fever."

He was glossy wet, his eyes half open, his lips slightly parted. His curly hair was slick against his head. Already there was a cold, grave hue to his skin. Julia, stunned, reached out to remove a trace of seaweed from his cheek. Kate flung her arms around him. She sobbed and Julia held her. Together they watched as the stretcher slid into the ambulance. The doors closed and the ambulance drove off, light flashing. Julia closed her eyes in silent prayer. Her tongue swelled in her mouth. She choked back tears. She asked, "My sister?"

"She's still in the boat," the Coast Guard official informed her. "Wouldn't ride with us." He paused, looking grim. "I imagine it all happened pretty fast. He must have been hauling in. Just keeled over the side, caught in the line. When we arrived she was still holding on to him."

Julia walked slowly around to the lobster boat. There was nearly a foot of water in it, spilled fish flopping about. Moira sat hunched in the stern. Julia called her by name to get her attention. Moira looked up. "He's gone," she said. They gazed helplessly at one another for a moment, then Julia took a deep breath and held out her hand.

Knit of the same coarse wool as Kate's old cardigan but never dyed blue, it might have been big enough to drape over the house if she had ever sewn the pieces together. Julia knit aimlessly, in installments of three yards, never taking care to keep the parts in order. Balled up in the corner of the porch over time, heavy

with sand from acting as a beach towel, packed into the closet
with the Chinese checkers and the empty terrarium and Michael's old monocle; the blanket was everywhere, a shroud. She
could sit all day long at the stove, teacups stacking up beside her,
balls of yarn unraveling at her feet. What did it matter? She was
done crying: a dozen handkerchiefs pinned to the drying line. And
she was finished writing thank-yous for the casseroles and bundt
cakes, finished apologizing in her next sentence for the fact that
no one had been invited back to the house after the funeral.

Julia had ironed so many handkerchiefs her wrist ached for
days after the ceremony. But she was glad she'd been prepared.
Tears streamed down her irritated cheeks throughout the eulogy.
Kate, too, had needed a handkerchief. It was virtually Kate's first
time inside a church and what with the organ wailing, the alter
awash in flowers, she couldn't have helped but feel it profoundly.
Helen was the one who had surprised Julia with her dry-eyed
sullenness, hunched at the end of the pew wearing one of her
father's old coats (she'd grown too tall for hand-me-downs). Helen
had come home from riding Tulip and had taken the news without a sound, except to say she did not want to go to the funeral
home to see the body. As for Moira, Julia was just relieved that
she'd attended the funeral service. They'd been late arriving at
the church on account of her. She had gone for a walk beforehand, returning with no time to spare. She announced with
aplomb that she'd gotten lost. Julia, frantically pulling the burrs
from Moira's hair, was aghast. "You know the woods like the back
of your hand!" Moira shrugged and said quietly, "Everything looks
different." Moira had sat closest to the aisle and the glistening
coffin. She had stared up at the ceiling. A swallow swooped in
the rafters. And, somehow, Julia felt, over the course of the cer-

emony Moira had become that swallow—walled off in a hard mud nest with a tiny opening, out of which she watched, later on, as he was laid to rest in the cemetery on the cliff with the blazing poppies.

After the funeral, in spite of Julia's attempts to convince her to wait until they were done grieving, Moira had cleared out Michael's closet and dresser drawers, boxing up clothes for the Saint Vincent de Paul. There was scarcely a sign of him about the house now. Except for his Bible and a few old photos, which Julia had managed to secure for herself, and the lingering scent of pipe tobacco—in the couch cushions mainly, and she was not beyond lying prone across the couch with her face in the pillows when no one else was around. Of course, she was forgetting for the moment the sketchbooks, all the imagery they might try one day to reassure themselves with. Not a day went by that Helen didn't mention her father's sketchbooks, but she was too timid to ask her mother for them. Moira had become fiercely protective of them. She spent entire days shut up in her room, poring over them. Eating nothing but oranges, as far as Julia could tell. Littering the rug with the peels. She wore her long johns, her hair unraveled, gone suddenly gray. She had not been out in the boat since the accident.

When the girls came home from school, Julia might rally and cook something, then coax Moira down the stairs for supper. Not that anyone besides Kate had much of an appetite. Mainly they sat at the kitchen table listening to Kate complain. Sick and tired of potato-leek soup. Sick of everyone feeling sorry for themselves.

It was startling how Kate insisted on calling a halt to the grieving. "Look at us," she would say, gesturing wildly at the unkempt rooms. "Who's going to buy our groceries?" Marching over to the desk and rifling through the stack of unopened mail, she finally tore open an envelope. Julia looked on uncertainly. Julia had never actually seen a bill up close before. It was remarkable the way the outside world kept track of people. Beneath Moira's name, the service or item purchased was listed and the corresponding sum total in a box.

"His coffin!" Julia gasped.

"It's a final notice," Kate sighed.

Moira got up from the table. They watched her go upstairs.

"She's hopeless," sighed Kate. She glanced at Julia. "I suppose *you've* never written a check before."

"Of course I have," Julia said defensively.

Kate pulled the checkbook from the drawer. "Well then, what are you waiting for?" Julia sat down at the desk. Kate handed her a pen. Julia drew up the check, signing Moira's name to it. "Not bad," Kate remarked, eyeing the forgery.

"I've had practice," Julia confessed. "I've written checks to my father."

"Really?" She paused. "In Arizona?"

Julia nodded her head. "We'd send him money every now and then."

"Well, don't go sending him any more money," Kate said. "We can't afford it. As it is, I should probably quit school and get a job."

"Now wait a minute," said Julia, but she wasn't in the mood to argue. She rested her face in her hands, her elbows on the desk. "Finish school for your father's sake," she said.

Kate figured she could have counted on a sizable gift, perhaps even a graduation party, if her father were still alive. Sitting in nervous anticipation with a few of the other girls on the sunny back steps of the gym, Kate gazed out at the parked cars, her father's pickup among them. He had been older than other fathers, his voice thick with Irish, and there were plenty of American customs—like wearing shoes in the house and smiling for a photograph—that he had never abided. Kate had even felt she needed to look out for him, for instance, if they were in a grocery store, or at a movie theater, or anywhere else that called for cultural know-how. Nevertheless, she looked up to him. She was still working for him after school three days a week when he died, stuffing her earnings into her new piggy bank with his words in mind: "If you save for something important, you'll understand what money is for, Kate." The bank had been a birthday present, a bit of a joke really, since they'd found that she had to be eighteen to open up her own account in town. She had broken into it to pay a speeding ticket and then again more recently for her cap-and-gown fee.

As she walked across the gym floor to shake the principal's hand that afternoon, Kate held back tears. She found her seat and peered up into the bleachers. Her mother, Julia, Skinny Roberts, and Helen were seated at the very top beneath the ski-team banner. She swallowed the lump in her throat and waved her diploma. After the graduation, everyone said it was up to Kate; they'd partake of the senior class picnic on the baseball diamond if she wanted. Kate took one look at them all—her mother's ratty hair, Julia's uncharacteristically dowdy housedress, and Helen's shy, downcast face—and said no, let's skip it for a cone at the Mr. Frostee. They drove to the ice-cream stand, with Skinny Roberts following in his car. Skinny insisted on treating. Kate got out to help him place the orders.

"What are you going to do now that you've graduated?" he asked Kate.

She shrugged. "Get a job—bait boy, maybe."

"Your ma won't like that, you working bait," Skinny warned.

"It isn't up to her!" Kate snapped. She handed two cones in through the truck window (Moira wasn't having any) and went back for hers. She felt angry. "My mother is hardly in charge these days, Skinny."

As it turned out, there weren't any fishermen who would hire a girl to set bait. Kate eventually came by a job in the accounting office of the marina, totaling sales on an adding machine. She knew she had been given the job out of sympathy, as Michael Sheehan's daughter, and so was eager to prove herself. She put in long hours, sitting at her desk by the window with her pencils, her sales receipts, a mug of hot coffee, gazing disdainfully out at her parents' boat from time to time. Sheathed in cold-weather tarpaulin, it was the only lobster boat around in the middle of the day. Michael Sheehan had been gone for almost a year now.

Kate made up her mind one day and posted a Boat for Sale notice on the marina bulletin board. Interested parties should contact her in the accounting office. On her desk the following Monday was a note from Denny LeClaire, who said he'd like to talk to her about the boat. She was pleased. She filled her coffee mug and chatted by the door with Skinny Roberts, who was in between deliveries at the packing plant. Skinny seemed to think she could get over a thousand dollars for the boat if she played her cards right. "Times is always tough," he said, "but a fisherman doesn't expect to skimp on his rig. Particular if he knows he's got competition."

Denny LeClaire showed up at her desk that afternoon, after helping unload his father's catch. Kate eyed him thoughtfully. He couldn't have been much older than she was, although he already had the fisherman's trademark bushy beard and sunburned face which made him look much older.

"Been wondering if you would ever sell," Denny said to her.

"Seems like a lot of people have been wondering that," said Kate.

"Oh?"

"Yeah." She laughed. "Get in line."

"You taking bids or something?"

"Exactly," she said, although she hadn't thought of that. She began tidying up her desk.

Denny shook his head, thinking. "Gotta get off my old man's boat. Know what I mean?"

Kate smiled mildly.

"That boat of yours, she have leakage of any sort?"

"Look," said Kate. "You know the boat."

"It's a good boat," Denny put in quickly.

"Well then," said Kate, pulling on her coat, "what else is there to talk about?"

He handed her a crumpled piece of paper from his pocket.

"What's this?"

"My bid," said Denny.

"Oh. Right," she said, slipping it into her pocket.

Denny LeClaire, Sr., telephoned the house that night to raise his son's bid five hundred dollars, which brought the total offer up to fifteen hundred. Kate was proud of herself, boasting of her business savvy at the supper table. Helen accused her of lacking sentimentality. Kate insisted there was no use paying the mooring

fees if no one was ever going fishing again. But there was one
thing she hadn't thought of. The title was in her father's name,
which meant the boat was Moira's now. Julia pointed this out.
"I'm afraid you can't up and rid us of it without your mother's
permission."

They all looked expectantly at Moira. She was sitting at the
far end of the table, hunched over her food. There was some
question in Kate's mind as to whether she was even listening.
"Ma?"

Moira lifted her gaze. "Don't you dare sell that boat, Kate."
She didn't care how much the LeClaires were offering. "Denny
LeClaire? He's no captain."

"Ma," pleaded Kate, "it's practically sold."

Moira glared at her. "It's my boat!"

Kate pushed back her chair. She grabbed the keys to the truck
and stormed out of the house.

Way back when Buddy Wentworth first felt her breast with his
mittened hand, Kate had fallen to her knees she was so shocked.
She had pulled him down on to the cold ground with her. Her
body rippled, burning up inside her ski jacket, and she heard the
wind whistle in her ears. Glancing up at the cloudy sky, pine
branches reaching across it, she could hardly believe herself. The
clearing with the red pine had been her and Buddy's secret place
until Helen carved that cross into the stump and made it feel
like a cemetery.

The night the LeClaire deal fell through, Kate and Buddy went
driving, out past the ferry terminal and the fish-packing plant,
cool dry wind whipping in. They drove and drove. Darkness closing in. Kate flipped on the headlights: glowing animal eyes on the

roadside, snatches of trees, bugs hitting the windshield. Kate pulled off onto the shoulder out on Calderwood Point and braked. Buddy sat up and smoothed back his hair. He leaned over and they started kissing. When a car came along and the lights shone on them, they stopped and sat apart. Buddy asked could he drive on the way back and she said just so long as he didn't speed, tossing him the keys. They each got out and walked around and, in the middle, the nearness of his whole upright body made her want to keep kissing. They leaned against the warm truck hood. She was filled with urgency, pressing into him. She climbed onto the hood and he climbed on top of her. Her fingers fumbling with his belt. He lasted just seconds inside her, which was fine since she could see headlights. It was the sheriff's cruiser, but it turned down the road to the beach instead of passing them. Kate sat up—she had changed her mind—and took back the keys.

She watched over her shoulder as Buddy plodded down his driveway in his hunting boots and lumberjack flannels, crew-cut hair barely visible beneath his baseball cap. Her breasts ached from his pawing. She gazed grimly out through the windshield at the starry night, thinking nostalgically of the red pine, its dark tip piercing the sky.

In July, nearly one full year after Michael died, Helen's horse Tulip unlatched her food bin and gorged herself sick. She lay on her side beneath the apple tree, legs stretched stiff and gut hugely bloated. It was too late to pump her stomach. Colic, the vet said, and he offered to send a truck to take the horse away, but Helen wanted to bury her. She plucked a green leaf from the tree and placed it over Tulip's gaping eye. She spent the rest of the day digging a hole on the edge of the yard over by the raspberries, but when Kate came home and saw what slow progress she was making and all the flies buzzing about the stiff horse, she said she'd call Buddy up, have him do them a favor. From the bedroom window, Helen looked on as Buddy Wentworth pushed the strange sallow horse to the edge of the yard with his snowplow, dumping her into the hole, pausing, before filling it in, to stuff his face with raspberries.

Once Tulip was gone, Helen began to hear things. Normal things at first: the smoke whistling up the stovepipe, a mouse scurrying across the kitchen floor, Julia's clickety-clacking knitting needles. She felt surrounded, trapped by the sounds, and was afraid to listen. When she listened, she heard everything, sometimes even things imaginary, like the dirt from her fist hitting her father's coffin, amplified to distortion. Or the sound of herself screaming at the top of her lungs in the middle of the night, which, once the lights were flicked on and Julia rushed in and Kate, too, was standing there at her bedside, she understood was quite real. She prayed, she prayed for peace and quiet and a good night's sleep, but it was terrifying to feel, as she did, that the cacophony kept God from hearing her. Often twice in one night, her fitful sleep woke the others. She was tangled in the sheets, shouting out nonsense. Kate hoisted her upright, Julia grabbed hold at her waist, and they walked her room to room while she trembled in their clutches. She came to, eventually. "I was dreaming," she might say, regarding them wearily, or "I need to use the bathroom," and they'd nod their heads encouragingly.

Julia dried and ground valerian leaves, boiled them in sugar, and made hard-candy drops for Helen to suck on before bed. Julia also made up her mind to talk to Moira about seeking professional advice for Helen. Skinny Roberts had gotten Moira a job at the fish-packing plant, which she'd started just last week. The job provided a little financial relief, and it got Moira out of the house, which was the best thing for her, Skinny and Julia had both agreed. The problem was that Moira took even less interest, which was to say none at all, in family affairs now. She went straight upstairs upon arriving home and reburied herself in the pages of Michael's sketchbooks. Her obssession with his drawings had become very irritating to Julia, particularly given how uninterested in his talent she'd always seemed.

"A doctor? Since when have you put your faith in doctors?" Moira asked.

"A specialist," Julia clarified, "a doctor of psychology." She looked plainly at Moira. "I'm at wit's end with Helen. She's barely making it to school."

Moira set aside the sketchbook. "I'm not denying she's troubled, but people can learn to live with their demons."

"Not without the help of example," Julia insisted.

Moira stared at the floor.

"She's lost her father," Julia said quietly. "She needs her mother."

"I've no hope to offer her," Moira said, sighing. She lifted her gaze. "And what's wrong with you?" she asked, her eyes flashing with anger. "Teach her to knit, for goodness' sake."

In the end, Julia felt that knitting needles were too dangerous, and knitting itself perhaps not far-reaching enough. She decided Helen should learn to type. This way, she'd have a marketable skill even if she didn't finish high school. Julia inquired about typewriters through an equipment rental agency, but became discouraged when she heard the rates. The checkbook register confirmed her feelings. They were barely making ends meet.

One afternoon, Julia was sprinkling holy water around the girls' bedroom—it had been Father Keane's suggestion in the confessional—when her gaze fell upon Kate's piggy bank on the bookshelf. All at once she was reaching out, as if propelled by a force greater than herself. The bank was knocked to the floor. It broke and a bevy of bills spilled out.

It was tough for Kate, certainly, since the bank had been a present from Michael, but Helen was the one Julia needed to worry about. Julia said she'd been clumsy. She apologized. Perhaps they could glue it back together? Kate was already wiping her eyes. Julia confided in Kate her hope of purchasing a typewriter for Helen. She thought she might borrow some money— unless, of course, Kate was saving for something more important than her sister's health and sanity. Kate shrugged. She didn't know what she was saving for, honestly.

Julia sat up late at night preparing practice charts, line after line of hopeful, uplifting Scripture printed out on cardboard. Helen had been to church only sporadically since her father's death. Somehow, after that, it made about as much sense for Helen to attend Mass every Sunday as it did for Julia to continue wearing a girdle and stockings under her housedresses. At the moment, it was not enough for Helen, a sensitive, dreamy girl of fifteen, to know that the obscurity of God's purpose was what made faith profound. Or to consider and seek solace in the symbiotic ways of all divine manifestations, the way Julia at a very young age had had to learn to do. "No redemption without strife, no satisfaction without want, no beginning without an end," Julia stated in a heavy tone. "Don't you see, child? Your heartache isn't fruitless." But Helen was deaf even to the poetry. Moira long ago had said that Helen's faith was not in God the Father, but in her own,

earthly father; certainly it was true that Helen had always identified strongly with Michael. Nevertheless, Julia had hoped that
Helen's confirmation was evidence of an independent commit-
ment. Helen's confirmation class had long since marched on with
their new names, while Teresa wallowed. Nothing to show for
herself but the figurine of Saint Francis of Assisi Michael had
given her (the Christian gift house in Portland didn't stock Saint
Teresa relics) and sorrow so great she could hear it.

The shiny black typewriter in its hard plastic suitcase turned
out to be the perfect distraction. Julia might have gone so far as to
say that typing restored Helen's faith. She took to it immediately,
if a bit compulsively, spending the entire day in her room perched
over the keys. The monotonous rat-a-tat-tat of the typewriter
comforted her as it drowned out other sounds. Eventually Julia
went ahead and glued the religious figurine to the typewriter
bridge like a masthead, and Helen took curious pleasure in
pounding the keys hard enough to make Saint Francis vibrate as
if possessed. She could type all night long if it weren't for Kate,
who refused to go to sleep with cotton balls in her ears the way
Julia, in the next room, was doing. Just as well, since Helen's fingers and wrists did need rest, and, no matter how many valerian
drops she ate, it was only when Kate was dozing off in the bed beside hers that Helen ever slept soundly.

Kate was two months' pregnant when she miscarried. No one
would have had to know, except that the bleeding didn't stop.
She became so weak she couldn't get up for work in the morning. She was shuffling to the bathroom and fainted. Moira, in
the kitchen, having her tea before work, heard the fall and
poked her head out. Kate had come to and was pushing herself

up off the floor. There was blood on her leg and on her nightgown. She glared at Moira, grabbing hold of the couch to steady herself. Her face was pale as a lily. "You've lost your sea legs," Moira observed. Kate didn't reply. Moira watched her go into the bathroom. "Kate," she warily called out, "it isn't just monthly blood, is it?" Kate glanced back at her. She shook her head, closing the door.

You're hemorrhaging," the nurse explained. She looked down at Kate. "You don't seem to want to close."

"But I do," said Kate. "Yes I do."

"I'm putting you on IV," said the nurse, already moving busily about the room setting it up. "Then the doctor will have a look at you." She had a friendly face and her white nursing shoes on the tile floor were perfectly silent. The IV needle burned as the nurse put it in Kate's arm. The sedative the nurse had given her began to take effect. It wasn't long before she caught sight of the wolf.

Broad-shouldered and slim-waisted, its coat was pure silver but for the gray muzzle and the narrow stretch of black-tipped hairs along the spine. The wolf was busy burying something, a scrap of food no doubt, in the shade of a huge pine tree. Kate marveled at how deftly it went about its work, pawing a neat hole in the forest floor, dropping the treasure in. The carcass of what tiny animal? she wondered. The wolf cast a wary eye in her direction, growling softly. It marked the spot with urine and disappeared into the wood.

Kate stole across the clearing to the big tree and hurriedly began digging. The pungent smell of the wolf pierced her nostrils. The earth was frozen, hard as glass, and, tearing into it, her fingers burned with feeling. She dug deeper and deeper, uncovering earthworms, beetles, the roots of the great tree. She dug farther, dug up bottles, bones, feathers, lapis, jade, and turquoise. A hard shell of granite, which she used her teeth to crack finally, gave way to miles of sticky black tar, hot to the touch, and the earth began to hollow out. Layers virtually slid away, huge chunks chipped off, and in the remaining empty space, still some distance away yet wholly visible now, she saw the pink glowing center and, choking back tears, reached out for it.

She heard the wolf snarl and turned abruptly to see the stiff tail and raised hackles. She cowered, backing up toward the hole. She knew she was really no match for a wolf, particularly since she had been caught red-handed, and thus would never be able to gain the offensive. She would either have to behave submissively or flee. The wolf bared its teeth. She stared in awe at the gleaming mouth.

"Now we wait for stabilization," Kate heard the doctor saying. He helped her sit up. Her body felt sober. She gazed across the room at her mother, sitting in a chair, absently clutching the string of rosary beads that had hung from the rearview mirror in the truck.

There were twelve sketchbooks in all. Pencil, charcoal, and rich oil-crayon drawings of babies, baby hands and feet. A lifetime featured in the kitchen stove and teakettle, his hip-high rubbers drying by the door, Julia's bifocals perched on the sewing machine, his pipe and pouch of tobacco. Sketches of the truck, the boat, the beach. The children swimming, the children asleep. The last of the summer's tomatoes ripening on the windowsill, a perspiring glass of iced tea, and canning jars cluttering the kitchen table. But it was a record of her loss as much as anything else, and she was trapped in it.

He had loved to draw lobster traps—a view through the slats and netting of the catch inside, or the whole big mountain of them stacked in the yard. Seals sunning themselves on Salmon Rock, a moose knee-deep in the marsh, a cardinal at the feeder, a skinned rabbit on a cutting board. No matter what she had said to dissuade him, he had drawn her, too: pregnant, gardening, reading the newspaper, combing her hair after a bath.

She was acutely aware of herself as she carried the pile of sketchbooks outside to the compost, an image she'd never seen before, so keenly drawn that, just for a moment, self-conscious-ness coursing through her, transfused, she wondered if it wasn't actually someone else watching and she glanced suspiciously back at the house. They would never forgive her, nor should they. She scraped a match against the flint, then held it to a roll of newspaper. Smoke billowed up from the torch into the June morning. She shut her eyes. She thought of Kate, fast asleep in her bed after getting home from the hospital, of the legacy she seemed to have inherited. She could almost feel time collapse. Survival knows no bounds, Heleen O'Leary used to say. Let it be a lesson to you. And she'd give an example of a wild animal, caught in a snare, gnawing through the flesh and bone of its own foot in order to free itself. Moira let go of the torch. It dropped onto the compost. She understood she could not go through with it. Instead, she rifled through the sketchbooks and tore out every last picture of herself, angrily feeding each one to the flames. She began to cry, gazing up at the morning sky. The sound of aban-donment she knew from long ago; ewes calling out to their lambs, penned in the fold.

IV

Crying Wolf

(1966–1969)

Matty O'Leary wouldn't have known his granddaughter. He was grateful for the photo Julia had sent ahead of her. Helen looked nothing like an O'Leary. Long and lanky, fair-skinned but dark-haired, with striking green eyes that met his with an unsettling interest. She was carrying a large rucksack on her back with a Boy Scout tent and sleeping bag tied on, but she came down off the bus like a foal being let loose to run and Matty thought to himself, Whooaah now, child.

He had been drunk on the phone. Pleasantly toasted on a gentleman's brand of whiskey after cashing the check sent in June from Julia and Moira. It was their first show of generosity in almost two years, and with it had come a note of explanation, which was how Matty learned that Michael Sheehan had died.

Rosita, his next-door neighbor who had read the note for him, let him use her telephone to place a call. On the other end, Helen answered. Hers was a sorrowful state of affairs, Matty soon gathered. Her sister had enrolled in nursing school, but Helen was doing nothing, nothing at all to keep herself from moping. The next thing Matty knew, he was inviting her to come visit him in Arizona.

My, but she was a strong one. Sheer foolishness for him to have insisted on carrying her rucksack on the walk home from the bus stop. He couldn't help commenting, as he flung the bag off and it landed heavily on the floor of his kitchen, "Is it full of bricks?"

"Nope." She laughed. "Books."

Her father's sketchbooks, stacked and tied with twine for the journey. He thought of Julia. She'd carried with her her mother's books when she'd left Ireland. Helen told Matty she'd brought the sketchbooks along with her because she couldn't trust Moira to take care of them. After hoarding the sketchbooks for months and months, her mother had finally relinquished them, depositing the stack of them, quite a bit worse for the wear, outside Helen's bedroom door one morning. Helen had soon discovered that Moira had torn certain pages out of the books and when she asked her what she'd done with these, Moira told her she'd burned them. "They were pictures of me. I had a right, didn't I?"

She spent a lot of time bad-mouthing her mother, Matty noticed. Moira, well, she was a hard nut all right, unforgiving, Matty agreed. But there wasn't reason to complain, not as far as he could see. "She's fed and clothed you, hasn't she?"

"So I shouldn't expect love, or understanding?" Helen replied pointedly. She had a quiet tone of voice, as disconcerting as her gaze. Was it worth the struggle was all he was asking. She sighed. She said she didn't know, "My mother's heart is made of stone."

"Well, stones don't break," said Matty.

He'd meant to spruce things up a bit before her arrival. The closet-sized kitchen was littered with dirty dishes, empty liquor bottles, and beer cans. Piles of *National Geographic* were strewn on the old couch and coffee table. The drapes were drawn but the sun shone through. There was a plastic crucifix on the wall, a glossy picture of the Pope wedged behind one arm of the cross and a photograph of President Kennedy torn from a magazine behind the other. The television flickered with the volume turned down. A black-and-white cat was curled on the seat of the recliner—one of Rosita's cats, come in through the window.

Right about now it was usually Matty, the cat in his lap, out cold. He could sit there all afternoon drinking and snoozing, if it weren't for Jimmy Spooner, the trailer park manager, who, heeding the complaints of the other residents, came banging on Matty's aluminum door every afternoon, threatening to call animal control if Matty didn't get off his duff and collect his goats. Rising from his stupor, Matty would fling open the door, swearing he'd shoot Jimmy if harm ever came to Billie and Babe. He'd drag his motor bike out from under the trailer and, holding his beer can in one hand, speed off to herd his goats.

Mother and daughter, but they looked exactly the same except for a scar on Babe's hind leg from a coyote. Matty showed Helen how to milk the goats, sitting on an overturned bucket, hand over hand, paying compliments to Billie so that she wouldn't be stingy. He sold his goat's milk to a few people in the trailer park, including his neighbor Rosita, the medicine woman, whom Matty credited with saving his liver. "I'm sick from the drink," confessed

Matty. Surely, he was different than Helen remembered him—sallow complexion, bone-thin, hunched over—but he still had a full head of hair and every last one of his teeth, he said, and bared them. One-quarter Navajo and one-tenth the price of any doctor Matty was likely to see, Rosita brewed up bitter teas for him every Sunday in her trailer, which doubled as a beauty parlor during the week. There wasn't any hocus-pocus involved, Matty claimed. Just straight herbs, a little prayer besides. The sort of thing Julia might prescribe.

Helen awoke one night to the sound of a shotgun going off. She climbed out of bed and quickly made her way down the hall to the other end of the trailer. The television screen cast an eerie glow. Matty was crouched on the couch (which was also his bed and had been long before she arrived), peering out the window. He held a bottle of scotch in one hand and a hunting rifle in the other. Helen's entrance startled him. He wheeled the gun around. "Ha," he laughed, lowering the rifle, "mistook you for a coyote."

Helen sat down cautiously on the arm of the recliner and let out a big breath.

"There's a pair of them," Matty mumbled, slumping down on the cushions. "Come down from the hills to raid the garbage Dumpster and harass my goats."

Just then, the cat pounced and Helen gave a little shriek. Matty chuckled. He poked the cat with his foot and it wrestled with him, biting his ankle. Helen went into the kitchen. She asked Matty if he was hungry, maybe she'd cook something. He said she shouldn't trouble herself. "It's no trouble," said Helen, peering into the fridge. Earlier that day, she had ridden Matty's motorbike into the town of Eager to buy groceries. Paying with food stamps, at his insistence, since that's what they were for and he couldn't use them at the liquor store. Upon arriving home, she'd found him sitting on the step of the trailer, plucking the feathers from a small bird. A grouse; he'd caught it out back in the long grass. "With my bare hands, mind you." Silent, keeping still as the desert itself until he pounced. He'd watched Rosita's cat to learn how. The bird froze in his clutch and he popped the head without fuss. "Are grouse good to eat?" Helen had asked, a bit skeptical. He shrugged. "Stewed with a few potatoes, a little pepper and salt?" Frowning later, at the supper table, at the small portion she helped herself to, to say nothing of how she spit out the tiny bones.

She was standing at the kitchen counter, stirring up eggs to dip bread in for French toast. Matty shuffled in and seated himself at the table. He began a game of jacks with a handful of bottle caps and a rubber-band ball, his free hand keeping the cat from interfering. Helen set two plates on the table. He said he bet she wondered how he survived on a diet of grouse, liquor, and boiled potatoes. But she was forgetting about the kefir, which he knew to be a youth elixir. He had some steeping on the radiator, if she wouldn't mind ladling it over his French toast.

Matty wasn't used to company; it was a novelty not to have to talk to himself. He enjoyed pointing out the things he did and didn't like in magazines and on television. His tastes were oddly charming. He adored any advertisement or commercial that featured redheaded children, families driving in a car, and cowboys. He wore a wide-brim straw hat when he rode around in the fields on his motorbike herding his goats. "A regular American cowboy," he joked. They discussed horses. She told him about Tulip and how she'd died. Her voice cracked and he was moved to unearth a very old and soiled drawing she'd done for him of a horse, years ago, although he could tell by the blank look on her face that she had no recollection of it. He said, "There's an Appaloosa ranch down the road. It costs an arm and a leg to ride for fifteen minutes." He scratched his whiskers. "I haven't sat in a saddle in ages."

She wore the baseball cap Julia had insisted on her packing and Matty wore his straw hat. The sun was burning a hole in the sky. Heat made a horse antsy, Matty claimed, and veered off the bridle path for the shade of the cedar trees. She shouldn't worry— getting lost in the desert wasn't easy. You could see so far and wide it was startling. Cacti were still in bloom in the fields at the edge of the cedar grove, enormous prickly stalks with blossoms like dragon tongues. Farther off, a rock ridge rose out of the earth without warning. They started off across the field toward the ridge. Helen said she wanted to see the view from the top. Matty opted to wait at the bottom with the horses, carefully dismounting, stretching out in the yellow grass with his face under his hat. The sting of a horse fly woke him with a start. He sat up, waving his hat. Then he set the hat on his head and peered up the steep rock, sighting Helen at the very top. She stood, gazing out. He knew well the view. It was wide open. It was limitless. Hugging herself in the wind.

She came across the tiny skeleton on her way back down. Its form had collapsed in her hands as she went to pick it up. Slender and stark white: the tiny bones of a rabbit. "Carried up there in the talons of a hawk," Matty said, and he eyed her curiously. "Whatever do you want with the bones?" he asked as she carefully wrapped them in her windbreaker. "I'm going to put them back together," she said, smiling. She clicked her tongue for her horse. Mounted without effort. Off she went through the long grass. Carefree and lovely, her horse responding enthusiastically, jumping over a rock. Matty was moved to follow. He dug his heels in. But when his horse took the jump, he slid out of the saddle and hit the ground with a thud. She came charging back to him. He had only had the wind knocked out of him. "Honest to God, child, save your tears." But she was unable to stop crying. She covered her face with her hands. Matty got to his feet. He gathered up his hat. The horses stood flank to flank in a brilliant patch of devil's paintbrush. "Enough," he told her gruffly, slapping the hat on his head, "When I go to meet my maker, it won't be an accident."

They were seated on the couch with a tube of epoxy glue and the bones of the rabbit spread out on the coffee table in front of them. Helen said that maybe she'd give that medicine woman a try and Matty nodded his head and sipped his beer, "Rosita? It couldn't hurt." He handed Helen one bone and then another, shrugging off her amazement; he'd skinned enough rabbits to know where the bones ought to go. She had a steady, patient hand, said Matty, watching her join the bones with the glue. It took several hours to complete the skeleton, the cat meowing and scratching furiously outside the window. Bone by bone, they recreated the little creature, hunched as it might have been on the verge of death. The sun was low in the sky by now. The light flooding the room was the color of ripe peaches. Matty let the cat in the window. The cat sniffed the little skeleton thoroughly and then seated itself in Matty's lap. He began stroking the cat so that it hummed. If truth be told, Matty'd never liked cats. Back on the farm, they had seemed to multiply like rabbits. He had taken it upon himself to drown a litter once, dreadful doing, years of bad luck. They'd been motley black and white just like this one warming his lap, which was perhaps why he indulged it, his guilt like a chill forever in him.

Helen asked him about Moira, what she was like as a girl. "Moira?" he hesitated, finding his tongue. "Stubborn as a new potato. Well, she was strong. Powerful, you might say. She could do the work of a man by the time she was fourteen." He glanced over at Helen. "Moira wore her hair plaited. It dropped straight down her back, the same as yours. Except your mother's hair was fair. Each of the three had a different shade of hair. Julia's was dark like her mother's. It's a crying shame, the bones of Julia's face getting squeezed. She would have been as pretty as Heleen." He paused to clear his throat. He ruffled his hair with his hand. "Now Ann, she took her auburn color from me, would you believe?"

"Ann?" asked Helen. "I never knew there were three children."

Matty looked at her. "Your mother and Julia don't ever speak of her?"

Helen shook her head.

"Well," said Matty, bewildered, "Ann was the third."

"What happened to her?"

"Your mother's never said a word?" All these years he'd been carrying Ann around, the hump in his back growing more and more pronounced such that lifting his gaze to the star-filled heavens was a struggle for him now and he hung his head as a matter of course. They couldn't have forgotten her. It struck him that his daughters' silence was the way they kept the peace. "Her mother died in having her," Matty said to Helen. "And Ann followed in her mother's path soon after."

"She was just a baby?"

"Aye," said Matty, "not much more than."

Rosita Lopez was a stout, solemn-faced woman in her fifties, wearing a pink smock and clutching a dustpan and broom in one hand. A strong smell of shampoo and brewing coffee filtered out through her door. "You want to use the phone, Matty?"

He said, "No. I've brought my granddaughter for a bit of medicine," nudging Helen up the steps.

Rosita said, "Fine, I was just finishing sweeping up the hair." She looked Helen over, beckoning her in. "You're Matty's kin." Helen glanced hopefully back at Matty. He could feel his throat swell and turned to go. Sadness was not easy to treat. Particularly when it was in your blood. In the arid meadow out behind the trailers, Matty caught sight of Babe and Billie romping about in the scraggly grass beside a rusted-out school bus. Farther off, in the copper twilight, a hawk was circling. He watched it hesitate in midair, then drop like a stone. What he'd realized after coming to America was that he'd never been able to face his daughters with his need for them. Anyway, their lives were richer without him. He had seen Michael Sheehan's sketchbooks. It was no wonder the drawings brought Helen security.

Matty squinted into the clouds of red dust stirred up by the bus. No sad farewells. He walked slowly home. A good swig from a bottle would go a long way right now, but lately he took pains to pour his whiskey into a glass first. Everyone said Helen had had a civilizing effect on him. Jimmy Spooner called her an angel of

mercy on account of the fact that she had appeared out of nowhere and helped him build a run for his goats out of sheets of
aluminum, which the goats couldn't chew through.

She was going to take her time heading home, see the sights
along the way, try to figure out what to make of herself. Matty
was always saying she ought to make something of herself. She
had talent, like her father. Shameful to waste it. She had stood
in front of the bathroom mirror earlier that morning with a pen
and sheet of paper. "Here, I've made something of myself," she
said to him after, handing over the portrait. When Matty got back
to the trailer, he took another look at the drawing. Helen had had
Rosita crop her long hair to her ears. Her smile practically jumped
off her face, the effect was so outstanding.

Helen had taken them all by surprise when she announced she
was going off to visit Matty. Julia would not have let her disappear
like that. She was filled with worry and misgiving, but Moira
insisted that they had no choice but to allow it. Helen was testing
them. Besides, Helen's mood had gone from bad to worse at
home; there was hope in her departure. It was true, Julia had
exhausted her own efforts to help Helen. In a way it was a relief
not to have to encounter Helen's downcast face at the breakfast
table first thing in the morning, but Julia's relief soon smacked
of shame. She grew lonely, useless really, having been a caretaker
her entire life. Julia had suffered only one flare-up since Michael
died, during which the possibility of prednisone treatment had
been a great temptation for her, but she persevered without it.
Somehow her relative good health only contributed to her feelings
of detachment, her lupus being a part of her, like a birthright.

Heleen O'Leary's swollen rhinoceros feet were the only physical aspect of her mother that hadn't faded from Julia's memory.

Julia passed the days roaming the house—tidying, straightening, rearranging, none of it satisfying. One morning she found herself in the girls' bedroom, gazing morosely at a well-worn book of fairy tales in the dusty bookshelf. She reached out and wistfully spun the globe that sat on top of the shelf. The wall calendar over Helen's bed was still set to August. Julia realized, as she was about to change it over, that the calendar was actually from two years ago. She left it as it was and backed away slowly.

A segment of the long, gray blanket Julia had occupied herself knitting after Michael's death in August 1964 was folded at the foot of Kate's bed. Julia unfurled it and wrapped herself in it. Felt a rush of blood to her head, the smell of the wool so painfully familiar her nostrils tingled. Oh, good God alive, there was no turning back now, was there? She studied her image in the dresser mirror. Julia was not accustomed to looking herself in the eye for anything more than a cursory good morning. She had grown up without a looking glass and with the understanding that her skull would never recover from the forceps (she had peered intently into the bucket as she drew it up from the well). She had gone on to work as a seamstress, wherein the reflection in the mirror she was concerned with—and certainly more comfortable with—was always someone else's. So, indeed, it was unnerving for her, but she stood her ground. She had recently passed her fifty-fifth birthday and yet she still showed very little gray. There was a pallor and a puffiness to her complexion, but no sign of irritation or rash. People used to tell her she had the same eyes as her mother, icy blue, lids curving downward at the corners, and she should smile more so that she wouldn't look so sad. Julia smiled, but it was wistful, fleeting, a smile embarrassed of itself. She was distracted by the autumn sun, which was filtering into the room as it broke through the morning cloud cover. Light fell across the desk and the shiny typewriter on top of it. Julia stared curiously, her fingers throbbing at the mere suggestion. She shook the blanket off her shoulders, letting it slide to the floor. Seating herself at the typewriter, she began.

Like everyone, I have been visited by loss from time to time. Yet the hand that lays itself heavily upon my shoulder each time is unfamiliar, a stranger's, and a surprise. And I ask myself is it so because I cannot endure another test of my faith? For what is faith—her fingers hovered over the keys—*but the manifestation of our greatest desire.*

Desire burned like oil inside Julia, and she forgot about her lunch and her afternoon tea, and didn't even pause to bring in the laundry, although the clouds had closed up again, promisingly. Over the course of these several hours, Julia became so deeply invested not only in the value of her words but also in the very act of bringing her words to bear on the paper in front of her. She felt each and every sentence. It was a startling, profound power in her. At last she made that final keystroke and, lifting her hands away, hung her head, as if in silent reverie.

If Michael were alive she would have certainly shown the composition to him, as if it were just another piece of her handiwork, reacting demurely when he praised it. A compliment from Michael was like a bushel of new potatoes in how Julia could make it last a season. But no matter what she pretended in her mind at times, he was her sister's husband. Her powerful, unwitting sister, who, simply by belching at the table, could render for Julia

Michael's high opinion of her suspect. With a mixture of excitement and dread, Julia realized she couldn't stand to keep the work to herself.

Moira was peeling carrots rapid-fire into the compost bucket and said she didn't welcome interruption at the moment. Julia pressed the typed pages on her nevertheless. With Julia hovering, Moira read, remarking now and again that *someone* was standing in her light. After she finished reading, she handed the papers back to Julia and picked up where she'd left off with the carrots.

"No comment?" said Julia.

Moira shrugged. "It's a bit personal for a church bulletin."

"I didn't compose it for the church bulletin!" replied Julia, affronted.

"Well, who did you write it for, then?"

Julia, flustered by the question, her pride smarting, insisted that her words could have wide appeal. "What with the convulsive changes that mark these times. Young people losing their bearings, turning to Lord knows what. I've a good mind to send it off as a guest editorial to the *Portland Gazette*."

And this was precisely what Julia did, following up her mailing one week later with a phone call to the editorial bureau. She spoke with an editor, Ed Bailey, who, with some prompting, recalled the piece she'd sent. He would be happy to pull it up if she would hold. A few minutes later, he was back and calling her letter intriguing. But his tone was noncommittal. She felt her dander rising and repeated the claim she'd made to Moira, that her words were sure to touch a cord. "With millions of readers," she insisted.

"Well, I'd say that's overstating it a bit," replied Ed Bailey, chuckling. "As it is, our readership only numbers in the thousands."

"Precisely because you're not printing work that speaks to the people!" retorted Julia.

It just so happened that Ed Bailey had leveled the very same criticism at his fellow editors earlier that week. He granted her request to come in and talk over the possibilities for publishing the piece.

The restaurant was on the wharf in Portland and frequented by fishermen, so perhaps Kate felt at home here, even if, as Julia pointed out to her, the tea was inferior and the sticky buns were stale. Julia was antsy, sitting at the counter strangling her tea bag. She wore a conservatively tailored skirt and jacket, her hair combed back severely and pinned into a bun. Leaning forward on her elbows, she complained to the young man flipping eggs at the grill that her pastry wasn't fresh. "See for yourself," she said.

To her surprise, he obliged her by sampling the sticky bun. "You're absolutely right. Can I scramble you some eggs instead?"

Julia shook her head. "No thank you," she replied, eyeing him with approval. He was sandy-haired and well-built, with an appealing, straight nose. No wonder this was Kate's favorite coffee shop. Julia said, "It's my niece here who has the morning appetite."

The young man glanced shyly at Kate. "How are your eggs?" he asked quietly.

Kate shrugged and said "Fine," never looking up from her book.

"You're blushing," Julia remarked to her after the young man had gone away.

"I'm agitated. I have a test today," Kate said defensively.

. . .

Kate dropped Julia off in front of the offices of the *Portland Gazette*. There were still five minutes or so before her appointment. She took a brisk walk around the building to collect herself. It was a crisp, clear September morning. Her new shoes smartly met the pavement. Her heart beat excitedly. How extraordinary that she should even be here today. Ed Bailey was not a pushover, and Julia's in-person impression of him confirmed it. A man in his fifties, barrel-chested, slightly bald, and wearing wire-rimmed glasses. His handshake was hearty and resonated with her. The presence of a wedding band was a bit puzzling, since the one photograph on his desk was of a sad-faced basset hound. Ed Bailey wore a pale yellow shirt, sleeves rolled, and a wide, unbecoming green tie. He seated himself behind his sprawling, untidy desk. She noticed a rumpled tweed jacket with false elbow patches thrown over the back of the chair.

"So, Julia O'Leary, what can I do for you?"

She was taken aback. Should she state the obvious? she wondered. "Short of publishing my editorial?" she asked.

He grinned. "It's sensitive writing. Touching in many respects. I'm just not sure we have a use for it."

"No use for it?"

"I'm not sure the appropriate venue for it is the *Gazette*."

"I don't understand," said Julia.

"It's a bit introspective for us." He hesitated before handing her back the essay inside the large envelope she had sent it in.

"Wait!" she cried out.

But he made as if to get up. "I'm afraid I've got another appointment."

She stood up, facing him. "Haven't *you* ever experienced loss, Mr. Bailey?"

He paused, his fingers drumming the desk edge. "I'm a widower."

"I see," she said. "I'm very sorry for you, then."

He shrugged. "It was several years ago now."

"Well, then you know it isn't true—what they say—that time heals."

Ed Bailey fell quiet. "I'll have another read," he finally said, holding his hand out to retrieve the envelope. She dropped it on his desk.

Ed Bailey telephoned Julia personally to let her know that her piece would appear as a guest editorial in that Sunday's paper. Ed Bailey made it sound as if he had been behind her all along, lobbying hard for the ed board's stamp of approval. She was delighted. She said she would look forward to Sunday. She hung up the phone. She didn't know quite what to do with herself. She had been making up Helen's bed when Ed called. Helen was arriving home on Sunday. In the nick of time, too, if she was planning on returning to high school. She had been gone the entire summer. Hitchhiking, Julia'd gathered, stretching the money they'd given her. She had been to a rodeo, eaten grits and red-eyed gravy. She had marched in a civil-rights rally in Washington and toured the oldest American pretzel factory. She had camped on the banks of the Black River and bathed in the crystal-clear quiet of Tomahawk Creek. Julia had scrutinized every postcard, locating in the road atlas the addresses on the postmarks. For each day Helen was away, Julia had said a rosary.

She went outside. Moira was on her hands and knees in the

vegetable garden. She wore a wide-brimmed straw hat but never gardening gloves, and when she reached out enthusiastically with her filthy fingers, urging a bite of a ripe tomato, Julia politely declined. Moira sat back on her heels, eating the tomato and talking about Helen. She wanted to know what time her bus was arriving, even though Julia had told her several times already, and she wanted to know if she thought they should both meet her at the station or if, perhaps, she should go alone to meet her. As for Julia, she was full to bursting with the news from the *Portland Gazette*, but as she entertained Moira's concerns, she felt her focus forcibly shifting, so that when she finally did open her mouth to speak it was to suggest that they throw Helen a small homecoming party. Come to think of it, she'd go ahead and cut the zinnias and the showiest dahlias for an arrangement.

Sunday morning found Julia racing barefoot through the dewy grass to collect the newspaper from the mailbox. She opened the paper directly to the editorial section and scanned the page for her own name. Color spilled into her cheeks: There it was. She stood marveling at how official and important her words looked. Why, her editorial was right next to a commentary on the disrepair of the state's lighthouses. The sun came through the pine trees and she felt it on her shoulders and lifted her face to the sky. They had edited slightly, but Ed Bailey had prepared her for the changes and she was taking his advice and not getting bogged down in the details.

As she carried the paper inside and laid it out on the kitchen table, her heart was pounding with anticipation. In the end, she had decided not to say anything to Moira about her editorial being published. Let her be surprised. She let the kettle whistle until her own ears were splitting, then made a pot of tea and sat waiting. By and by, Julia realized that she could hear water running outside. She went to the window and, sure enough, caught sight of the hose stretched across the lawn. Her gaze followed the line of the hose out to the garden, where she found Moira, in her rubber boots, watering, a cup of tea already in hand, suggesting she'd been up for a while since Julia hadn't felt any warmth in the kettle.

Julia decided to go and get dressed for church. She chose a blue linen dress, which she usually reserved for wearing on Easter, and a smart pillbox hat. When she returned to the kitchen, Kate was standing at the table, reading the funnies. She had poured herself a cup of tea. Julia said to her gamely, "Will you have a look at your aunt's first published work, Kate?" Kate barely stirred. Perhaps she hadn't heard. "Shall I cook you some eggs, Kate?" Julia said, more loudly.

Kate glanced up. "Oh, no thanks. I'm going to the library. I'll stop off at the diner first, probably."

"Your sister's coming home today," Julia said, after a moment. "Don't be late." She watched Kate gulp down her tea.

Kate grabbed up her books, leaving the newspaper be. "Need a ride to church?"

Julia shook her head. "Skinny is driving," she replied, a lump in her throat suddenly.

Thank goodness for Skinny Roberts. He'd read the paper and had seen Julia's letter, called it the best darn guest editorial he'd read in weeks. She beamed. Father Keane had also seen it, as well as Ralph and Sue Pelletier and several others. Julia was showered with praise during doughnuts and coffee. She was as gracious as could be, prickling with humility. By the time she returned home, she was in good spirits. She kept her composure as she walked into the kitchen and saw the paper pushed aside to make room for the party preparations. Moira was busying about in one of Julia's aprons, measuring cup in one hand, wooden spoon in the other, stopping up short to glare at the *Joy of Cooking*. Helen's bus wasn't due to arrive until three, Julia reminded her. She should slow down—have a cup of tea, look at the paper. But Moira wasn't listening. She was attempting to separate an egg, making a fool mess of it. She looked suddenly to Julia, lamenting, "I'm afraid I won't ever get it right." Julia gathered she wasn't really speaking of the cake she was making, but she went and tied on an apron straightaway.

Julia spread a tablecloth over the picnic table and set the vase with the flowers in the center. There was roast chicken, potato salad, corn on the cob, ripe scarlet tomatoes, and strong, tart lemonade spiced with rosemary. Kate had drummed up several of Helen's old friends from 4-H to invite but Helen hadn't really been friendly with any of these girls since Tulip had died. And Helen had never relished being the center of attention. She seemed shyer than ever. It was a bit awkward to start. Then, thankfully, Kate arrived. Late, in a cloud of dust. Helen's face brightened as she ran out to meet the truck. Julia choked back hot tears as she watched the two of them hug.

Kate had brought along a few of her nursing school pals and that fellow from the diner with the ponytail. Jim Martinson was his name. The mood soon picked up. Kate organized all the young people into a softball game. Moira and Julia sat on the sidelines, talking back and forth about Helen, how she seemed generally revived by her trip. Didn't she look like her father with her hair cut short, remarked Julia, and Moira shook her head in over-whelming agreement. Her rangy, bosomless daughter. So like Michael. It was the first thing that had struck her at the bus station earlier. Like hugging a ghost, almost. "Quit staring at me," Helen had said to her. Moira turned the key in the ignition, muttering an apology. They drove through town. Helen said she was hankering for a lobster roll—could they stop off at the Gull? Moira bit her tongue about all the food waiting at home, since the party was supposed to be a surprise. They sat on a wooden bench on the promenade and watched the men working in the lobster pound.

"Ever think about putting to sea again?" Helen had asked her. Moira shook her head, denying it. "I've lost my mate."

"Life goes on," Helen said pointedly.

"I'm glad to hear it," Moira replied.

Moira and Julia carried the dishes inside. What a day. Moira sighed. She slumped down at the kitchen table while the sink was filling. She yawned. Hadn't even had a chance to look at the paper today. She reached across the table for it, and Julia froze where she stood. In all the commotion of Helen's homecoming, she had practically forgotten her own claim to the day. Newsprint crackled and shifted. Julia's cheeks were burning, her palms turned clammy. She bit her lip in irritation with herself and held her hands under the faucet. She could hear the crack of the bat out on the lawn, the kids erupting in cheers and laughter, and she turned vacantly to the waning light outside the window. The game had apparently just ended. Everyone was settling themselves on the blankets. Someone had a guitar and they were lighting a fire in the old barbecue pit. It hadn't been used in God knew how long, since it was against Park Service rules. The smoke would probably bring the sheriff, but in the meantime let them enjoy. She could hear the singing, and for a moment felt that her sister's opinion might not even matter. She glanced over her shoulder. Moira had dozed off, her head resting on her arms on top of the newspaper.

That first editorial *did* make a certain splash in the greater Portland community. Ed Bailey was calling it an explosive piece; what kept the presses rolling was the author's poignancy and honesty in accounting her efforts to help herself recover from repeated hardship. After four successive guest editorials in which Julia O'Leary expanded her scope of personal interest and experience to include subjects such as the women's movement and nipping the winter head cold in the bud, the *Gazette* determined that there was no rhyme, reason, or foreseeable end to her appeal. Her candid eloquence and her unwavering faith in the truth—if not the objective truth, then a truth that made more sense to people—was a welcome change of pace to a readership shaken by news of war, riot, and disorder.

"Plain and Simple" was the name of the weekly column Julia was officially hired on to write for the *Portland Gazette* as of the first of the year, 1967. Ed Bailey prided himself on having discovered Julia O'Leary. He liked to call her up and chew her out for not stopping by to pick up her fan mail. He also liked to get the scoop ahead of time on what she was working on for Sunday.

"Planning a wedding in a pinch," she told him.

"That's it?" asked Ed.

She paused. "For a pregnant bride."

"Ah," said Ed. "There's the twist."

"Now if you'll excuse me," Julia said, hanging up on him.

She was often cutting him off like that. He sighed with exasperation. There were several things he needed to discuss with her. He was her editor, after all. Good relations were essential. She had been on staff five months now. Ed Bailey scratched his bald head. He rifled through his desk drawers for the notebook in which he had written her address. Unity was a good forty minutes from Portland. He glanced at the clock, guzzling the lukewarm coffee in his mug. Maybe he'd call it quits a little early today.

He was no fisherman, in his wrinkled tweeds and wide tie. Still, Ed Bailey knew the marina was the hub of towns like Unity, so he stopped off to ask the way. No one was willing to oblige him with exact directions.

"Just up the hill," Marty Sklor said.

"Up top," said Denny LeClaire, gesturing.

"Thanks," Ed said. Thanks for nothing. He wandered back out to his car. Never expected this to be difficult. Not for an old newshound like himself. He drove along the streets of Unity, window down, asking every person he saw if he was headed the right way. Which was how Julia found out he was coming. Sue Pelletier finished rolling in the Calico Cat awning, then went back inside the shop and telephoned Julia. Julia had time to take off her apron and comb her hair. She had time to put away thesaurus and dictionary. She was exchanging her slippers for a pair of sandals as Ed's car pulled into the driveway.

He picked a bunch of lilacs for her from one of the bushes out front. She took them from him awkwardly, reluctantly, knowing how demanding cut lilacs could be. He also had a pile of mail for her from her readers, which was one of the reasons he'd

made the trip, he said. She thanked him. She did make an effort
to read each and every letter, although doing so often depressed
her. Ed handed her the letters and she noticed the sweat in
crescent moons under his arms. They stood in stiff silence on the
porch. Finally, Julia asked him what was the other reason he'd
come and he squirmed a bit inside his jacket, his broad cheeks
quivering, and he coughed, "Curiosity."

"I see," said Julia, although she didn't really.

Suddenly the screen door swung open behind them and there
stood Kate and her pregnant belly. Kate stopped short. "Oh. I
didn't know you had company. I had a question about appliqué."

Julia introduced Kate, who reached out gamely to shake Ed's
hand. A certain tension dissolving. Julia said, "Come in for a glass
of iced tea, Ed?"

Kate's wedding dress was cut from several yards of yellow taffeta.
A seam was sewn high above the waist and wide pleats were set
to drape down the front, softening a sixth-month bulge. As a way
of showing Julia gratitude for sewing the dress, Kate said she was
going to name the child Louise if it was a girl. Louise was Julia's
middle name, but it was no less mortifying to Julia than if Kate
had chosen Julia itself. As fair-minded as she often managed to
come across in her newspaper column—for instance, she was
espousing the importance of the wedding celebration for young
couples who were still taking the plunge, even under scandalous
circumstances, or, as she put it, "under the inevitable trappings
of a modern attitude toward love"—Julia O'Leary was far more
righteous than her authorial self. Necessarily so, for if it weren't
for the higher ground that she occupied in real life she would
not be able to summon forth such generosity, such understand-

ing, for the outside world when she sat down at the desk in her spartan little room to write.

Back when she first learned the extent of Kate and Jim Martinson's engagement news, Julia said to Moira, "She wasn't raised Catholic. What do you expect?" And that pretty much summed up her attitude toward her readership, too. But the idea of an illegitimate child sharing her name made Julia's blood boil. Maybe it would be a boy. That's what Ed had said, sitting in the kitchen drinking iced tea earlier in the week, the table strewn with scraps of colorful fabric. Kate was hard at work on a quilt for the baby. In fact, she was quilting to the exclusion of everything else, including nursing school. She sat with the square she was working on spread out on her round belly, the rest of the pieces strewn across the kitchen table.

"Doing every inch of it by hand," Ed had remarked, impressed.

"Julia says it's the only proper way to do a quilt," Kate had replied.

Julia handed Ed his iced tea. He emptied his glass in a few swallows, set the glass down. He said, "I'm guessing it's a boy."

"What makes you think so?" Kate asked him.

Ed shrugged. "It's got to be one or the other, right?"

"So scientific," said Julia.

Kate was refusing to wear a veil and train. Just as well, perhaps; such delicate work was taxing. Julia stared into the waves of shimmery yellow fabric. She didn't disapprove of Jim Martinson; she simply felt, as she did about all young people today, that he lacked self-control. He'd lost his mother to heart disease earlier in the year and there was no father in the picture, so he was on his own. Fortunately, he was hardworking and painstakingly thrifty—she had once watched him remove an uncanceled stamp by suspending the envelope over the spray of steam from the kettle. He had warm brown eyes, a strong jaw, and there was talk that he might cut his hair for the wedding. He was also deaf in one ear as a result of a childhood infection, and had been classified 1F by the draft examiners.

Kate and Jim were going to be married at the courthouse in Portland, with a reception afterward at the diner where Jim worked. Hardly the perfect venue for a wedding, Julia felt, and she'd tried to sell Kate on the grange (Tom Yardley could play the wedding march on his bagpipes) or even on their own backyard (azalea and rhododendron in high bloom now), but Kate was adamant that she wasn't going to get married in Unity. It was, Kate claimed, a small-minded place; everybody knew everybody's business, there was no privacy, a fact that was clearly painful to her these days, as evidenced by her pulling a rain slicker over her body to go grocery shopping. Julia couldn't help but marvel at how differently she felt about the town. Julia'd been involved in the church since it opened, served two terms on the PTA, donated old clothes to the local AmVets, facilitated knitting night at the Calico Cat for Sue Pelletier—she could go on in this vein forever—and she still felt virtually anonymous walking down the street in Unity.

Julia sighed, removing her sewing glasses to massage her tired eyes. She sat back in the chair and looked vacantly about the room. Her gaze came to rest on the pile of wedding invitations on the hutch. Getting up abruptly, she went in search of a pen. She addressed an invitation to Edward Bailey, in care of the *Portland Gazette*, writing her name and return address boldly in the corner. Her fingers were tingling with purpose, and somehow she knew that this sensation would be lost as soon as she returned to hemming Kate's dress. She stood there a moment longer, just holding the pen.

Three days before her wedding day, on the twenty-first of June, 1967, Kate miscarried. Jim drove her to the emergency room in Portland. She was sedated for the delivery and dreamed she could hear the baby crying. She was running through a field of poppies, her breasts swinging heavily from side to side. Poppy petals fluttered into the air like butterflies in her wake. She could no longer hear the child, but there were clues—trampled brush, upturned stones, a scent as strong as her own—which she followed. She came upon a wolf cub curled in the flowers, and looked curiously at the furry creature. It was clearly too young to be out on its own. She picked it up carefully, delighting in its softness, and guided it to her arching nipple.

The child, a boy, was no bigger than an eggplant. He was alarming looking; redheaded and pointy-eared, with disproportionately long fingers and toes. She insisted to the point of tears that she be allowed to hold him. The nurse cleaned him up first, then settled his lifeless body gently in Kate's arms. She stared intently, wondering what on earth she'd have called him.

They were stopped at one of various rest stops that Julia, unaccustomed to riding in a car for any length of time, obliged Helen to pull off into. Helen and Julia had spent the day at the Portland hospital. Moira had been unable to find a work replacement on such short notice. She was apologetic about it, but Julia could see that she was secretly relieved. It was especially disturbing because throughout the day Kate kept saying how much she wished her mother were there.

A good stroll around the perimeter of the picnic ground, Julia told herself. A spot of tea poured from the Thermos into a paper cup afterward. She made Helen promise to be terse when Moira asked about Kate. News wasn't free; it came with responsibility. Let Moira go to Portland and see for herself the circles under Kate's eyes and the baby bootie she was clenching. Julia yanked at the seat belt repeatedly before realizing she'd closed a piece of it in the door. She bubbled over with her frustration. "It's shameful, if you want to know the truth. Your mother not coming. She's the one who has always mattered to Kate."

Helen reached across Julia, opening the door for her. Julia retrieved the belt. She fastened the buckle. She sniffled. "She weaned you too early, starved you for attention." She pulled a tissue from the box she had bestowed on the dashboard for the trip, and vigorously blew her nose. "I have never understood my sister. It is very, very difficult to love someone so puzzling"—she sniffled again—"yet so certain of herself!" She fell silent, staring out the window. She was not accustomed to confiding in either of the girls. She glanced shyly over at Helen before continuing. "I was always rather in awe of my sister. As a girl, she worked in the fields with our father. She could whistle through her teeth and the whole band, one hundred head of sheep, would turn a perfect circle 'round her." An unexpected tear slid down Julia's cheek. She brushed it away. When she spoke again it was in a seemingly detached and summarial tone. "There is really nothing worse than having to bury a child."

Helen gazed out the windshield. She remembered the night

last winter that she and Kate had gone skating on the iced-over clearing. They had carried a hurricane lantern into the woods with them, ice skates slung over their shoulders, and a broom to sweep off the snow. They had sat on the old tree stump to lace up their skates. Kate sailed out across the ice and Helen followed, laughing. The tassel of her hat blowing. The sharp swift sound of her skates, and her sister's ahead of hers. Helen had reached out for Kate's hand. They circled around and around. Helen glimpsed the serene pleasure on her sister's face in the lantern light. As they paused to catch their breath, staring up at the black branches, Kate asked could Helen keep a secret. In her next breath, she confessed her pregnancy. Helen was shocked. "You're not even married!" As if that were news to Kate. Dark as a bruise, the sky seemed.

Julia and Helen arrived home from Portland to find Moira lying on her back on a blanket on the lawn. "Aurora borealis," she told them, and they joined her on the blanket, the silence hanging heavily. High above, soft green lights undulated in flickering waves across the sky. "God, it's beautiful," Helen murmured, but otherwise they were quiet, in contemplation, each alone with the subconscious sense that this tumultuous evening was a reflection. The longer you looked the more lost you felt, and yet it was hardly uncomfortable. The breeze smelled of lilies. The crickets throbbed. By and by, Helen decided she'd save her question about the sister that died for another time. "Good night," she whispered; she was heading in to bed, pausing on the porch to look over her shoulder at the two of them lying side by side.

. . .

The departure of God from Moira's life when she was not much more than a child, admittedly, had left a gap, but she'd been adamant, iron-willed, covering it over with hard work. It had not been easy, particularly in full view of her sister. And, it was not as if she didn't ever have cause to wonder, and to wish there *was* a God. But she didn't like it when this kind of contemplation crept up on her or took her by surprise. (It was like coming upon an old acquaintance in the street—that is to say, a situation she dreaded and would otherwise go to great lengths, darting shame-lessly down alleys, to avoid.) She had succumbed to calling out to God in those cold, final moments on the boat. Michael was sliding out of her hands and, like a rush of blood to the head, the prayers came back to her. Hail Mary, she'd prayed. Full of desperate, fleeting hope.

No matter what careless or hapless turns Kate's life thus far had taken, Moira had always felt she was better off for having been raised free of religion. But when Kate lost the baby, Moira's confidence suffered. In some essential way, she felt it was her fault. And she felt ill-equipt to argue with Julia who claimed the burial would be sorely lacking without a priest and called up Father Keane. Moira's thoughts returned to her sister Ann and, in turn, to Heleen O'Leary, whom she'd known to be smart-minded, practical, capable of distilling the intrinsic usefulness from a gooseberry as well as from her religion. But Heleen O'Leary had not buried her own mother at the age of twelve. (She had been eighteen when Hanora Sullivan died, also in child-birth.) There was no one and nothing to dissuade Moira from deciding, at age twelve, that death was simpler and easier when it possessed no meaning.

They had first noticed the cemetery from the boat, years ago. A fine place to be buried, Michael had declared. With a view to the north of the islands, and a constant breeze. It had been idle conversation but, when the time came, she had made out as if it was his will, in order to avoid burying him in the Catholic cemetery. She rather liked visiting the graves on the bluff, with its windswept yellow grass in need of mowing. On Sundays and holy days she made a point of staying away, since Julia was known to hire a taxi to drive her out to the cemetery after church. Once, before Moira had become aware of this routine, she bumped into Julia at the cemetery. Julia was leaving just as Moira was arriving. It was a strange, awkward moment, with neither one of them saying anything. Moira had wheeled her bicycle past, nodding cordially.

Whosoever liveth and believeth in me shall never die," read Father Keane, and Moira gazed moodily up at the vaporous sky. The fog was so thick today they had carried flashlights. There were flowers from just about everybody who'd been invited to the wedding, and they had brought the bouquets with them to the cemetery. The colors were brilliant in the gray mist.

Moira looked on as Kate sobbed in Jim's arms. She felt a painful urge to join their embrace, but she could hardly picture it: the three of them, holding on for dear life. Such a gesture might mean a lot to Kate. But it would be completely out of character for Moira, and clumsy, her cold hands groping. And what would she do with the bag she was carrying? She was stymied by Julia's ginger loaf. Julia had wrapped several pieces for the ride home

from the cemetery, a comfort to eat something. Moira had been
left to carry it since everyone else was occupied with the flower
bouquets. Her heart pounding, she walked slowly over to where
Kate and Jim were standing. Kate turned to her and there was
such familiar sadness, such desperation, on her face that Moira
panicked—holding her hands out, foolishly offering the cake.
Kate shook her head, no thanks.

Walking back across the misty field in the direction of the
waiting headlights, they heard the gulls' cries. For the child's
spirit, an offering it may have seemed when, after removing the
cellophane, she had set the ginger loaf beside the grave site, but
Moira had had in mind the birds the whole time. A flutter of
wings over the grave, as over the boat on its way to harbor at the
end of the day. Out of nowhere seagulls always came.

Julia and Ed Bailey became a couple, quietly, in the wake of
Kate's misfortune. Ed had taken the liberty of driving up to Unity
to drop off an orchid corsage he had originally ordered with the
intention of bestowing it on Julia at the wedding. Julia was
touched by the gesture but it also worried her, and at first she
declined to let him pin it to her chest, regarding it as too festive
to be worn in mourning. The orchid was so stiff it looked
starched, but at least he wasn't making the mistake he'd made
with the lilacs. Ed prevailed on her finally, claiming he hadn't
driven all the way from Portland so the flower could sit in its box.
Besides which, an orchid's beauty was stately, in good taste no
matter the occasion. Personally, Julia had always felt they were
a pretentious flower, but she said nothing, held her breath as Ed
pinned it to her dress. In the bathroom later, she'd take a moment
to straighten it. They sat together on the porch and he listened

to her concerns about Kate, who was considering going ahead
with the marriage (albeit not a wedding reception) in spite of
everything. As Julia was talking, a green Park Service truck pulled
up and two brown-shirted park volunteers got out of the truck
carrying paint cans. The volunteers waved and Julia nodded her
head at them. Every year, she told Ed, they repainted the trail
markers at the edges of the property. She would mention their
coming to paint the next time she talked with Kate. It was just
this sort of mundane detail that confirmed the continuum of life,
wasn't it? Ed reached out and she felt his hand on hers. It was
cool and moist from holding a water glass. She was quite taken
aback by the gesture, and did her best to dissuade him.

"I am hardly an exciting personality, Mr. Bailey."

Ed paused. "You excite me."

Julia blushed deeply.

He apologized, "I'm an editor. I don't mince words."

She bit her lip. "No, indeed."

It was late September before he kissed her. She was standing in
her herb garden explaining the medicinal uses of certain plants
to him when he abruptly took her in his arms. She let go of the
garden hose. Cool water seeped through her sandals. The kiss
was as sweet as parsley. Later that evening, as she was getting
ready for bed, Julia discovered the key to her hope chest missing.
She deduced that it must have slipped out of her apron pocket
in the heat of passion in the garden. She would find it in the
morning, surely, and took pains to focus on her bedtime rituals
the same as any other night: a cup of raspberry leaf tea, calendula
ointment rubbed up and down her legs, and a few moments at
her desk to read over what she'd written during the day. Never-

theless, she was in a quandary. She remained sleepless half the night and was up, out of the house, at the first sign of light. She raced across the grass in her flannel nightgown, her heart leaping at the sight of something glittering in the sunlight. A chunk of mica in the rock, only. She was practically in tears. And yet she felt so foolish because, in fact, the key itself meant nothing. She couldn't remember the last time she had opened the hope chest, but the missing key upset her sense of security, and she blamed Ed Bailey.

She subsequently tried to refrain from passionate kissing. Ed was forced to satisfy himself with short, fierce pecks and warm bear hugs while Julia silently invoked the Virgin to give her strength. Cloaked in cornflower blue, placid as the afternoon. A kiss was not just a kiss, the way popular culture claimed. She'd seen what it could lead to. At the same time, she had never known the comfort she knew at Ed's side—whether they were at the movies (hunched over a bucket of popcorn, second-guessing the plot in each other's ears) or driving home in the car with the sun setting, Ed in those funny sunglasses, her own eyes resting, closed. She'd never thought she'd be so trusting as to fall asleep in a moving vehicle.

That earnest look of Ed's, that plucky tone of voice. She had never before thought of Ed Bailey as sweet—the way Helen described him—but he was, wasn't he? Was he too sweet for her, perhaps? She was swimming in doubt sometimes. She could become so distracted it was a struggle to write. Julia had never told Ed about her attraction to Michael Sheehan, about her habit of comparing her feelings for each man, coming up short, generally, not because Ed wasn't lovable, but because Ed was possible.

When Julia prayed to the Lord, she asked Him for clarity, but

He was elusive on this matter. She even wondered if He weren't slightly angry with her. She had less time for her prayers now, what with Ed and she going out several nights a week. For the most part, though, Julia believed that God wanted her to be happy and although, at an earlier point in her life, marrying a Protestant would have precluded such happiness, she was in too deep now to be dogmatic. Of course Ed hadn't said anything about marriage (they had only been official since September), but, from Julia's way of looking at it, kissing and marrying were almost synonymous.

She had long believed that marriage was a unique arrangement, and spent long moments picturing Ed's toothbrush standing up-right in a rinsing cup with hers and his coffee mug and her teacup set opposite one another on the breakfast table. And she imagined there was nothing quite so pleasing as the sound of a loved one breathing beside you in bed. She thought daringly of lovemaking, her flesh crawling with pleasure merely imagining. She would lie awake at night, silent, staring at the water glass on the night table. Twenty minutes, an hour, even two might pass before she'd hike herself up on her elbow to drain the glass in long, thirsty gulps. This stupor, this mindless depth she sank to in considering losing her virginity, scared her, and she spent the last of her waking moments vigorously playing the alphabet game with herself.

Julia, Moira, and Ed Bailey were all sitting in the living room discussing the *Portland Gazette*'s coverage of the impending strike at the Unity fish-packing plant. Moira called it biased, while Ed defended it as responsible reporting of both sides of the story. Helen came in, back from visiting her sister and Jim at their apartment in Portland. She helped herself to a piece of the blackberry cobbler on the table. The afternoon sun faded, a cold November wind rattled the windows, and Ed glanced at his watch. He knew enough to keep his mouth shut about the time, about his desire to get on the road before it started to snow if they were going to make it to Portland in time for the play. Julia was never in a hurry to leave the house, Ed had noticed, particularly if her sister was home. Tonight she claimed she had a headache. Finally, he coaxed her into her coat. They sped down the highway through the flurries.

By intermission, Julia's headache had grown into a fever. Ed regretted having brought her. She looked so ill. He helped her out of the auditorium. After a long hiatus it was not uncommon for her lupus to flare up with a vengeance. While Ed retrieved the coats, she made her way into the ladies' room. Her head was pounding. She sat down gingerly on the backs of her hands. When she was finished, she stood up too quickly. The room whirled and she fell, slamming her head against the sink.

A head wound always bled like the dickens, she explained, but Ed was overwhelmed by the sight of her pressing a clump of bloody paper towels to her forehead. He had a frenzied look on his face as he hunched over the steering wheel and peered out through the freezing rain. The wipers whipped back and forth. The car crawled through the icy streets. He'd never get her home at this rate. He panicked and changed direction, his hand reaching across the seat. "Almost there now." He squeezed her fingers fiercely. She looked curiously out the window. They weren't near the highway. Stopped at a light, Ed nervously drumming the wheel, the lights of the hospital came into view. "Where are you taking me?" she asked abruptly. The light turned and Ed gunned the car down the avenue.

• • •

Moira watched from the window as Ed pushed the wheelchair up to the house. Even though Ed had warned her over the phone ("she doesn't look like herself, just so you know") Moira was not prepared for the sight of her sister's pumpkin face and bloodshot eyes. Julia had been given massive doses of steroids, which had relieved the pain and inflammation considerably (though her face swelled hideously as a result) but had also proved crippling. In one fell swoop, the cortisone was decimating years of carefully maintained tissue—or so Julia explained her weakened condition to Moira. She was certain she was dying. And she was angry at Ed. She could never forgive him, she said. He should go now that she was home. Leave her to her death! Her sister would care for her. Her sister would never have offered her up like a sacrificial lamb to the hospital!

"You were a bit hard on him," Moira said after Ed left.

Julia shrugged, sullen. She asked for a cup of hot water with rosemary and to have a look at the day's *Gazette*. She turned first to the obituaries. It was not easy to make the right final impression, was it? Julia set the newspaper aside. Perhaps she really *was* dying. It would make so much sense, in a way. Even the happiness she had felt of late, the wonderful warmth inside as she held Ed tight, as she gasped for air and looked boldly into his eyes, possessed a final quality. Certainly the no-place she drifted off into, lying awake at night with her private fears about marriage, felt as lonely as the end of time. "You're glowing," he had whispered to her as they were leaving the house last night. It was the fever presumably, flush in her cheeks. He had pulled her close, turning his face to hers. The heat of his breath causing her lips to pulse. While she lay against the pillows daydreaming, she began to feel the very same fogginess creeping over her. She fought off her fear with curiosity. So intrigued did she become, so watchful and awake, that the fog dissolved rapidly.

It would be far easier to die anonymously, far more consistent with her life up until recently. Julia had been named Golden Pen columnist last month, her photograph appearing in a little box beside the award announcement, and she could not help feeling that her readers, in the event of her death, should be allowed to pay their respects. A wake would be in order. Humble but tasteful: no chrysanthemums and, for refreshment, tea and cookies of the shortbread variety. For the funeral Mass, she would want the thirtieth psalm read, even though it was not the crowd-pleaser the twenty-third was. She might even abide a short passage from Job. It occurred to her that there was no one in the family to partake of the Eucharist, except possibly for Helen, and not without trembling, not without a substantive visit to the confessional first. Helen went to church solely on holidays; better than not at all, Julia consoled herself.

Julia's earlier declaration of loyalty to Moira notwithstanding, Ed Bailey proved to be a more dedicated bedside companion. Ed was compliant, servile, remaining with her despite everything—her poor humor, flatulence, and regular visits from Father Keane. "What's wrong with you that you can't join me in my hour of need?" Julia badgered Moira. "Ed's a Protestant, yet he partakes. Well, not of the sacrament, but he's there with me—he prays."

"Thank God for Ed," Moira said.

"I certainly do," said Julia.

She had reconciled with Ed over the telephone the day after

he had brought her home from the hospital. It didn't make sense to hold a grudge given that she was dying. Besides which, she was possessed of a Christian spirit and understood that he had been frightened. He'd admitted as much over the phone. "I was scared. I didn't know what else to do. I'm sorry, Jules."

"I'm sorry too," she replied, meaning sorry for herself.

Her condition worsened through the winter. Christmas was celebrated around her bed. Helen turned eighteen that New Year's, 1968, but Julia was too weak to participate. She was asleep long before the paper airplanes and the eggnog. She didn't get out of bed for Eugene McCarthy's campaign stop. (She was crazy to miss it, Helen said, but Julia replied that she'd wait for Bobby Kennedy.) And she didn't go to the Memorial Day parade, even though she'd dreamed the night before of cotton candy.

Spring tulips on Julia's night table were replaced with irises. Wild irises, infinitely more delicate than the cultivated kind. But the dark, intricate veins demanded too much of her at times. She would grow dizzy from looking at the flowers and have to turn her head away. When half the irises rotted before ever fully opening, she was secretly relieved. There were daylilies afterwards, in endless supply—ivory, mauve, lemon yellow—until Ed confessed he found them depressing. Daisies he could tolerate; they were simple, genial—though they weren't very fragrant, were they? Roses, they both agreed, now there was a flower that had everything. She thought she might like to have Ed plant a rosebush on her grave site, but she didn't tell him this directly since he scared so easily. A floribunda. She would add it to her will, including directions for pruning: "Start at the tips and snip a few inches at a time until the stem centers show white. Go to work on anything that looks dead, but don't always assume that the brown and brittle isn't full of life inside."

By the time the rosebushes were in high bloom, it was July. With Julia's permission, Helen had begun taking photographs of her. Helen had unearthed Michael's old camera and had enrolled in a summer photography course up in Rockport. "These are meant to be candids," she complained as Julia reached for a hairbrush. Unlike her mother, Helen did not behave as if Julia was an alarmist; in fact, quite the opposite, she was very serious about documenting Julia's illness. Intent on capturing every detail, she photographed ankle-dressing preparations on the night table, bottled herbs and tubs of salve lining the bookshelves, even the bedpan. Moira came in with a vase full of the roses Julia had requested. Gorgeous fiery pink, on the window ledge. Helen snapped the picture.

Julia was still writing her weekly column, dictating it on a tape recorder because her fingers were too sore to consider using the typewriter. "Plain and Simple" began to bear the weight of Julia's doom. First there was the piece on the seventeen-year cicada hatching over in Alna, then there was the story on the three-clawed lobster a fisherman out on Cushing hauled up. When the Saco flooded, Julia devoted two inches to description of the bloated forms of dead cows. There was a heavy, moralistic undercurrent to pull her readers along now. There was a rash of blue lobsters, feral cats on Loon Island, and the drowning of Billie Watts on his annual swim round Scully's Point.

As her editor, Ed warned that readers would become discouraged. But Julia insisted she was telling it like it was. If her popularity suffered as a result, so be it. Maybe she was outgrowing the *Portland Gazette*. Maybe she didn't care to spend what precious little time she had left slaving to please an unsympathetic audience! There was something fundamentally dislikable and undeserving about a readership. She was forever compromising her words on their account. Dumbing things down. No reader ever read a story the way they were intended to.

Julia's fatalism penetrated her everyday life as well. "Kindly split this carton of eggs for me," she told the dairy man at the back door one morning. "I couldn't stand the thought of eggs rotting if I were to pass on suddenly." She canceled her subscriptions to the *Homeopathy Circular* and the *Catholic Digest*, and every time Moira drove her to the clinic for dialysis, she sighed wistfully as if it were surely her last time on the streets of Unity.

"Stop it," Moira snapped at her. "Stop the nonsense, Julia. I have never known anyone so afraid of being happy."

"I'm not unhappy," Julia defended, "even if I am dying."

Moira snorted. She turned the truck into the clinic parking lot.

The trips into Free Harbor for treatment involved so much fuss with the stairs and the wheelchair that eventually they opted to administer dialysis at home. Kate, in her final semester of nursing school and interning at the Portland hospital, volunteered to come by the house to show Moira what to do. Like Helen, Kate also took Julia's condition seriously and entertained her concerns about the possibility of death from stroke.

"Stroke!" exclaimed Moira.

Kate shrugged. "It's possible."

Moira scoffed. "Like man on the moon!" She walked out.

"Just you wait," Julia called after her.

Julia was delighted to see Kate. She looked so well. Recovered, if

that were possible. She was wearing her nursing shoes, smiling easily. She was pregnant again, she divulged. Julia's jaw dropped open
on hearing this news. Like a rabbit, she said to herself, but she mus-
tered up a more considerate appraisal: "You're a brave girl, Kate."

Kate laughed. "Well, it wasn't intentional."

Julia had read about strokes, how a stroke could alter one's
personality, and had become convinced it was her destiny to go
this way. It was not a threatening prospect for her, since the hand
of God was believed to be involved. He would take her, little by
little relieve her of herself. Certainly, it would be frustrating to
lose the weight and density of being, but perhaps she would no
longer be the sort to complain. In the quiet of the morning when
no one else was home, Julia daydreamed her final moments. It
was a comfort to her somehow, and helpful in convincing her
that her death was as real as she wanted it to be and not, as
Moira claimed, a product of invention and insecurity.

Moira simply didn't understand! After the stroke, Julia should
try to convey to her how much better she felt. Honestly, soft and
round as a cloud. The pain had been so cavernous before, ago-
nizing, unimaginable. But the stroke—swift, lightning quick—
would lift Julia out of herself and she would see, then, Moira at
her bedside, lowly witness to this epiphany. Fumbling with the
catheter, distilling meds through cheesecloth, rubbing salve on
the sores. Overcome with sweetness, truly as if her blood had
turned to syrup, Julia would feel such charity! And perhaps forgive Moira the past, *forgive her finally*, if she could only find the
words to speak. Words having all but floated out of reach by this
time, Julia would be conscious nevertheless of their unformed
breath, their history, a history evident on Moira's stubborn face.

Apparent in the window light and in the shadow of the heavy-headed roses. Pungent as the scent of grass after a good rain. Rich, luscious as a snail-shaped ice cream brought to her from Bantry.

The telephone rang and Julia was shaken from her reverie. At her request, the phone had been moved into her room so that it would be within easy reach in case of need when no one was home. She pushed herself up on the pillows. The caller was Rosita Lopez, who apparently was some sort of healer in addition to being Matty's neighbor. Julia listened in disbelief to what she was saying.

"His liver up and quit. There wasn't anything I could do for him."

"Lord knows it's called the *liver* for a reason." Julia sighed.

"He went quickly," Rosita assured her, "and he looked peaceful once he was cleaned up."

Julia said thank you, stiffly, soon hanging up the phone. She inhaled deeply. It struck her that her father's death had eclipsed hers. But wasn't it fitting? Julia lay back on the pillows. For a moment, she felt frustrated. But the sun was filtering through the curtains, warmth washing over her. She did not notice the months of gloomy apprehension melting. She was listening for her sister. The screen door swung shut and Moira's robust shout soon followed. "Julia? Are you with us still?" Julia drew back the quilt and carefully slid her legs over the side of the bed. Another big breath and she pushed herself up. She was standing. She placed one foot carefully in front of the other, shuffling out past the wheelchair, to tell her sister the news.

One April evening, 1969. Moira stepped out onto the porch for a look at the moon while she waited for the kettle to boil. A soft green mist was rolling in over the trees, temporarily obscuring the starry sky. She bristled suddenly, alert to the presence of something out on the lawn—rabbits nosing their way under the cold frame, or perhaps it was her father's ghost manifesting for the second time today. Earlier that morning, teaching Helen the boat, Moira had felt unnerved by the roll of the water beneath her feet. As for Helen, she had done beautifully for her first time out. She seemed undaunted by the chop, and she possessed what Moira considered to be a talent for discerning her direction without the use of radar. Stray hairs had whipped across Moira's face; wind blowing from the north, buffeting solidly up against her spine. Then a trick image of Matty appeared out of the corner of her eye, and her head began to spin. A feeling like that of wind picking up offshore, wind that choked words back into the throat, tore shutters off the house, wrenched up trees and dumped them in the sea. It came over her unexpectedly, a raging nor'easter riding in on twenty-foot waves. A fisherman's undoing. She hung over the port side, blinking back the salt spray, and retched into the waves.

Moira was still feeling a bit chagrined that she had been the one to get seasick. From the porch, she watched the fog closely. She had a hunch that Matty wasn't going to let her be until she made a decision about what to do with his ashes. But if it *was* a rabbit, she ought to fetch the slingshot. Just then, the kettle whistled.

She sat in the rocker with her cup of tea, one ear cocked for Ed Bailey's car coming up the road. As a Catholic, Julia had been opposed to the cremation ("Goodness me!" she had exclaimed, looking shocked, when Moira first mentioned it back in September. As if, despite all the hours she'd spent in gloomy contemplation of her own death, she had never heard anything so morbid). Moira claimed it wasn't worth paying a lot of money to have Matty sent to Maine in a coffin when he wouldn't give a damn one way or the other. All things considered, cremation was cheaper. It would be foolish not to consider costs, since the plant workers were on strike again and there was no telling when she'd see another paycheck.

When the box containing Matty's ashes had first arrived, it sat in the middle of the kitchen table for half the day, Julia and Moira both conducting their tea and biscuits around it. It was Julia who finally broke the silence. "Well, what now?" she had said, looking expectantly from the box to her sister. "I'm not sure," Moira confessed. And that was how they had left it, except that Julia did move the box eventually, to the shelf in the cupboard where the popsicle molds, plastic picnic utensils, and other miscellany were kept.

Moira could taste the ocean salt on her lips. It had been a test run only, precipitated primarily by Helen's acceptance into the art school in Portland for the fall. She had received a partial scholarship, and had hatched a plan to spend the summer lobstering as a way of coming up with the rest of the money. It was true, people paid an arm and a leg now for lobster. But it had never been solely about making money. Moira had insisted Helen understand: even if she did agree to launch the boat, it did not necessarily mean she was returning to lobstering. Michael Sheehan's boat had been sitting under a tarpaulin in Skinny Roberts' barn ever since Moira had prohibited Kate from selling it. Skinny had generously offered to store the boat so that they wouldn't incur the mooring fees. He knew Moira wouldn't be able to bear the look of it, idle, in her own backyard. Skinny had smiled when Moira told him, just as she'd told Helen, that she was just testing the waters. "Oh, I know better than that," said Skinny as he walked the circumference of the boat, gauging how they could best load it onto the trailer. "Well," she'd confessed, "maybe it is the missing piece."

Driving home from the harbor today, sunlit road in front of her, Moira was too tired to speak. But she was wondering whether any of their old lobster pots would still pass muster. No sooner had she and Helen arrived home than the telephone began ringing. It was Kate, calling to say it was time. Helen shot up off the couch and went to pack an overnight bag. As planned, she was going to drive down to Portland for the birth. She flew about the house gathering provisions, Moira marveling at her energy. Moira stayed sitting after Helen drove off. Her mind wandering in circles, and every which way she went she was bumping up against another big taut wiggling belly. She thought of her own mother, Heleen O'Leary. Endless generations! An ocean full. Bobbing in the waves like porpoises, shiny-eyed, curiously trailing the boat. The sun had gone down but it was a long time before Moira had roused herself to get up and turn a light on and, while she was at it, see about a cup of tea for herself.

When she heard the crunch of tires on the gravel, Moira set down her teacup. She switched on the porch light and flung open the door. A chipmunk scurried into a hole in the porch floor. "So it's you, finally," Moira called to Julia as she and Ed came across the lawn. "The baby's coming!"

Julia's face lit up. "None too soon," she said excitedly. She turned to Ed. "Will you come in for a spot of tea?"

He shook his head, affably declining: "I'll leave the Easter vigil to you two."

Julia smiled. He kissed her forehead. She and Moira went inside.

"I was going to have a bite to eat," Moira said.

"I'm fasting since Good Friday," Julia pointedly replied. She had been at church throughout the afternoon. Ed had met her afterward for a walk on the beach, which had become their Saturday night outing ever since she'd given up the cinema for Lent. Julia sat at the kitchen table playing nervously with her engagement ring while Moira went about spreading butter and jam on her toast. At Christmastime, when Ed presented the ring to Julia, her fingers were still too swollen for it. She had been wearing it for over a month now, although Moira still hadn't said anything. Julia glanced at the clock. There was no telling how long the birth would take. Especially since Kate's obstetrician had discouraged her from drinking the blue cohosh tea that Julia recommended to speed the labor. Julia sighed audibly. "Go and pray," Moira said, locking eyes with her. Julia nodded her head, getting up directly. Yes, of course, what was she waiting for?

By the time Moira went up to bed, the sky was clear, and she watched for a while out her bedroom window at the boat lights down in the harbor and at the stars dotting the black sky above. There was a deep fear inside, her mind flooding with the memory of her mother on her hands and knees, belly touching the floor, scouring out the hearth of all things, the day before Ann was born. How Matty had come home and taken one look at his wife, up to her elbows in soot and ash, and remarked that the baby wouldn't be long now, Heleen had the nesting instinct. But it wasn't until Moira was a grown woman, herself, driven to plant her garden up until the very moment her waters broke, that she understood that Heleen O'Leary had been acting on a desire to feel resolved. "Ash to ash," Moira murmured. She had been staring so intently out the window, by now there was no longer a distinction between what was a star and what was a boat light.

Just waves," said Kate. "Big waves, little waves. I don't know what to think."

Her doctor felt they shouldn't wait any longer. The nurse wheeled her into the delivery room, Jim and Helen in tow. "We're right here—we're with you, Kate." Jim helped her climb onto the table. A contraction clamped her jaw shut. She tried to focus on the nurse prepping the room. Honestly, she couldn't have stood this whale's body, the swollen veins, the pendulum boobs forever. Yet the moment of truth was daunting. She could see right through Jim's enthusiastic coaching and caressing. He was as meek as she. The two of them uncertain suddenly.

Kate gripped Helen's hand and squeezed. Her body was howling. Warm sunshine, bright light. Beads of sweat raced down her face. "I'm looking straight into the sun," she moaned. A pain like no other jolted far inside and she shut her eyes against the white. In front of her, she saw a grasshopper. A sun-soaked snake. Tobacco hung to dry. Wind was blowing, turning everything cold. Snowy. Then, suddenly, she spied the wolf loping across the ice. Steady, tireless, determined in its motion. Over the sparkling field and into the forest, the wolf was tracking something. She was fearful, watching. When it turned to her, she remembered having seen it before and grew angry, protective. She sat up wide-eyed, growling, startling the doctor who had made the incision.

Jim fainted at the sight. He could not remember blacking out. He remembered waking with alarm, fear of not knowing what had come of her. "A boy," the nurse told him. A boy, Jim told himself, when they held up the creature. A vast shudder, every inch of his being relieved.

Helen bought a cup of coffee and a roll of film for her camera and tried to phone Unity. She went into the hospital chapel and sat contemplatively with her coffee. There were several potted Easter lilies on the altar. She couldn't help thinking of her mother. Moira had worn a white lily in her hair when she married Michael Sheehan. Helen had seen the photograph. Last summer, while Helen was earnestly documenting history with her father's old camera, she had complained frequently about the dearth of family photos. Helen suspected that her mother had thrown them away after her father's death, but one day Julia mentioned almost wistfully that there was an envelope of old photographs in the hope chest. Unfortunately, said Julia, the hope chest was locked and the key lost. Helen had gone in search of a hammer. She had pounded the lock until it broke. Julia sat up on the pillows, watching from her bed as Helen muscled up the trunk lid. The first thing they saw was a blue, child-size cardigan. Helen lifted the sweater out. There were piles of musty old books underneath and, as well, a couple of library books that had never been re- turned. There were bags of gray wool, beeswax candles, and an old flower press. There was also an old book of commercial dress patterns, which Julia said surprised her since she'd never once succumbed to sewing from a pattern. "Give it here," she ordered. Helen handed her the pattern book. Leafing through it, Julia dis- covered one of Michael Sheehan's drawings tucked between the pages. She smiled. It was the first portrait Michael had ever done of Moira, on the boat before he even knew her name. Julia showed it to Helen. "Do you recognize your mother?"

"She was pretty," Helen said. "So young!"

"Yes," Julia sighed. "Young. Uncertain. Afraid. No wonder Moira never liked it."

Julia said Helen should keep the drawing. They had gone on to look at old buttons, Michael's letters from the war, and newspaper clippings about the shipwrecked ocean liner on which Matty had sailed. They had sorted through the old photographs. The expression of unrivaled joy on her mother's face in her wedding day photo had taken Helen's breath away. It had been a hopeful afternoon. Julia had posed for a picture holding her United States citizenship certificate. The shot later won an award in the Rockport student show.

Kate's sleep was so deep and captivating she didn't hear a thing. Voices, a child's cry, but all as soft as cotton. It stuffed up Kate's ears and she went right on sleeping. The nurse helped Jim wake her finally, handing her the baby. "He's got to eat." She was wary. Except for the weight, surprisingly dense and solid in her arms, he did not seem real. Then his lips found her. She sat up, watched him suckle. She was calling him Michael.

Jim had smoked the only cigar of his life and his head was spinning. It had been all he could do to stumble back to the right room with the bag of chocolate eggs she'd asked for. He sat down on the bed, gazed quietly out the window. Helen wandered in with her camera. She said, "I tried phoning. They must be out."

Kate unwrapped the silver foil and popped the chocolate into her mouth. "Out celebrating."

"Yes," said Helen, gazing through the camera lens at the baby. "It's Easter Sunday."

Earlier that morning, still no word from Portland, Julia had gone off to Easter services. Moira had watched the clock while she cracked and peeled a few of the colored eggs to make sandwiches. She packed the lunch in her bicycle basket, along with the box of her father's ashes. She wheeled the bicycle out of the road. It was a fresh, lovely morning, daffodils and tulips leaning in the breeze. She coasted down the hill, her braid blowing like a kite tail. She passed the Park Service Center, which was the old Francoeur farmhouse renovated and painted. Shingled homes appeared as she neared town, lobster traps stacked high in the yards. She rode past the fish market, nautical map and gear stores, and the old marina, now a restaurant. At the church of Saint Francis, Mass had already let out. The church bell tolled. People flooded the sidewalk, children in Easter bonnets played tag on the church lawn, but she did not see Julia. Perhaps she had already gone on. Moira stood up off her seat and pumped as the road began to wind steeply up. She pumped and pumped. It was a fierce struggle, but she reached the top. She stopped short to collect her breath. A barbed-wire fence lined the road on one side, behind it the new power plant and a sprawling employee parking lot. She pedaled on, at last arriving at the entrance to the cemetery. She dismounted, still breathing hard, and wiped her forehead with her sleeve. She left her bicycle leaning against the gate, collected her things from the basket and walked toward the graves.

. . .

Julia was sitting on the grass in her blue Easter dress, her back resting against Michael Sheehan's gravestone. She was lost in thought, working her engagement ring, and was startled by Moira's arrival. She got to her feet, asking anxiously was there news of Kate. Moira, a bit awkwardly, said no, holding up the box to explain her intrusion.

"Da's ashes," Julia said with surprise.

"Yes," Moira said. "It's bad luck to be holding on to them."

They would have some lunch first. Julia settled herself back down on the grass. Moira unstrapped the bag and took out the milk bottle. She helped herself, then passed the bottle to Julia, but Julia, having yet to break her fast, was more interested in a sandwich.

"I brought you two," said Moira.

"Thank you."

They ate the sandwiches, Moira's gaze wandering over to the small gravestone beside Michael's. The crocuses Kate and Jim had planted were up. An interested gull set down on the stone. Moira tossed it a morsel. Clearing her throat, she said, "Julia, remember back when Ann died?"

"I remember."

"Da told you I fell asleep."

"Yes," said Julia. "It wasn't the truth he told."

Moira paused. "He didn't think you'd ever forgive me."

Julia held out her hand for the milk bottle. She swallowed hard. They sat for a while, the breeze moving through the long grass. The ocean pounding like a heart against the rocks. Then

Moirareachedfortheboxwiththeashes.Shewalkeddowntothe
gate cliff edge. Julia followed her. They opened the box and un-
sealed the lining. The ash in their hands was softer than feathers.
On the count of three, they agreed, and flung their arms out.